Confrontations out East

I gave the guy the sort of smile that means nothing and said, "This is a local Guild, or is it part of a larger Guild throughout the country?"

He gave me what I'm sure he thought was a Penetrating Stare. "Why would you want to know that?"

"Just curious."

"Why do you want to know that?" Loiosh thought at me.

"Just curious."

It was interesting, though. Last night, there was someone who had just assumed I was an aristocrat; and now this guy just assumed I was some sort of thug, or criminal. I hate it when people make those kind of assumptions about me. It makes me want to break their legs.

I said, "Does the name Merss mean anything to you?"

His scowl deepened. "Are you threatening me?"

"No."

"I don't respond to threats, young man."

"That's good, because I don't issue them."

"I think you had best leave my establishment."

Establishment. He had an establishment.

I shrugged and walked out because I didn't think staying would be productive, and because that was probably the last thing he expected me to do.

"That," I told Loiosh, *"was one of the more interesting conversations I've had in a life full of interesting conversations."*

"Meaning you have no idea what just happened, right?"

"Right. Only something did. Didn't it?"

"Sure, Boss. Is there a reason you think it might be connected with what you're looking for?"

"Loiosh, I mentioned the name of my family and he thought I was threatening him."

He didn't answer.

BOOKS BY STEVEN BRUST

THE DRAGAERAN NOVELS

Brokedown Palace

THE KHAAVREN ROMANCES

The Phoenix Guards
Five Hundred Years After
The Viscount of Adrilankha,
which comprises
The Paths of the Dead,
The Lord of Castle Black,
and
Sethra Lavode

THE VLAD TALTOS NOVELS

Jhereg	*Athyra*
Yendi	*Orca*
Teckla	*Dragon*
Taltos	*Issola*
Phoenix	*Dzur*

Jhegaala

OTHER NOVELS

To Reign in Hell
The Sun, the Moon, and the Stars
Agyar
Cowboy Feng's Space Bar and Grille
The Gypsy (with Megan Lindholm)
Freedom and Necessity (with Emma Bull)

STEVEN BRUST

JHEGAALA

TOR®
fantasy

A TOM DOHERTY ASSOCIATES BOOK

NEW YORK

This is a work of fiction. All of the characters, organizations, and events portrayed in this novel are either products of the author's imagination or are used fictitiously.

JHEGAALA

Copyright © 2008 by Steven Brust

All rights reserved.

Edited by Teresa Nielsen Hayden

Diagram copyright © 2007 by Kere'sa "Silver" Croft

A Tor Book
Published by Tom Doherty Associates, LLC
175 Fifth Avenue
New York, NY 10010

www.tor-forge.com

Tor® is a registered trademark of Tom Doherty Associates, LLC.

ISBN 978-0-7653-4155-6

First Edition: July 2008
First Mass Market Edition: July 2009

Printed in the United States of America

0 9 8 7 6 5 4 3 2 1

To Anika and Miklos

THE CYCLE

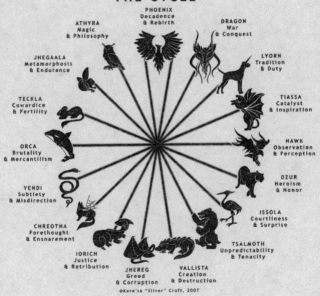

PHOENIX
Decadence
& Rebirth

DRAGON
War
& Conquest

ATHYRA
Magic
& Philosophy

LYORN
Tradition
& Duty

JHEGAALA
Metamorphosis
& Endurance

TIASSA
Catalyst
& Inspiration

TECKLA
Cowardice
& Fertility

HAWK
Observation
& Perception

ORCA
Brutality
& Mercantilism

DZUR
Heroism
& Honor

YENDI
Subtlety
& Misdirection

ISSOLA
Courtliness
& Surprise

CHREOTHA
Forethought
& Ensnarement

TSALMOTH
Unpredictability
& Tenacity

IORICH
Justice
& Retribution

VALLISTA
Creation
& Destruction

JHEREG
Greed
& Corruption

@Kere'sa "Silver" Croft, 2007

Part One

EGG

Incubation time is short—eight or nine days—during which the egg is vulnerable. While the mother is able to protect the eggs after completing her metamorphosis (see Chapter 19), that still leaves between thirty-five and forty hours during which the eggs would be entirely without protection, were it not for the help of a male who has undergone his own metamorphosis after fertilizing the eggs (see Chapter 18) and now returns, as it were, to stand guard while the mother is helpless, as will be covered in more detail during the discussion of the levidopt.

It must be stressed that it is not, in particular, the father who returns to guard the eggs, but rather the first unattached male levidopt to pass within fifty feet or so of the transforming mother. Exactly how the male levidopt finds the eggs . . .

—Oscaani: Fauna of the Middle South: A Brief Survey, Volume 6, Chapter 15

PROLOGUE

There is a place in the mountain called Saestara where, according to the locals, you can look east and see the past, and look west and see the future. I suppose it has its origins in some migration in pre-history, or some invasion, or some mystical rubbish built of thin air—plenty of that in the mountains, at any rate. I don't know, but the locals seem to believe it.

And, if it's true, I was going backward. Looking west, I remembered lots of painful scrabbling up paths that were made by and for mountain goats; looking east, I foresaw more of the same going down.

Some distance behind me was a lake called Szurke, on the edge of a forest. I owned the lake and a little bit of the forest and the big manor house near it, courtesy of the Empire and thanks to "extraordinary service." That's a laugh. I didn't dare stay there, courtesy of the House of the Jhereg and thanks to "extraordinary misdeeds." That's not such a laugh.

I'd installed my grandfather as regent. As I told him, "I prefer nepotism to despotism." He hadn't been amused; he didn't much like the idea of being a despot himself, having pretty much always hated the aristocracy with a sort of mild dispassionate hate that had its origins in a past of which I'd never gotten more than hints.

He and I had both been worried during my visit. He was worried because the poaching in his part of the forest had gotten out of hand when the poachers realized he didn't have the heart to enforce the laws against it. I was worried that the Jhereg might be mad enough at me to take it out on him. I didn't think they would—what I'd done hadn't been as bad as, say, giving evidence to the Empire—but it caused me some concern.

We talked about that, and Noish-pa wasn't worried. The Jhereg is capable, perhaps, of making use of a human witch, no matter how much they scorn the magic of "Easterners," but they'd be hard pressed to find one as skilled as my grandfather. And give him a little time with all the animals, and even the trees and plants in this area, and he would create a security network and defensive perimeter I'd defy Mario to break through.

We had a long talk about the trouble I was in, and his troubles with poachers (which translated to hating having to tell anyone what to do), and where I was going to go from here. He didn't want to know, because he figured that what he didn't know the Jhereg couldn't force him to tell. I was going to explain that the Jhereg didn't do things like that, but, well, sometimes they do.

I played with Ambrus, his familiar; and Noish-pa and Loiosh, my familiar, got reacquainted. I stayed for a week and he cooked for me and we talked about many things, especially how he could continue as regent without actually running anything. We came up with some ideas to at least cut down on the orders he would have to give, and he seemed happy.

One night, over Fenarian brandy, I said, "Noish-pa, is there anything you can tell me about my mother?"

He sighed. "She studied the Art, Vladimir, and that made my son, may he find peace, unhappy. And so I saw her little."

"Eh, why?"

"You know how your father felt about the Art, Vladimir. He didn't want the two of us speaking of it. I hardly saw my son after his marriage, save when he brought you over after your mother passed on. I wish I could tell you what she was like, Vladimir. I remember she had a kind face and a soft voice, yes?"

I nodded; that much was more than I'd had before.

He said, "You know that, like me, she was not long in this land of elfs. I came from Fenario when—when I had to leave. But her father came, either before she was born, or when she was only in arms."

"Why did he leave?"

"She never said."

I nodded. "What was her name? I mean, before she was married?"

"I don't know," he said. "No—" He frowned. "Yes, I may know at that. A moment, Vladimir, while I search."

He left the room—a cozy little alcove that Noish-pa had turned into his library—and was gone for about half an hour. When he returned, he was holding a piece of parchment-cloth. He said, "I had this note of her. I have often puzzled over it."

I took it. It smelled the way cloth gets to smell when it's been in a drawer for years and years; it had yellowed a little. I studied it and frowned. "You can't read it either?"

"Oh, I can read it, Vladimir. It is a runic writing that is very, very old in Fenario. Some say it goes back to before the Fenarians settled there. It is still sometimes found in old tomes of the Art, which is why I learned it. I should have taught you."

"Well, if you can read it, what's the puzzle?"

He smiled the smile I knew so well: eyes twinkling with secrets that were fun, rather than secrets that could cut. He took it back; he had to hold it just a little farther away from his eyes than he had a few years before. He cleared his throat and read: "Father, the food was good and the evening delightful. Please accept my thanks on behalf of myself and Pishta. We both very much look forward to seeing you again. With love, Marishka Merss Taltos."

"Merss," I said.

He nodded.

Then I frowned. "Wait. What is puzzling about it?"

"Eh, Vladimir? You tell me." His eyes were twinkling again.

"Umm," I said. "Well, is it what it seems? I mean, did it come after a meal?"

He nodded.

"Then what—oh." It took me a moment, but I got it; first one piece, then the other. "In the first place, why did she use her full name when writing a thank-you note? In the second, why write a thank-you note in an ancient runic script?"

He nodded. "I still wonder."

I said, "Do you remember the dinner?"

"Oh, yes. Not often did your father visit me at that time."

"Noish-pa?"

"Hmm?"

"Was my mother pregnant when she wrote that?"

He frowned and his eyes narrowed and shifted up and to the right as his memory worked. After a moment he nodded.

I smiled. "It was meant for me, Noish-pa. To answer my questions, in case I lived and she died. She knew my father—"

He was grinning and nodding. "Yes. It must be!"

"I wonder where she was from?" I said.

He shrugged. "Merss, it is not a common name. Do you know its meaning?"

I shook my head.

"Pulper," he said. "And what is a pulper?"

"Um, it has something to do with wood. With making paper out of wood, I think."

He nodded and frowned. "I know of a town where much paper came from, in the west of Fenario where the River of Faerie is young and strong. Burz, it is called."

I laughed. "Burz? They named their town Burz?"

"Eh, perhaps making paper makes not such a pretty smell?"

"Maybe," I said.

A town called Burz with a paper factory and a bad smell, on the River—that was where my mother might have come from. And me with nothing to do except stay out of the clutches of the Jhereg. There would be all sorts of advantages to going East to the homeland of my mother and father. For one thing, a Dragaeran would stand out there even more than I stood out among the Dragaerans. For another, I had the strong feeling that they were going to use a Morganti weapon on me. And bringing such a weapon in among a group of witches would alert every one of them within a quarter of a mile. There are special sheaths made to conceal the effects of such a blade from a sorcerer—I knew, I'd used them a couple of times. But even if it were possible to construct a sheath to hide the psychic emanations a witch would feel, the Jhereg wouldn't know how to go about it. In fact, they might well not even be aware they needed to.

No question, it would be safer for me in the East.

And I could find my mother's family.

The conversation passed on to other things, and I never told him I was going East, but over the next several days I received lectures, in the same tones I remembered from when I was studying the Art, about Eastern customs, the political structures of Fenario, and the culture. He also began speaking Fenarian and demanded I did, too. He was very picky about my pronunciation, and even pickier about my accent.

Guilds and Covens.

We talked a lot about Guilds and Covens, and it was good that we did, because—but no, I'm getting ahead of myself. But I'll tell you some of it now, so that later you'll understand. Well, understand at least as well as I did, which wasn't very.

Guilds, I was told, were for trades—craftsmen—and were a means to have some way of defending themselves against the merchants who often sold their goods as middlemen. In some parts of Fenario, the craftsmen sold things directly, so there were fewer Guilds. In other parts, there were Guilds that took in large areas (well, relatively large; Fenario itself is a pretty small kingdom by my standards).

And nearly every town, no matter how small, had its Coven, occasionally open, but more often with its members secret. The Coven functioned as a Guild for witches, sometimes combining their powers into common spells, sometimes simply using the threat of their abilities to look out for the members' interests.

I asked him, "Are all witches usually members?"

"Vladimir, in Fenario, there are, ah, well, nearly all peasants know some little spell or another."

"Then who joins a Coven?"

"Those who use the Art a great deal. Many will sell their services, you know. And others, who gather and prepare the herbs."

"Like you. You'd be in a Coven if you were back there."

He nodded. "Many places, you can't help it. Those who do not join, but should . . ." He trailed off, leaving to my imagination what a Coven might do to an individual witch they didn't like.

"Is there ever more than one Coven?"

"Not for long," he said.

Guilds and Covens, Covens and Guilds. Yeah, it's a good thing he took the time to explain those to me.

We drank more brandy and ate more food, and finally, the day after Spring Balance day, I embraced him and said good-bye, which was how it came to be that I stood in the pass of Saestara, looking behind me into the future and before me into the past.

Below, at some vague point, was the end of the Empire, and the border of Fenario, land of ignorance and knowledge, superstition and science. Okay, well, maybe not so much with the science. But what do you call it when the superstitions might be true?

Loiosh on my right shoulder, Rocza on my left, I started down the mountain.

Part Two

APOPTERA

This stage will last from the moment of hatching until the layer of fat has been entirely consumed—usually four to five weeks. During this period, the apoptera, its fins fully grown by the time it has hatched, will remain entirely in the water while its basic organs develop. Curiously, the last of these is sight; the apoptera is blind until nearly the moment of transformation. Indeed, it is speculated by some natural philosophers (cf. Hidna, Corventra) that it is the first sensation of light that triggers its metamorphosis. . . .

Much remains unknown about the memory of the apoptera. Most of the assumptions in previous work about the "astonishing memory" at this stage are based on Leroni's work documenting its determination to explore every corner of its limited world. While its inquisitive nature cannot be denied, it has never been positively established that there is any memorization as such that carries on to later stages. Indeed, there is some indication to the contrary (see Appendix D this volume).

> —Oscaani: *Fauna of the Middle South: A Brief Survey,*
> Volume 6, Chapter 16

1

BORAAN: *A candle! As you love the Gods, a candle!*
NURSE: *But we have no candles!*
BORAAN: *How, no candles?*
NURSE: *They were all burned up in the flood.*
DAGLER: *Permit me to sell you this beeswax.*
  [Boraan strikes Dagler with candlestick]
  [Exit Dagler, holding his head]

—Miersen, *Six Parts Water*
Day One, Act IV, Scene 4

The transition from mountain to forest was so gradual, I wasn't entirely sure I was out of the mountains for a while even after I had turned north; and this in spite of them towering over me to my left. But eventually, I became convinced that I wasn't getting much lower, and soon enough, there was no question that I was in deep woods, with trees I can't name so close together I sometimes had to squeeze past them and with branches so low I had to duck to avoid getting hit in the face. The combination seemed unfair.

After that I felt more confident as I headed north, giving thanks for the occasional clearing, even though in the clearings I could see the Furnace, and it hurt my eyes.

I don't like forests. I hate the trees, and I hate the bushes, and I'm not even that fond of the paths, because they have a way of either suddenly heading off in directions you don't want to go, or just stopping without giving you any explanation for their conduct. When I was running my territory for the Jhereg, if any of my people had acted like that I'd have had their legs broken.

In the Pushta, you can usually see a good distance around you; you just have to keep an eye on what might be moving through the grasses. In the mountain, at least the mountains I've been on, you can see for miles in at least a couple of directions. In the city, you might not be able to see very far, but you can identify where anyone who might want to do you harm could be lurking. Forests are thick, and anything can come from anywhere; I never feel safe.

And sleeping is the worst. I spent about three nights in the forest after I came down from the mountains, and I didn't get a good night's sleep the entire time, in spite of the fact that Loiosh and Rocza were watching for me. I just couldn't relax. When I become ruler of the world, I'm going to have inns put up along every little road and trail in that place. I would certainly have gotten lost if it weren't for Loiosh and an occasional sight of the mountain.

I waded over several brooks and streams, one of which showed signs of becoming a river soon: it seemed to be in a terrible hurry, and had a lot of force for being only a foot or so deep and maybe ten feet wide. I didn't much care for that, either.

In spite of the annoyances, I was never in any danger so far as I know (though I'm told Dzur sometimes hunt the forests). I made it through; leave it at that. The trees became lower, sparser, and the grass taller, with large, jagged boulders intruding on the landscape as if the mountain were encroaching.

"Well, for marching blind, I guess we did all right, Loiosh."

"We sure did, Boss. And only modesty forbids me from saying how we managed."

"Heh."

An hour or so later we found a road. A real road. I could have danced, if I could dance. It was getting on toward evening, and the Furnace was sinking behind the mountains. The shadows—remarkably sharp, looking almost tangible—were long, and a certain chill was coming into the air on a breeze from behind me.

"That way," said my familiar, indicating down the road to the right. Since the mountains were to the left, I'd have figured that one out on my own, but I didn't say anything. I set out.

After mountain and forest, it was a positive luxury to walk on a road; even a rutted, gouged, untended road like this. My feet thanked me, as did my left elbow, which was no longer being cracked by my sword's pommel when I raised my left leg to climb onto a rock.

For an hour or so, I saw no one and nothing save a lone farmhouse far across a field. The shadows lengthened and Loiosh was silent and my mind wandered.

I thought about Cawti, of course. A few weeks ago, I'd been married. A few weeks before that, happily married; or at least I thought so. Anyone can make a mistake.

But what was odd was how little I was feeling it. It was pleasant walking down the road, and I was in good shape from all the climbing, and the evening wasn't too cold. I knew the whole thing was going to hit me—I mean, I *knew* it. It was like seeing an out-of-control team barreling down on you, and watching it come closer, and knowing it's going to flatten you. Here it comes, yep, I'm about to be either killed or messed up. Any second now. How interesting.

I could even be sort of dispassionate about it. I pondered whether I could convince her to take me back, and, if so, how? I ran through the arguments in my head, and they seemed very persuasive. I suspected they'd be less so when I actually tried them on her. And, even if she was convinced, I'd still have to deal with her politics, which is what had gotten between us in the first place.

And there was still the big problem, which was that circumstances had conspired to force me to save her. I don't know if I could have forgiven her if she had saved me; I didn't see how she could forgive me for saving her. It's an ugly burden. Eventually, I was going to have to try to overcome it.

And in the meantime, I was heading in the opposite direction, while somewhere behind there were people who wanted to get rich by putting the shine on me.

No, it didn't look good.

How interesting.

"We getting close to the water, Loiosh?"

"Wind shifted, Boss. I don't know."

"All right."

I should mention that nothing so far was at all familiar from my previous journey to Fenario, but that had been years before, and I wasn't paying all that much attention to my surroundings then.

With an abruptness that caught me by surprise, it was dark—I mean completely dark. There were small pinpoints of light in the sky, but they provided no illumination. Maybe they should have; I was told by a human physicker once that I had poor night vision. I could have had it corrected, but the process is painful, and a spell to compensate is absurdly easy. Except, of course, when you are unable to cast the simplest of spells for fear of removing the protections that keep the bad guys from finding you. So for now, little points of light or no, I was effectively blind. I wondered if failing to have that fixed when I could would end up being what did me in. Come to think of it, I still wonder.

I stepped a few paces off the road, and, having no better idea, took off my pack, spread out my blanket, and lay down. Loiosh and Rocza, I knew, would take care of any annoying beasts, and wake me if there were any dangerous ones. It wasn't until I was prone that I became aware of the sound of night insects all around me. I wondered if they were the sort that bit; then sleep took me.

Evidently they weren't the sort that bit.

I'd been walking about two hours the next day before I passed a young man driving a wagon filled with hay. I hailed him, and he stopped the horse—one of the biggest I'd ever seen—and greeted me. I had the impression he was a bit disconcerted by the jhereg on my shoulders, but was too polite to say anything.

"Which way to Burz?" I asked him.

He pointed the way I was going. "Over the bridge," he said, "in a while the road will fork, and there's a sign. You'll likely smell it after that."

"Good enough," I told him, and gave him a couple of copper pennies. He tapped his forehead, which I took as a gesture of thanks, and continued on his way.

I suddenly felt as if I was too relaxed, not paying enough attention, and resolved to stay a little more on my guard. Then it hit me that I had now made that resolution around a dozen times since coming down out of the mountains.

"I'm feeling safe, Loiosh. As if I'm out of danger. I can't decide if I should trust that feeling."

"I'm not sure, Boss, but I've been feeling the same way."

"Like we're out of their reach?"

"Yeah."

"Well, we probably are, but let's not trust it too much."

I found the bridge—it spanned a stream maybe twenty feet wide—and went "a while," which turned out to be most of the rest of the day. Once over the bridge, the road abruptly improved, showing signs of regular maintenance. I stopped a couple of times to eat bread, cheese, and sausage I'd gotten in Saestara (the village, not the mountain). The bread was getting stale, but it was still better than the hardtack. As I walked, I noticed that the forest, which I had thought was left behind me, seemed to be returning on my right; or maybe it was a different forest. I ought to have tried to find a map, I suppose, but I'm told they are hard to come by and rarely reliable.

Over the next several hours, the forest seemed to come closer, but avoided the road (I know, the road was dug around the forest, but I'm telling you how it looked, all right?). Eventually, I found the fork, and there was a sign just as there was supposed to be, on a stout wooden pole.

I followed it, and the road bent closer to the forest. It took us over low hills, and in places there were crops I didn't recognize in neat rows. More farmhouses appeared. The outbuildings were in good shape, and well painted. I tried not to look down on the locals for building everything out of wood; I knew that just came from living among Dragaerans. From an unbiased viewpoint, this seemed to be a more prosperous area than similar regions near Adrilankha. I wondered what Cawti would say if I made that observation to her.

The shadows lengthened, as the Furnace prepared to vanish behind the mountains, still looming up behind me. Presently, I became aware of a low rumble to my right, and I saw that the road had been joined by a fairly respectable river.

The Furnace plunged below the mountains, and it became significantly darker; still somewhat lit by the glow behind me, but—I was going to have to get used to how much more quickly it became dark, and how very much darker it was here. It had never occurred to me that the permanent overcast above the Empire might somehow provide a bit of ambient light, but apparently it does. I went another mile or so, and realized sadly that I was probably going to have to spend another night on the road.

The road curved as I came to the top of a hill, and below, still some distance away, was a very faint light. "*Check it out, Loiosh.*"

It was a long way away; I must have covered half a mile before he returned, and from what I could see it could still be anything from a bonfire to—

"*Just what you want, Boss. A nice little inn. And just beyond it, a nice little town. And, to judge from the smell, it is just the nice little town you're looking for.*"

"*You are hereby forgiven for the last nine things that require forgiving.*"

"*Speaking of smells, I think they have real food at the inn there, Boss. Just don't forget who your friends are.*"

It was full dark by the time I reached the door to the place. The light I'd seen came from two windows of oiled paper, and wasn't enough to let me see the sign. But I didn't need it by then. There was talking and laughing and the smell of bad beer and good food, stronger than the stench from—I presumed— the paper factory that I'd started to notice during the last few hundred yards.

I forced myself to ignore the growling of my stomach for a few minutes, while I stood near a window and let my eyes adjust; then I opened the thick door and stepped inside, moving at once to the side. I got a couple of glances, and Loiosh and Rocza got a couple more as I looked around. It was a two-story building, with doors in the back, but this room occupied most of the structure. A long, polished bar ran about half the length of the wall to my right, and there were a few score of people—

Easterners—humans—sitting at tables, leaning on the bar, or standing against walls.

I went up to the bar, and eventually a middle-aged human came over to me. He had a pot belly and wore a sleeveless brown tunic; his arm muscles were truly impressive. Before I could say anything, he gestured toward my familiars with his chin and said, "Get them out of here."

I studied him. He looked strong, but not very fast. His eyes were brown. After a moment, he looked away. I said, "Brandy. I also want some food." He barely nodded, poured, and said, "See one of the girls about the food." He retreated to the other end of the bar. I left him a couple of coins, then went over to find a blank piece of wall.

"*Ignorant prejudice, Boss. It's shameful—*"

"*Stay alert.*"

"*Yeah, yeah.*"

Eventually a young lady came by. She was dressed in red and blue and yellow and had nice ankles as well as a tray full of mugs and pitchers. "Food," I said as she passed by.

She stopped, noticed the reptiles on my shoulders, and seemed to consider whether she ought to be upset. Eventually she decided not to be, because she said, "There are some fowls roasting, lamb stew, and a hunter's stew."

"The hunter's stew."

She nodded, then looked around. "I don't think there's any place to sit."

"I can stand."

She made an effort at smiling, then turned and walked away. I used my finely honed powers of observation to make sure the ankles looked as good from the back. They did.

It was about then I noticed that, full as the room was, there were no women there at all except the three barmaids. I wasn't sure what that meant, but it was interesting.

I picked up bits and pieces of conversation. Not much was interesting, but they were speaking Fenarian, and the purity of the accent made me miss my grandfather although it had been only days since I'd seen him.

Presently, the ankles returned with a large bowl of hunter's stew, a big spoon, and a loaf of black bread that could have fed a family in South Adrilankha for a week. I set my drink down on a shelf against the wall—probably made for that purpose—paid her, and collected the food. She inspected the Dragaeran copper carefully, but accepted it without complaint.

The stew was pork (no, I don't know why they'd call something made with pork "hunter's stew," unless it was the tenderest wild boar in the history of cooking) and onions, and a delightful variety of mushroom I'd never had before and three kinds of peppers, peas, carrots, and some other sort of legume. The bread was still warm from the oven and it was perfect. I got a few looks as I fed bits to the jhereg, but no one seemed inclined to comment—maybe because I was the only one in the place openly carrying a weapon.

I was about halfway through the bowl when a table opened up in front of me and I was able to sit down. That was better. The place was beginning to clear out a bit. By the time I'd finished eating, there were only about a dozen left, all having quiet conversations. Most of them were elderly. The hard-core drinkers. I knew the type; I'd be willing to bet thirty hours from now I'd see the same faces in here.

I called a barmaid over. This one also had nice ankles; it seemed to be a requirement of the profession. I said, "Is it possible to get a room for the night?"

She had deep violet eyes, unusual for a Fenarian. She nodded and said, "You'll have to see the host."

"I will then," I said. "In the meantime, another brandy."

She headed off to get it while I relaxed and started realizing how tired I was getting. The thought of a real bed, the second since I'd left Noish-pa's, was enchanting.

I drank the brandy slowly, after it was delivered, enjoying the feeling that I was very tired and would soon rest. Then I went up to the host and asked about a room. He glanced at the jhereg on my shoulders, then nodded grudgingly, accepted a silver orb, and pointed toward a door in the back of the room.

The door led to a stairway, which ended in a hall, beyond which were doors. I opened the first one on the right, saw the bed, smiled, and stretched out on it. I gave a sigh of contentment and that's all I remember for a while.

The host was there the next morning when I came downstairs. He glanced at me, then returned to wiping down the bar. I walked out the door and took my first breath, which was no fun. Verra's tits and toenails, but it stank!

"Boss—"

"I know."

"Rocza doesn't like it."

"We'll get used to it."

"I hope not."

I tried to ignore the stench, and took a good look around.

The sign over my head showed a long pointed hat painted with red and white stripes. I didn't want to guess what they called the place. To the left was nothing. Well, okay, fields planted with wheat, and the road. To the right was a small town: a few score buildings and houses, and I could see some side streets heading off. Between some houses I could make out a river, with docks jutting out into it, and boats and barges tied to the docks, and the Furnace, bright enough that I had some trouble seeing the rest. I headed in that direction.

Not many people were on the streets; one woman in a faded blue dress and absurdly bright yellow shoes carried an infant into a shop; two old men sat on a low stone wall in front of a narrow house—I think they'd been in the inn last night; a young man wearing a battered silk hat drove a pushcart full of bits of iron, and seemed to be in no hurry to get where he was going.

As I passed the two old men, they stopped their conversation, and politely stared at me. No, I'm not sure how they did that. I turned right on a winding, narrow road, aiming for the docks. Two men were strolling in the same direction. One said, "How are things, Janchi?" to which the other replied, "Dreaming small," if I heard him right. Then they heard my footsteps, glanced back, and stood aside while I passed. I nodded to them. They nodded back, then stared politely.

The breeze was in my face as I approached the docks, and I could now see a large brick structure on the other side of the river, belching smoke. There were docks there too, and several barges. I stopped and watched for a while. There was an affair upstream of the dock that, after some study, I realized was a log corral; at least, that's all I can think to call it. It was a sort of slatted fence, complete with gate, and through the slats I could see logs floating.

The river was of respectable girth; I'd say a good quarter of a mile across. I watched it for a while. There is something calming about watching a river. I know some people get that feeling from watching the ocean, but I prefer a nice river. When I was a kid, I used to stand on the Chain Bridge and watch the Adrilankha River float by under me for hours at a time. This river didn't have any such pretensions; it didn't even have any river traffic, at least while I was watching just then. But it was soothing. I had never asked Cawti how she felt about rivers; it had somehow never come up.

I left my dignity there, then walked out to the end of the dock in front of me and sat down. The river was a sort of dingy brown, but if there was any smell to it, it couldn't penetrate the rotting-vegetation smell of the factory. I watched the river as if I had a reason to, as if I were on a job. But I wasn't. I didn't have anything I really had to do. I had idle curiosity about my mother's family, and a bit of a clue to follow up on, but it wasn't important. I'd maybe ask a few questions, and see if anyone could tell me anything, but beyond that, my life was focused around not letting the Jhereg get to me. I was going from, not toward. It was a new experience. I wasn't certain if it would come to bother me, someday in the future when I would start to feel things again. I wondered where I would be when that happened. Alone, I hoped.

I suddenly wished I had a handful of pebbles to throw into the water one at a time, to listen to them plunk and watch the ripples.

I must have sat there for a couple of hours; then I got up and went back to the inn, where the host was convinced to feed me some of yesterday's bread with a goat's milk cheese, smoked sausage, and some coffee with warmed cream, chocolate, and beet sugar. It was a little stuffy inside, and for just an instant I was going to ask him to open a window, when I realized why it was closed.

I finished eating and went back to the host, who was sitting on a tall stool behind the bar, his head back against the wall and his eyes closed. He opened them when my footsteps approached. I said, "My name is Vlad."

He hesitated, then said, "Inchay."

I nodded, and decided that was enough sociability for the moment; I headed back out into the stench.

You don't need to hear about the next several hours. I walked around, nodding to a few people and getting to know the town. It was big, as such places go, with a couple hundred identical shacks at the far end, a shoemaker and a dry goods store to support them, and a spot for the market to set up come

Endweek. The area around the shacks was a lot filthier than the farms I'd seen. And I saw other things, nothing worth noting.

As the shadows became long, I returned to the inn and had them feed me on a roasted fowl basted with sweet wine. As I was eating, two of the barmaids appeared wearing simple peasant gowns. They vanished into a room in the back of the inn, then emerged a few minutes later with their ankles showing and their breasts stretched taut against yellow or blue fabric. The one with curly, dark hair asked if I needed anything, and I accepted a glass of the local red wine, which was a bit acidic, but drinkable.

As it grew dark outside, the place filled up again. I was seated along the back wall, and this time, I suppose because I wasn't hungry and exhausted, I paid more attention to the people around me.

I realized that I knew at once those who worked at the paper factory, because they wore simpler clothing than the peasants who had dressed up to spend an evening drinking and wore bright blues and reds and yellows; those who worked in the mill wore simple clothing of dark green or brown. The young ones had long hair and were clean shaven; the older ones had mustaches or neatly trimmed beards. There were only a couple of small groups of these; most of the patrons were obviously peasants, some of them too young to shave. And there were still no women in the place, save the barmaids. The more I sat there, the stranger it seemed that it was so easy to identify which group they were part of, and that they all held so rigidly to their style. The groups didn't mix with each other, either.

To be sure, there were a few who didn't belong to any group: One fellow with bright, teary eyes who grinned a lot through several missing teeth and wore black pants and a white shirt with a blue coat and several rings. And another who had high red boots and mustaches that fell well below his chin. And the barrel-chested one in the blue felt vest with inky black hair that fell behind his shoulder in thick curls.

"What do you think of those three, Loiosh?"

"Dunno, Boss. If we were home, I'd take the toothy one and the mustached one as merchants. Couldn't guess about Curly."

"That's what I was thinking as well. How come there are no women in this place?"

"I couldn't guess, Boss. Ask someone?"

"I think I will."

While I was deciding what to ask, who to ask it of, and how to approach it, the problem was taken out of my hands by the guy in the blue felt vest, who came up to my table, glanced at the jhereg on my shoulders, and said, "Mind if I join you?"

I nodded at one of the empty chairs.

He sat down smoothly and held up a hand; in a few minutes, a barmaid came over and brought him a tiny porcelain cup, which he lifted in my direction. "Barash Orbahn. Call me Orbahn."

"Merss Vladimir," I lied, lifting my own. "Vlad."

He frowned a little. "Merss? An unusual name."

"Yes," I said.

He downed his drink and winced, shivered, shook his head, and smiled. I sipped from mine. "What are you drinking?"

"Rakia. Plum brandy."

"Ah. I should have guessed. My grandfather used to look like that when he drank it."

He nodded. "It's imported from the South. I don't know why we import it, or why anyone drinks it. A test of manhood, maybe." He grinned. He had all of his teeth, and they were very white.

I chuckled. "The local palinka is good, and I think safer."

"A wise man," he said. Then, "If you'll forgive me, you have a trace of something foreign in your speech."

I nodded. "I've come here from some distance away."

"And yet, your name is distinctly local."

"Is it?" I said. "I hadn't realized."

He nodded.

"Not surprising," I said after a moment. "I have family from here."

"Family? Or kin?"

In Fenarian, those are different words, with rather more of a difference than in the Northwestern language. "Kin," I said. "Think you might know anyone I might be related to?"

"Hmm. I'll have to think about it. This is a pretty big town, you know."

No, it wasn't. "Yes, it is."

After a moment I said, "No offense to your town, but it stinks."

He smiled. "Yes, I suppose. Believe it or not, after a while you don't notice it at all."

"You can get used to anything, I suppose."

"Indeed."

"Maybe you can tell me something else."

"Sure."

"Why aren't there any women in here?"

His eyes widened. "Women go into taverns where you're from?"

"If they want a drink."

"I see. That, ah, doesn't happen here."

"Why not?"

"Well, because . . ." He frowned and seemed to be searching for words. "Because it wouldn't be right," he finally said.

I nodded and didn't push it. "What do you do?"

"Beg pardon? Oh. I import and export liquor."

"So the rakia is your fault?"

He smiled and nodded. "I drink it as a sort of penance."

"A man of high moral character, I see."

"Not that high; I'm a trader." He signaled the barmaid and she brought him another. "So, ask me your next question; it seems I am today the man with the answers."

"All right," I said. "Why are the streets so wide?"

"Eh? Are they?"

"Wider than I'm used to. A lot wider."

"Hmmm. Well, the streets you're used to—why are they so narrow?"

"A fair question," I said, "only you claimed to be the one with the answers."

He smiled his smile—it was the sort that makes you think that by smiling he was losing a round. His drink came. He raised it and said, "Welcome to our city and our country, *boyore*."

I felt my eyebrows climb. "*Boyore?* Why do you call me that?"

"It's as clear as Doroatya's ankles. You're used to giving orders, and expecting them to be obeyed."

"Am I?" I said. "Interesting."

"Not to mention the rather long piece of steel at your side."

"Yes, I guess that's unusual around here."

"I'll not pass it around, if you don't wish me to; but unless you begin to walk differently, and start looking down a bit more, you can expect the peasants to bow and call you 'my lord' and stand aside when they meet you on the street. But then," he added, "perhaps they'll not meet you at all, what with the streets being so wide."

He laughed a little as if deucedly pleased with his cleverness. I smiled and nodded and sipped my wine.

"Where are you from that women go into bars, and streets are narrow?"

"Oh. Sorry, I'd thought it was obvious. I live on the other side of the mountain, the Dragaeran Empire."

"Ah. Yes, I sort of suspected that, but I wasn't sure, and I didn't know if you'd want it known."

"Why not? I can't be the first human to come back here."

"Here? Yes, you're the first one I know of. I've seen a few others in my travels, but they don't stop in Burz. And they don't seem as, well, as aristocratic as you. At least, not until they reach Fenario, or Esania, or Arenthia, and find out they have magic no one else has."

"Mmm. I hadn't thought about that."

"Hadn't you? I assume you have the same sort of magic."

"You seem pretty blasé about magic."

He shrugged. "Not everyone is. You know about the Art we practice; I see signs of it about you. Is it really so different?"

Yes, it was. "No, not really," I said.

He nodded. "I can't tell if you follow the light or the darkness, of course; they, too, aren't as different as many think."

I nodded, wondering what he was talking about. I said, "What generally happens to these people you mention, the ones with the magic no one else has?"

"Usually they set themselves up as minor lordlings until someone, ah, puts them down, if you know what I mean. No one has done that around here, though; at least, not in my lifetime. Which is good, because the King never turns his attention this far west, and sometimes the King has to be the one to deal with them."

I nodded. "Well, if that's what you're worried about, you don't need to. I'm not especially interested in becoming a minor lordling. Or a major one, for that matter."

He studied me. "No, I don't imagine you are." I wasn't at all sure how to take that, so I just let it go past.

We drank for a few minutes, and then he said, "It's getting late; I should be going."

I said, "Is there any chance you might be able to find out anything about my people?"

"Sure," he said. "I'll ask a few questions, see what I can learn."

"I'd take that as a great kindness," I said. "Where and when shall I meet you?"

"Right here is good. Say, sometime around noon?"

"Lunch is on me," I told him.

He smiled and stood up. "See you then," he said.

As he walked away, I drank more wine and considered.

"What do you suppose he is, Loiosh?"

"Not sure, Boss. I suppose there is always the possibility that he's just what he claims to be."

"No," I said. *"There isn't."*

2

LEFITT: *But that's a body!*

BORAAN: *I had already come to the same conclusion, my dear.*

LEFITT: *But, how long has it been there?*

BORAAN: *Oh, not more than a week, I should say. Two at the outside.*

LEFITT: *A week? How can it have been here for a week?*

BORAAN: *Well, the servants must have been dusting it, or you would certainly have noticed and spoken to them quite sharply about it.*

—Miersen, *Six Parts Water*
Day One, Act I, Scene 1

Loiosh was silent for a moment, and then he said, "*Okay, Boss. What did you see that I didn't?*"

"Not saw; heard. Or rather, what I didn't hear. What he didn't ask."

It took him a few seconds. Then he said, "*Oh. Right. He should have asked what you were doing here.*"

"Exactly."

"*Maybe he's just polite.*"

"Loiosh, no one who lives in a small, out-of-the-way town can have a conversation with a stranger without asking what brings him there. It defies the laws of nature."

"Which means he knows, or he thinks he does. You're pretty smart for a mammal."

"Thank you ever so much."

"The Jhereg, you think?"

"I intend to assume so until I have a reason not to."

"So, then, what about tomorrow?"

"What's your guess, Loiosh?"

"What we should do is be out of here tonight. But knowing you—"

"And then we'd have him after us and not know where we stood. No. I want him where I can keep an eye on him."

"You're the boss, Boss."

I got up and walked out into the stench and the dark streets, mostly to see if he'd have me followed. As soon as we were outside, Loiosh and Rocza took to the air. I didn't need to tell my familiar what I was doing; we'd been together for a while. My rapier tapped reassuringly at my side. I'd had to reduce the weight I carried before trying the mountains, but I still had a few little surprises concealed about my person; I didn't plan on being easy prey.

The street was pretty quiet, and looked entirely different in the dark. Not sinister, but, well, more like it had secrets it wanted to keep. Lights came from the houses, diffused by the oiled paper. Many were entirely dark, either because there was no light within, or because here in the East, where it is so much brighter during the day, they had perfected shutters. I could hear the tap-crunch of my boots against the well-packed stony dirt of the street. The reek from the paper factory had diminished, though it was still present; it had probably seeped into all the walls and the dirt of the road itself.

"Anyone?"

"Not a soul, Boss."

"Good."

Sometime while I was walking the wind shifted, and the smell, while still present, became easier to bear. In the stillness, I heard the river lapping against the docks not far away, and chittering of insects. I shivered a little.

This was where my mother had come from; or her people, at any rate. Why had they left? Famine? Disease? Tyranny? Powerful enemies? But whatever had made them leave, this is where they were from, and in a sense, this is where I was from.

And it seemed those who wanted to kill me had tracked me here. How nice.

I found that I was fingering the hilt of the dagger in my left sleeve and stopped doing it. I did, however, touch Spellbreaker, wrapped around my left wrist; where there are Dragaerans, there is sorcery. Spellbreaker's presence was reassuring in spite of the gold Phoenix Stone I bore around my neck, which ought to protect me even if I weren't paying attention. When my life is involved, I like over-protection.

Well, if anyone carried a Morganti blade around here, every witch would know about it. And if a Jhereg—or any Dragaeran— showed up, he'd stand out like Dzur Mountain. I'd once been told that my friend Morrolan had been raised somewhere in human lands, and hadn't known he was Dragaeran—just thought he was a very tall human. I'd never asked him if it was true, but I didn't believe it; the differences were too obvious. No, if a Jhereg showed up in town, I'd know it.

I walked to the other end of the town—it wasn't far, maybe an hour's walk. I reached the tavern I'd noticed earlier; it had a small, neat sign showing a small animal I couldn't identify in the dim light. I didn't go in, but made a note of it for later. No one came out as I walked by.

"Hey, Boss, remember a couple of days ago, you said you were getting too comfortable?"

"Yeah, I guess we don't have to worry about that anymore, do we?"

As far as I could tell, the town just stopped; all of a sudden there were no shops, no buildings, just the road going on, parallel to the river. I turned around and walked back. By the time I returned to my inn, the place was pretty quiet and the guy in the blue vest had gone. I went up to my room and slept.

I was awoken the next morning by a horrid light in my eyes, which I eventually figured out was the Furnace; I had neglected to close the shutters. Shutters are much more important in the East than they are back home.

I stumbled out of bed and dressed. I checked the garrote in the collar of my cloak (wondering why I still carried that; I'd never used a garrote in my life, and wasn't even sure I knew how), the throwing knives and shuriken in its lining, and the few daggers I still carried. After some thought, thinking over what Orbahn had said, I left my rapier in the room. I had enough hardware on me without it, and I wanted to see what would happen if I were less overtly dangerous.

Morning: the Furnace slanting down more sharply than my knives; a few kids playing in the street; the occasional woman, with or without a babe in her arms, visiting a shop; lots of people heading off to work in order to produce ugly smells for miles around. I wondered how much paper they produced at that place. They must ship whole bargefuls of it down the river. Who needed that much paper? And for what?

Loiosh and Rocza took their places on my shoulders—Loiosh taking the left today. I never knew how they picked who was where, and I wouldn't give Loiosh the satisfaction of asking. I had once thought it was a complicated division of labor; now I'm inclined to think they do it just to make me wonder.

As I walked, I gave some thought to how I was going to go about finding my family. Excuse me, my "kin." Two months ago, it would have been easy. I'd have said, "Kragar, find out if I have any family in this village." He'd have made a couple of snide remarks, and a few people would have been bribed, and a few threatened or slapped around, and I'd have had my answers. Now I had to do it myself. I had an image of walking through the area stopping at every peasant's shack and saying, "Ever heard the name 'Merss' before?" I didn't like it much. A few untended kethna wandered around on their under-sized cloven hooves, snorting and snuffling and looking for victuals. Presumably, they were owned by various people; I wondered how their owners told them apart. Were kethna smart enough to know where home was? If so, and given their ultimate fate, were they smart enough not to go there?

Across the street, a chubby guy with a fringe of white hair was raising a wooden awning, supported on two posts, and it came to me that this was so people could stand in front of his shop without the light of the Furnace blinding them. I guess I was just beginning to realize how much having the Furnace blazing down affects everything you do. I would have to try to stay aware of that.

I crossed over to him. He gave me the usual merchant appraising glance, the one where he's decided if you might actually buy something. He didn't seem especially excited by me, but managed a nod. Hanging from hooks and sitting on sturdy tables were teapots, coffeepots, hinges, cups, boilers, and even some engraved plates, all of them in that reddish gold color. I warmed to him; I always admire people who can make things.

"You're a tinsmith," I said.

He raised an eyebrow and sniffed. "Hardly. I'm a respectable merchant and a member of the Guild. All of the tinsmiths sell through this shop, or they don't sell around here."

Suddenly I wanted to see how many coffeepots I could shove down his throat. I said, "I see," and continued looking around the shop. He watched me like I was going to steal something. I was tempted to, just on principle.

"Boss, remind me again why you won't kill an Easterner."

"I never said I wouldn't kill an Easterner. I said I won't accept money to kill an Easterner."

"In that case—"

"I am not killing him, and no, you may not eat him even if I do. Besides, that much fat would be bad for you."

I studied the wares, careful not to touch anything, because if he'd said anything about "handling the goods" I would have killed him.

"The Guild," I repeated.

"Yes, young man. So watch your step."

"I'm new in town. What guild is that?"

He sniffed. "The Merchants' Guild, of course."

"Ah. Of course."

"Boss—"

"Hush. I'm working." I gave the guy the sort of smile that means nothing and said, "This is a local Guild, or is it part of a larger Guild throughout the country?"

He gave me what I'm sure he thought was a Penetrating Stare. "Why would you want to know that?"

"Just curious."

"Why do you want to know that?"

"Just curious."

It was interesting, though. Last night, there was someone who had just assumed I was an aristocrat; and now this guy just assumed I was some sort of thug, or criminal. I hate it when people make those kinds of assumptions about me. It makes me want to break their legs.

I said, "Does the name Merss mean anything to you?"

His scowl deepened. "Are you threatening me?"

"No."

"I don't respond to threats, young man."

"That's good, because I don't issue them."

"I think you had best leave my establishment."

Establishment. He had an establishment.

I shrugged and walked out because I didn't think staying would be productive, and because that was probably the last thing he expected me to do.

"That," I told Loiosh, *"was one of the more interesting conversations I've had in a life full of interesting conversations."*

"Meaning you have no idea what just happened, right?"

"Right. Only something did. Didn't it?"

"Sure, Boss. Is there a reason you think it might be connected with what you're looking for?"

"Loiosh, I mentioned the name of my family and he thought I was threatening him."

He didn't answer.

I walked down the street about ten paces before I was hit with a wave of nostalgia like I hadn't thought I could feel. I was standing in front of a tiny little place, with what looked like a fresh coat of dark green stain on the thin-looking exterior, and no window, and a doorway covered by a thick curtain of pale wool. Hanging from the low eaves were herbs: mistletoe, koelsch, thyme, spinnerseed, eddieberry. My grandfather's shop had looked different, but smelled the same. I stood outside for a moment, feeling the smile on my lips, then pushed aside the curtain and went in.

It was dark inside, a smoky, flickering lamp at either end making the pottery on shelves and plants on hangers jump and twitch. As I stood there, my eyes adjusting to the darkness, the flickering subsided.

The fellow in the shop was nothing like my grandfather. He

had one of those faces that looked like someone had grabbed hold of the chin and pulled, with a high domed forehead and a receding hairline to increase the effect. He wore a sweat-stained singlet that had once been blue and loose pantaloons of brown. I couldn't guess his age within thirty years. He looked me up and down with pale brown eyes and an expression that reminded me of the guy I'd just been speaking with. It was obvious he didn't like me. Maybe it was the jhereg on my shoulders. Then again, maybe it was just me. I refrained from breaking his left kneecap and right instep. I didn't even think about it.

He dipped his head in a bow so perfunctory he could have taught Morrolan a few things about being rudely polite, and waited for me to say something. I finally settled on, "Have you any shaba-salt?"

"No," he said.

I paused, then decided on the direct approach. "What's the problem?"

"No problem," he said, tight-lipped. "I don't have any, that's all."

"Not that. Your attitude. What have I done to you? You don't like how I'm dressed or something?"

"You're a witch," he said.

Now, that I gotta explain. "Witch" is the only way to translate it, but what he actually used was a Fenarian word, *erdergbassor*, that means, sort of, "witch who does nasty things to people," or maybe, "witch who studies things nice people don't talk about." Something like that. It was a word I knew, but not one I'd ever expected to hear directed at my sweet, lovable self.

I spoke to my familiar, who had picked up the translation from my mind. *"Loiosh? Any ideas?"*

"Color me stunned, Boss. Not a clue."

I drew a little circle on the counter with my finger, while looking at the merchant—I call him a merchant because I had trouble thinking of him as a witch. "I've never been called that before," I told him.

"Don't threaten me, young man. I'm a mem—"

"Member of the Guild," I said it with him. "Yeah. So, what is it that makes me a witch?" I asked him, using that same word.

He just glared at me. I wondered how long I could go without needing to hurt someone. It was odd: while surrounded by Dragaerans, I was never tempted to start messing with humans; but here, with no Dragaerans around, the idea didn't bother me a bit. In fact, it was getting more tempting by the minute. The last time I had been in this land, years before, I hadn't met all that many people, but those I'd met had been pleasant. I guess between that and the stories of my grandfather, I'd built it up in my head as some sort of paradise. Yeah, well.

"I'm serious," I said. "What makes you think—"

"Young man," he said, "either you are a fool, or you think I am. I know a familiar when I see one."

Oh. Well. So it was Loiosh after all. Who knew? But there were implications in there that hurt my head to think about. So I said, "All right. Do you know a family named Merss?"

"The door is that way, young man."

And, once again, it was either walk out the door or use violence. I was sure I'd come up with some good remark to use on him tomorrow; meanwhile I pushed my way past the curtain and back into the street.

The next place was a shoemaker's, and the smell of leather and oils overpowered even the stench of the town. I'll spare you the details; the results were no better. These people just flat out didn't like me. I felt myself starting to get angry, and sat on the feeling; right now that wouldn't do any good. I needed to figure out what was going on.

"Three in a row, Boss. Convinced?"

"Yeah, only I'm not sure what I'm convinced of exactly."

He wasn't able to enlighten me, so I took us back to the inn, glancing at other shops as we walked, but not going in any. The shutters were open this time, and I concluded it must have to do with wind direction. Orbahn wasn't there when I arrived—in fact, I nearly had the place to myself—so I found a corner and a glass of strong red wine (actually, it looked more purple to me) and settled in to wait for him. The wine was decent.

After an hour or so I got a plate of lamb stew with leeks and garlic and a dollop of sour cream, and some thick-crusted bread. An hour after that Orbahn showed up. He didn't waste any time; he looked around, saw me, and came right over.

"And how has your day been?" he asked me, signaling to the barmaid.

"Interesting," I said. He ordered a drink, and I reminded him that I was buying lunch, so he got a bowl of the same stew I was having. "I'm not sure where to begin. Any idea why I might have been called an *erdergbassor?*"

His eyebrows climbed a little. "Hmmm. Who called you that?"

"The fellow that owns the witchcraft supply shop."

"Oh. Him." He shrugged. "I'll talk to him."

"No, no. Don't bother. I'm just curious. He seemed to think, either because my familiar is a jhereg, or because I have a familiar, that—"

"It's because your familiars are jhereg," he said. "A lot of people here think that means you follow the dark way, that those who follow the light have birds or cats, occasionally ferrets. Not reptiles."

"Oh. Odd."

"It is odd. It's a strictly local belief."

"This is a peculiar town."

He shrugged. "Just be careful here."

"Eh? What do you mean?"

"I mean, don't ask too many questions."

"Why? I came here to find some things out."

"I know. But, well, just be careful, all right? There are people here—"

"The Guild?"

He stopped in mid-sentence. "Ah," he said. "You've found out about that?"

"I've found out it exists, and that it isn't like any other guild I've ever heard of."

He rubbed his chin. "I was born here, you know."

"All right."

"And I need to do business here."

"I understand."

"If you get on the wrong side of the Guild, don't expect me to help you. Or even say hello when we pass on the street."

"All right. That's clear enough. But, until then, what can you tell me about it?"

He hesitated, then shrugged. "It's old, it's powerful."

"And all-inclusive? That is, no merchant is going to survive without being in the Guild?"

He nodded.

I said, "And this is strictly local?"

"Other towns have Guilds; most of them do. But this one is, ah, unique."

"How did it come about?"

"I don't know; it's been around as long as anyone can remember."

"Who is in charge?"

"There's a leader of the Guild. His name is Chayoor."

"Of course it is. Where does he live?"

"Why?"

"If I'm going to avoid trouble with the Guild, that would seem like the place to start."

He shook his head. "It's up to you, but I wouldn't. I think you ought to stay as far from it as you can."

I sipped my wine, wondering just how far I could trust this guy. Loiosh sort of shifted on my shoulder; he was wondering too. I decided not very far, for now. I don't trust people easily. I guess that surprises you.

"All right," I said. "I'll keep that in mind. I really just want to find my family, if there are any still here. Then I plan to move on. There isn't a lot for me in this town."

He nodded. "I had no luck with that," he said. "Wish I could help you."

"Thanks for trying."

He nodded. "I think this town isn't good for you. I don't mean that as a threat," he said quickly, I guess seeing some look on my face. "I have nothing against you. It's just a warning. If you keep poking around, it's going to get less comfortable. I'm sort of outside of things, I'm not involved as much as a lot of others because I travel so much. I don't have to be as, well, protective of the interests of the town. But I'm still part of it, know what I mean?"

"In fact," I said, "I haven't the least idea. But I'm curious."

"Mmm," he said. He drank about half of his glass, showing no more expression than if it had been water, and looked thoughtful. "I guess what I'm saying is that I can warn you, but if you get into trouble, I can't protect you."

"Oh," I said. "All right. Fair enough. I've only spoken to merchants, so far. I trust the common folk are not in the Guild. I'll ask among them later."

He shook his head. "You'll do as you wish, of course. But I think it would be a mistake."

"You think the Guild will notice?"

"Unless you're pretty careful. And you do stand out here, you know."

There was something amusing about the idea that I, a human, could blend into a crowd of Dragaerans without being seen, but here, among my own people, I stood out. Still, he was probably right.

"Why are you helping me?" I asked him. Sometimes a blunt question can shock someone into an honest answer.

He shrugged. "You seem an all-right fellow. If you saw a stranger going for a stroll in a direction where you knew there was a nasty bog, wouldn't you mention it?"

Probably not. "I suppose so," I said.

"Well, Loiosh? What do you think?"

"Boss?"

"Is he warning me away for my own good, or because he doesn't want me learning something?"

"How should I know? Could be both."

"Mmmm. Good point."

"Can I buy you another drink?" I asked him.

"No, I'm fine. I need to be running anyway. I need to make sure the people preparing my next shipment aren't lightening the burden by drinking it all." He grinned and stood up.

"Okay," I said. "Thanks for the information, and the advice. I owe you." Exactly what I owed him was still to be determined.

He made a dismissing gesture and walked out of the inn.

I sat there for a while, watching my fingers draw circles in the moisture on the table. One thing just wouldn't leave my head: When I had asked the tradesman if he knew anyone named Merss, he had thought I was threatening him. That was just too intriguing to pass up. Sitting and thinking about it would tell me nothing.

Presently I got up and went out.

3

The smell wasn't as bad. There was a wind from the west and it was cold, too cold for mid-spring. I pulled my cloak around me and thought about going back to my room to get warmer stuff, but then I'd have to put up with remarks from Loiosh, and it didn't seem worth it.

"Boss?"

"Yeah?"

"What now?"

"Now I find someone who'll talk to me."

"So, you don't trust him?"

"Yes. No. I don't know. I need to know more. And, dammit, I want to find them."

"Why?"

"Loiosh—"

"No, Boss, really. When we came over the mountain, it was something to do since we were here anyway. Now it's become this thing you have to do. Why?"

Part of his job is asking me the hard questions.

While I was trying to think up a good answer, my feet carried me over to the pier. If you've lost track, it was the middle of the day. The factory across the river was belching gray smoke into the air. The wind was coming from the mountains (which I'm told is unusual) so at least the stench wasn't bad. People—not many, mostly mothers with children in arms—were walking along the streets behind me. I didn't worry about them, because Loiosh was—

"Someone's coming, Boss. Woman, doesn't seem threatening, and doesn't seem to be walking up to you in particular."

"Okay."

I didn't turn around, and presently there were footfalls behind and to my right. Soft-soled shoes that quietly "sa-wooshed," probably darr skin or something like it. I saw her out of the corner of my eye, about ten feet away, and turned and nodded. She nodded back. She was around my age, maybe a bit older. Her eyes, which I noticed first, were an intriguing gray; her hair was black, I suspected dyed, and fell in long ringlets well past her shoulders. Her nose was straight, her form very pleasant, curvy; some time in my past I'd have been interested, and that part of me must not have been completely dead or I'd not have noticed. She wore long silvery ear-rings, and several rings on her fingers. Her dress was forest green, with a low, square neckline, and large obvious ties down the front; it didn't quite reach her ankles and the red ruffle of her flaisl* was just visible below the hem. She wore slippers the same color as her eyes.

I turned back to studying the smoke from the factory. She seemed to be doing the same. After a few minutes she said, "Looking for a little fun?"

"No thanks," I said. "I hate fun. Never wanted any. Even as a child, I'd run and hide if it looked like someone wanted me to have fun. I was pleased to grow up, because now I can go through the rest of my life without ever having fun."

She laughed perfunctorily then gave a sort of sigh and continued watching the factory. I figured her work-day would likely begin when the place closed for the evening.

"Is the Guild in charge of your profession too?" I asked her.

You never know how tags will react to questions about their work. Sometimes they'll talk about it the way you'd talk about the prospective harvest if the frost didn't come early; sometimes they'd give a sort of haughty glance as if figuring you were getting excited by asking; sometimes they'd become angry as if any question about how they made their daily bread was more personal than the act itself—which I guess maybe it was.

She just said, "The Guild runs everything."

"I was getting that impression. I'm Vlad."

She looked at me, then looked back across the river. "Well met, Vlad. I'm Tereza. What in the name of the Three Sisters would bring you to *this* crappy little town?"

There were lines in the corners of her eyes and on her forehead that she hadn't quite managed to conceal with her

---

*A flaisl, it turns out, is a warm, abstract-pattern fabric used by prairie prostitutes for colorful yet comfortable petticoats during the cold winters. Thanks to K. Christie for finding that out for me.—SB

makeup, but I guess the makeup wasn't expected to function in full light. The lines made her more attractive.

"I came for the aroma."

A smile flickered quickly.

"In fact," I went on, "I've been standing here asking myself the same question. Mostly, I'm passing through on the way to somewhere else. Or I guess from somewhere else. But I understand I have kin somewhere around here, and I'd like to find them."

"Oh. Who?"

"The name is Merss."

She turned her head and gave me a long, measuring look. I waited.

"I can't help you," she said at last.

I nodded. "I'm beginning to suspect they aren't here at all," I said, because a good lie can loosen tongues better than a bad truth.

"I know who would be will—that is, able to tell you many things about this town," she said.

"Oh? Well, that's the most hopeful thing I've heard today."

She hesitated, then said, "It'll cost you."

I looked at her.

She sighed. "Oh, all right. There's a public house called the Cellar Mouse."

"Yes, I saw it."

"In back of it are stables. Most nights, there will be a man there named Zollie. He's the coachman for Count Saekeresh. He knows everyone and everything, and he's the Lord's coachman so no one can touch him; or at least so he thinks. Get him liquored up a bit and he'll tell you anything."

I dug an imperial out, walked over and put it into her palm. She did that thing people do when judging the weight of a coin, and said, "Is it gold?"

"Pure. Don't spend it all in one place."

She laughed. "I owe you, Vlad. Fenario, here I come!" She grinned and kissed my cheek. She was nearly as tall as I was. She was much more attractive when she was smiling. I watched as she walked away, a nice spring in her step.

After a bit, I took myself over to the Cellar Mouse, which was a lot like the Pointy Hat (as I'd started calling the other place in my head) except the room was longer and the ceiling a bit higher. The tables were all small and round. After the usual reserved but not-unfriendly nods, I took a glass of wine to a small table and set in to nursing it until the evening.

The place started filling up quickly as dark came, mostly with men who had both the look and the smell of the factory across the river. There were also a few girls, all of whom wore gowns with obvious ties down the front and ankles uncovered. Sometimes one would leave with a workman, heading into the back. A couple of them looked at me, but none came over.

I studied the people, for lack of anything else to do, and worked on memorizing the faces for no reason except that it's good practice. Eventually, I made my way out the door and around back. The stable was directly to the rear about fifty feet, and, from what I could see, connected to a sort of paddock. Outside of it was a tall coach, and even in the dim light that leaked out of the inn it seemed to glisten. There was a marking of some sort on the door, and no horses were attached. Where there was a coach, there would be a coachman. And where there's a coachman, there are stories. And where there are stories, there are answers to questions, and maybe even the right ones.

I went in.

It smelled of fresh hay, old hay, wet hay, moldy hay, and manure. It was a big improvement. There were ten stalls, four of which were occupied by horses of various colors and sizes, the fifth by a skinny fellow wearing black, with a high-domed forehead over thick brows, making him look, well, a bit ridiculous. His hands were folded over his stomach, and there were several odd white scars crisscrossing the backs of them. He sat on a low stool, and his eyes were closed, but opened as I came closer; I saw no trace of sleep in them, nor sign of drunkenness—the latter being unusual, if you believe all you've heard about coachmen.

"If you've come for a ride to the manor," he said in a clear voice, somewhat higher pitched than you'd guess from looking at him, "you're too late. If you've come for a story, you're too early. If you've come to buy me a drink, your timing could not be improved."

"I have questions and money," I said.

"Make the money liquid, and I'll answer the questions."

"Good enough. What do you wish?"

"Wine. White wine. And the better it is, the better your answers will be."

"I'll be back directly."

He nodded and closed his eyes.

He opened them a few minutes later when I returned with his wine as well as something red for myself. He sniffed his, drank it, nodded, and said, "Grab a stool." There were a few low three-legged stools like a cobbler uses; I took one and sat on it opposite him. The horses shifted around, and one of them eyed me suspiciously as I walked in front of him. Or her. Or it. Or maybe it was looking at Loiosh and Rocza.

I sat down and said, "My name is Vlad."

He nodded. "They just call me Zollie, Kahchish, or Chish." He took some more wine. "Good choice. All right, Vlad. You had questions?"

"Many, many, many."

His smile was friendly. I believed it, provisionally. So, where to start?

"Do you know a family called Merss?"

"Sure," he said. "About six miles north, the little road past the walnut trees. Big white house that looks like it's been added to a lot. Unless you mean the cousins; they moved away some years ago. I don't know where, but probably to Fenario. The city, I mean."

"Oh," I said. "Thanks."

"It's about a half-hour ride."

"I don't ride."

He looked genuinely startled. "You've never been on a horse?"

"I have been; that's why I don't ride."

"Mmmm. Very well. What else?"

"Why wouldn't anyone else answer my question about them?"

"They're scared of the Guild."

"Yeah," I said. "The Guild. That would be my next question."

"It's everyone's question. Mine too. No one quite knows how it came to be what it is."

"You must know some of the history."

He finished his wine and held the mug out to me. "Some," he said.

"Keep it," I told him. "I'll be back with a jug."

"I'll be here," he said.

The place had filled up a bit, so it took me about ten minutes to get back. I handed him the jug and settled down again. "All right," I said. "The Guild."

"Yes. The Guild." He studied me for a bit. "Why the interest?"

"I kept running into them while I was trying to learn about the Merss family."

He studied me more carefully. "They're kin, aren't they?"

"I always thought I took after my father."

"The way your nostrils flare. Most of them have that. Is that what brings you to Burz?"

"Yes and no," I said.

He waited for me to continue, and when I didn't he just shrugged.

"Fenario is old kingdom, Vlad. Very old. Two thousand years, the same people, in the same land."

I didn't comment on how short two thousand years would seem to Morrolan or Aliera, much less to Sethra; I just nodded.

He continued, "The borders have shifted a bit over the years, and other things have changed." I nodded, because he seemed to expect it. He continued. "For the last few hundreds of years, the King hasn't been too concerned with the outlying provinces. He's done what he's had to to make sure the borders are secure, and other than that, pretty much left it up to the local Count to do as he would."

"Except for his taxes, I suppose."

"Sometimes yes, sometimes no."

"Mmm."

He shrugged. "Believe me, or not. As often as not, the King doesn't seem to care if the taxes are collected. At least, this far west. I suppose if he demands too much, he'll only encourage smuggling."

"All right," I said.

"So when things happened, we were on our own."

"What things?"

"The story is that the Count, the old Count, my Lord's grandfather, went off his head. Started thinking all the witches were trying to kill him or something."

"Were they?"

"Eventually."

"Hmmm."

"I don't know the whole story, of course. No one does. But somehow, the local witches split themselves into those who wanted to hide from the Count until his madness passed, and those who wanted to do something."

"Something like . . . ?"

"I don't know. Kill him? Cure him? What's the difference?"

"You remind me of some people I know."

He poured more wine into his mug. "So there was a long time—ten years? twenty? thirty?—when all the Count was doing was fighting witches. There are songs that list the diseases he contracted and was cured of. They probably aren't true either, but I imagine he was pretty busy. Still, things had to be managed, so it ended up with the Merchants' Guild more or less running things."

"Well, and later Counts? Didn't they have anything to say about that?"

"As I understand it, the old Count's son settled things for good and all."

"How did he do that?"

"Made a deal. You don't hurt me, I won't hurt you. Usually the Count is happy to get his silver and sit at home complaining about poachers."

"Strange."

"It's a strange town."

"Yes, you can smell that much."

He nodded. "The peasants don't like the stench from the factory, and they don't like all of their sons leaving the land to work indoors, but the factory is how the Count gets his silver, so the merchants make sure nothing interferes with it. They don't want the Count complaining to Fenario, you see, because there just might someday be a King who actually cares what's going on."

"A strange town," I repeated. "What's the difference between those witches who fought the Count and those who didn't?"

"Eh?"

"I mean, how has that changed?"

"Oh. I've no idea. No one except witches ever talk about it,

and I've never studied the Art. Some say that those who were
loyal to the Count only have birds and mice as familiars. I don't
know if that's true."

"Is any of what you've told me true?"

He considered that. "I'm telling you a story. If you want history, go, ah, elsewhere. I don't know if it's true. We pass these
things on, we coachmen."

"So, none of what you're telling me might actually have
happened?"

"I'm sure some of it is related to what happened, somehow."

I noticed I hadn't had any wine in a while so I drained about
half of my mug while I thought things over.

"Then I take it," I said slowly, "that the Merss family is associated with the, ah, the dark forces of the Art."

He nodded.

"Hmmm. And yet, they're still around."

"A few. They're stubborn."

I smiled. That pleased me.

"And," he added, "they mostly keep to themselves, and
don't offend anyone."

"Just like me," I said dryly.

He either missed the irony, or chose to ignore it. "So then,
Vlad, have I answered all of your questions?"

I laughed. "Sure. And generated a hundred more."

"That's how it usually works."

"The Count, how is he called?"

"My lord will do."

"No, no. His name."

"Oh. Veodric. His family name is Saekeresh."

"Thank you. Tell me, Zollie, what brings you here?"

"I was born here," he said.

"No, I mean, why are you at the inn, instead of at the manor
with your Good Count Saekeresh Veodric?"

He laughed. "Good Count Veodric, aside from being a bad-tempered spoiled child who can speak of nothing but his aches and pains, is three and eighty years old," he said. "Once a year he leaves the manor to attend the Planting Festival, and once a year he leaves to judge at the horse show. This isn't either of those days, and the company here is better."

I looked around. "The horses?" He smiled and winked at me. "Oh," I said. "Expecting someone?"

"Sooner or later," he said.

"Then I'll leave you with the wine and my thanks."

"It has been a pleasure, Merss Vlad. I trust I'll see you again."

"I hope so," I told him. "I'll have more questions after I've thought things over."

"And more wine, I trust."

"And more wine."

It had gotten late while we spoke, and there seemed to be little sound coming from the inn. I made my way back across the small village, Loiosh and Rocza keeping close watch, because I was suddenly nervous. Nevertheless, nothing happened; I made it back and was let in to the Pointy Hat by the host, Inchay, who gave me a sour look (the place was empty; I guess he'd been about to retire).

"Well, that was useful, eh, Boss?"

"What are you being sarcastic about now? It was useful."

"How? He said everything he told you might be made up!"

"True or not, there are many who believe it."

"Oh, well, everything's solved then."

"He also said there's truth behind it, somewhere."

"Good luck finding it."

"Oh, shut up. I'm tired."

Some pleasures never get old, and taking off your boots at the end of a long day is one of those. I took off my cloak and outer layer of clothing, remembered to close the shutters, and stretched out on the bed. I was pleased that I hadn't had cause to regret leaving my sword here, and I decided not to do that ever again.

"Well, Boss, I hope it's progress. I'd like to be done and out of here."

"This town makes you nervous, does it?"

"What, it doesn't make you nervous?"

"Yeah, I guess it does at that. Good night."

4

LEFITT: *But the fact is, that is the body of Lord Chartis!*

MAGISTRATE: *The Gods! It is impossible!*

BORAAN (to Lefitt): *My love, you make the classic error. That is not a fact, that is a conclusion drawn from facts.*

LEFITT: *You mean, it is not Chartis?*

BORAAN: *Oh, no. It is certainly Chartis. I was merely objecting to your choice of words.*

—Miersen, *Six Parts Water*
Day Two, Act IV, Scene 3

I remember thinking, the night before, how nice it was to sleep in an actual bed. It was still nice.

I slept late, and felt rested when I got up and stumbled down the hall to splash water on my face and so on. I returned to the room, dressed, and took a bit of extra care looking over my weapons as I strapped them on and secured them. Then I went down to eat bread and cheese and drink coffee. A lot of bread and a lot of cheese—I was going to be walking again today. Not so much coffee; foul, nasty, bitter stuff made bearable only by heavy cream and glops of honey.

It was still morning when I set out. I stood outside of the Pointy Hat (I still hadn't heard what the locals called it) and sent Loiosh scouting to find a road south. It took him about five minutes. I followed his directions around a three-story red brick building that I guessed to be some sort of merchants' exchange, and started walking, pacing myself. Loiosh rejoined me, on my right shoulder this time, and had a conversation with Rocza that was none of my business.

The morning was fine and clear; the sky a bright, clear blue dotted with puffy bits of white. That was going to take some time to get used to. It came to me that over the last couple of days I had been half-consciously avoiding looking up. If you've never been in a place where all of a sudden the sky looks entirely different from what you're used to you probably won't understand, but it messes with your head. It makes you think of those stories about people who step through holes in a cave wall and find themselves in Upside Down Land or Walk Backward Land or Everything Too Big Land.

Or Mud Land. I was glad there hadn't been a lot of rain lately; I hate walking through mud.

A wagon, pulled by a young and spry-looking horse—at least, it seemed young and spry to me—passed me going the other way. The peasant gave me a hesitant half nod, which I returned. He wore a wide-brimmed straw hat. Lots of the people I'd seen in town had worn hats. The Furnace again, I imagine. Maybe I should get myself a hat. The Furnace was bright on my right side.

"Should I get a hat, Loiosh?"

"Yeah, Boss. It'll give me something to play with when I'm bored."

Okay, skip the hat.

There was a small hut, probably a farmhouse, set back a long ways from the road. Why build so small when there is so much room? Were there laws about it? If so, why?

The Furnace had climbed up noticeably higher in the sky, and I was starting to sweat a little. I stopped, opened a water bottle, and drank, then poured some into my palm for Loiosh and Rocza. Rocza still couldn't drink out of my palm without tickling me with her tongue.

I passed a few clumps of trees—thin, with the branches far over my head and forming a high awning—but other than that, there were just the gently rolling farmlands, like an ocean in all directions, with stuff growing in neat rows. Sometimes there would be something that was almost a hill, and there the rows would be along the hill, rather than up and down it, which looked to me as if someone went to a lot of extra work, but no doubt there were reasons having to do with the sort of witch-craft all peasants knew in this land.

I guessed I'd been walking well over an hour now, maybe two. I tried to check the time on the Imperial Clock, and of course I couldn't; it was just habit. I didn't notice exactly the point where I was far enough from the Orb that the effect of the amulet prevented me from getting the time, but it's odd how, once I became aware of it, it made me uncomfortable. It isn't like I *needed* to know the time anymore; it just made me twitchy that I couldn't find out whenever I wanted. No doubt those who lived here could tell the time pretty effectively by how high the Furnace was in the sky. I looked at it, then looked away. There was a thin wisp of smoke ahead and off to my left, probably some peasant burning rubble.

"Boss, those are walnut trees on the left."

"Ah. Good. I'm glad one of us recognizes them."

"You could have asked the coachman to describe them."

"I was too embarrassed."

Just past the trees was a gravel road, looking impressively well-maintained. I took it, and the thin plume of smoke was now directly in front of me, and I suddenly got a bad feeling.

"Loiosh—"

"On my way, Boss."

I tapped my rapier and kept walking.

It took him about three minutes.

"It's the house, Boss. Burned to nothing. And—"

"Are there bodies?"

"Six so far. Two of them small."

I fought back an inclination to run; I was obviously hours too late already. I also told myself to shut up because my brain was busily constructing scenarios in which this wasn't my fault. Yeah, get real.

By the time I was fifty yards away I was able to see that they'd made a proper job of it. There was a brick chimney, and smoking rubble; that's it. There was a medium-sized barn nearby, and a few smaller outbuildings that hadn't been touched, but the house itself was cinders and ash: I don't think there was piece of wood left as big as my fist.

I kept walking. I couldn't get too close—it was still bloody hot. But I saw a body. This one was whole, and unburned, just outside the scorched area. She was facedown. I turned her over, but there didn't seem to be any obvious marks on her. The expression on her face wasn't pretty. She was middle-aged. We'd been related—maybe she was my aunt, or great-aunt.

"Boss—"

"You know, I don't even know what my own people do with bodies."

The wind shifted and smoke got into my eyes. I backed away.

"Boss—"

"*Go find the direction of the nearest neighbors, Loiosh.*"

"*Sure, Boss,*" he said, and flew off. Rocza went with him.

I'm not sure how long it was, but presently he said, "*Not far, Boss. About a mile. Start west and you'll see it.*"

I turned my back on the Furnace—it was still morning—and started walking. My feet felt numb, which was odd.

I did, indeed, see the place—a neat little cottage; it looked cozy. Loiosh and Rocza rejoined me and we approached the place. By the time we reached it, there were two people waiting for us, one holding a scythe, the other some sort of small curved cutting implement I wasn't familiar with. One was a little older than me, the other quite a bit younger, maybe around sixteen or so.

"That's close enough," said the older one. "Another step closer and I'll—"

I kept walking. Loiosh flew into the young one's face; the older one started to turn, stopped, and by that time he was on his back with my foot on his weapon-hand. He made a pleasing "whump" as he hit the ground. The other, I assume his son, turned back toward me as Loiosh flew away, by which time I was holding a dagger at his throat. There was a stifled scream from the cottage.

"Don't threaten me," I said. "I don't care for it."

They both glared at me. The younger one did it better, but maybe that's because he was still on his feet. I took a step back and made the dagger vanish. "You can get up," I said, "but if either of you look like you're trying to hurt me, you'll both bleed. Then I'll go inside."

He stood up slowly, dusted himself off, and looked at me. Yeah, he could glare better standing. I could have given him a lesson in manners, but that wasn't what I was there for.

I gestured over my shoulder without letting my eyes leave them. I knew the smoke was quite visible from here.

"Did either of you see what happened?"

They both shook their heads.

"If you had, would you tell me?"

They glared, but gave no other response.

I took a deep breath, and let it out slowly. I knew the only reason I wanted to take it out on this pair was that they were the ones in front of me; but that didn't help all that much.

Yeah, I got my temper under control.

I looked at the two of them, then finally focused on the presumed father. "My name is Merss Vladimir. You see the smoke. Someone burned that house down either before or after killing everyone who lived there. I don't know how many bodies there are, because I couldn't get close enough to count, but at least six. And at least two of them are children. They were my kin. I want to know who did it. If you know, and you don't tell me, I will hurt you badly."

He dropped his eyes, and his mouth worked. "We didn't see," he said. "I sent K—I sent my boy over to look, and he saw what you did. We were talking about what to do about it when you, when you showed up."

"All right," I said. "I'm not from here. What is customary to do with bodies, to show respect?"

"Eh?"

"What do you do with the bodies of those who die?"

"We bury them," he said, as if I were an idiot.

"What else?"

"What . . . sometimes Father Noij will ask the Demon Goddess to look after their souls. Sometimes not. Depends on if, well, if they were known to follow Her."

"Were they?"

He nodded.

I turned to the younger one. "Go get Father Noij. Have him meet me there. And I'll need a shovel."

The father's mouth worked again. "I have two shovels," he said. "I'll help."

"Were they friends?"

He nodded. "I heard that they, well I heard things. I didn't care. They never bothered me. And one winter—"

"All right. You can help."

"I'm sorry I—"

"Forget it."

I turned and walked the long, long mile back to the Merss place.

In what had once, I guess, been the back yard there was what I thought was a maple tree. I sat down and rested my back against it while I waited. Swirls of smoke came from the rubble of what had been the house, and I could see at least three blackened shapes that had once been people.

I sat there and tried to face it that I had almost certainly caused this. Or instigated it. Someone else had caused it. I would find out who that was and I would do bad things to him. Whatever was going on, this shouldn't have happened.

The shadow of the tree had shortened considerably when Loiosh said, *"I think someone's coming."* A minute or so later, I heard footsteps. I stood up and dusted myself off. The peasant had a pair of shovels over his shoulder.

He walked up to me and nodded, handed me one of the shovels.

"My name is Vaski," he said. "I'm a free farmer."

"All right," I said. "Where should we dig?"

"Under the maple. They always liked that maple."

See? I knew it was a maple.

"All right. How big should the holes be?"

"About as deep as a man's height. We lay them on their backs."

"All right," I said. I took off my cloak and folded it, then removed my shirt. He pointed to a spot and we started digging.

Ever heard someone tell you that hard physical labor can be soothing? Can take your mind off your problems? Can leave you feeling better? I'd heard that. In my opinion, hard physical labor gives you blisters, and the only real distraction I got was trying to remember the spells I'd once known for curing them. He was much better than me, by the way; turns out there is even skill involved in digging holes. Who knew?

We were partway into it when a wagon drawn by a small cream-colored horse pulled up with the son and someone who introduced himself as Father Noij. He was short and fat, with brown curly hair around his ears.

"Merss Vladimir ," I told him.

"I'm sorry for your loss, sir," he said. "What, exactly, was your relationship to the family?"

"My mother was a Merss. I took her name. I'm not certain beyond that; I was young when she died."

"And your father—?"

"He's dead too." I left it at that, and he nodded.

"You came here to find them?"

"Yes. Did you know them well?"

He nodded.

"Tell me about them."

He did, but a lot of it I'm not sharing with you, whoever you are. Some things should stay private, and it wouldn't help you understand what happened anyway. He talked, mostly about Vilmoth, whom he described as sour and stubborn, but a loving father. As he spoke, Vaski's son looked through one of the outbuildings and found another shovel.

The digging went faster with three of us.

When Father Noij had at last finished, he said, "What of the stock?"

"Who inherits?" I said.

He shrugged.

Vaski said, "If there were a will, it's burned up by now."

"No other family?"

"There were once; they've moved away to get away from—"
He broke off and glanced at Father Noij. "—from things," he
concluded. "Or changed their name."

"Changed their name?"

"That means they disinherit themselves."

Yeah.

"You may be the nearest relative," said Father Noij. "Perhaps you should decide what to do with what is left."

"Pretty casual about this stuff, aren't you?"

"Anyone who wants to object can always see the Count."

"Not the Guild?" I said.

He stiffened a little, then relaxed. "It would fall under the
purview of the county, not the town."

"All right. I'll look things over, see if there are any docu-
ments or keepsakes that have survived. Other than those, if it's
up to me, these people can have the stock."

Vaski grunted a thanks.

It turned out there needed to be seven holes, not six; one of
them very very small. It made me sick. If I had still had my Organization, it would have been the work of a day to confirm that
the Guild was behind it, and two more days to demolish the
Guild so that no trace of it remained. I thought about that as
I worked my shovel and sweated.

The shadows had grown short and then long again when all
the holes were dug; neat rectangles, each with a pile of dirt next
to it.

"All right," said Vaski. "Let's get the bodies."

That's something else you don't need to hear about. Let's just say that most of them were no longer recognizable, and it was as bad as you'd think. I'd spent a lot of my life around death, and seen my share of corpses, also your share, and your uncle's share; but Vaski handled it better than I did. By the time we were done, it was all I could do not to show how badly shaken I was.

We filled in the holes one at a time, while Father Noij intoned softly in a language I didn't know, but from which I could occasionally pick out a name; usually Verra's but sometimes that of a corpse. He passed his hands over the holes, making cabalistic gestures, and from each picked up some dirt which he whispered over before replacing. I didn't feel any magic, but with the amulet I was wearing, I probably wouldn't. I wondered if the Demon Goddess was actually paying attention.

Partway through the service, we were joined by three more people, who proved to be Vaski's wife, daughter, around twelve, and youngest son, I'd guess at six or seven. His wife was carrying a basket, which made me realize that I hadn't eaten since I broke my fast that morning, and it was now late afternoon. With everything, all the different emotions warring in my skull, my stomach was still demanding attention. It's enough to make you laugh or cry or something.

Eventually, the last hole was filled in, the last of the rituals completed. It was still late afternoon. It seemed like it should have been much later.

Vaski and I went through the charred remains of the house, then briefly through the outbuildings, but didn't find anything of interest. When it was time to eat, Father Noij insisted we draw water and carefully wash our hands. There was a touch of ritual about that, I guess because we'd been handling dead people. There was still some light when the basket was opened, and we ate chewy, sweet dark bread, a harsh goat cheese, dried kethna, and a white liqueur that tasted of cherries but was oddly refreshing. I found I was eating slowly, in spite of my hunger. No one spoke while we ate; it was like that was part of the ritual, too. Maybe it was.

It had become pretty dark by the time we finished. I nodded to Vaski. Father Noij said, "I can drive you to your inn, if you wish."

"I'd like that," I said. "Ah, is it customary to pay you for such services?"

"The burial, or the ride?" he asked, and then chuckled. "A pittance as a gesture would not be improper."

I gave him a few copper pennies, and he nodded. He went over and said a few words to Vaski and his family, then climbed into the wagon. The horse shook its head and made some sort of horse sound as I climbed up next to Father Noij. He turned the wagon around and started us back to town. I'm no judge, but it seemed that he knew how to handle the horse and the wagon.

It was a long ride back to town after a long day. I started to drowse off, and I might have fallen asleep if he hadn't said, "Feel free to rest; I will wake you when we reach your inn." I hadn't told him which inn I was staying at. No, that didn't really mean anything, but it made me nervous enough that I stayed awake for the rest of the journey.

"Thank you for the ride," I told Father Noij as we reached my inn.

"You are welcome, Merss Vladimir," he told me. "And I am sorry that this happened."

"Thank you," I said. "Someone else will be, too."

He shook his head. "That is no way to think."

I stared at him. "What are you talking about?"

"Revenge is self-destructive."

"I thought you were a priest of Verra."

"And if I am?"

"When has the Demon Goddess frowned on vengeance?"

"I do not speak for the Goddess, Merss Vladimir. Though I serve her, and the people of this town through her, I cannot make such a claim. I speak as one man to another. Your desire for vengeance will—"

"You're bloody serious, aren't you?"

"Yes," he said.

"Amazing."

He said, "I once knew a man who spent thirty years—*thirty years*, attempting to—"

"Feh. That's not about vengeance, that's obsession."

"Nevertheless—"

"Thank you for the ride, Father," I told him. I hopped down from the wagon and entered the inn, Loiosh hissing laughter in my ear.

What surprised me when I walked into the Pointy Hat was how busy it was; I guess it was only then I realized that, by most standards, it was still early in the evening. I took a quick look to see if Orbahn was in. He wasn't. If I wanted to, I could decide that was suspicious, but it was too much work just then.

I took myself up to my room, removed my boots and cloak, and stretched out on the bed.

A part of it hadn't hit me until that moment: the realization that I wasn't going to be able to speak to them, to get to know them, to ask them who my mother was, and why she had left. A big piece of my past had just been lopped off. I was going to find who had done it, and I was going to find out why, and I was going to hurt somebody very, very badly.

"*Loiosh?*"

"*Yes, Boss?*"

"*We need to find a safe place tomorrow to take the amulet off long enough for me to do something about these blisters.*"

"*Safe? Boss—*"

"*Safer. Sort of safe.*"

"There is no such time or place."

"Think it's safe for me to be wandering around with my hands blistered?"

"Aren't there other ways to cure it that don't involve letting the Jhereg find you?"

"Sure. That should only take a week or so."

"We can hide for a week."

"Yes, but we aren't going to."

"Okay, Boss."

He fell silent, and I stared up the ceiling for a long time, remembering the bodies in the ruins the house, and wrapping sheets around them so we could drag them to the holes we'd dug. Oddly, my dreams weren't about that, they were about digging the holes; I dug them over and over in my sleep.

But I did sleep; I guess that's the important thing.

Part Three

STEMINASTRIA

The steminastria, which can last for several weeks depending on food supply, is the most active of stages, in the sense that it is constantly moving, and constantly eating, never leaving the pond in which it was born. In seasons where there is great competition, or little food, the steminastria will often die rather than transform. . . . One of the more unusual features of the steminastria is that at this stage, when it eats far more than at any other stage (at least nine times its own weight every day), it is a pure vegetarian—living on the underwater plants and lichen. We still do not know exactly what triggers the transition to its next stage, unless it is simply that the enormous quantity of food it consumes causes it to reach a point where it must transform before it literally bursts. . . .

High on the list of the steminastria's natural enemies must be itself, when considering its reckless disregard for the size and characteristics of its predators, even when based on its own experiences. . . .

—Oscaani: *Fauna of the Middle South: A Brief Survey*,
Volume 6, Chapter 17

5

BORAAN (DETERMINED): *Search! Hunt! Find it!*
FIRST STUDENT (frightened): *What if it isn't anywhere?*
LEFITT (calm): *Then it will take rather longer.*
—Miersen, *Six Parts Water*
Day Two, Act III, Scene 5

When I woke up, I hurt.

My shoulders, my arms, my back, my legs.

Why my legs? I don't know. What do I look like, a physicker?

I lay in bed moaning for what seemed a long time. If the Jhereg had found me then, they'd have had an easy target. I'm not even sure I'd have minded.

Eventually I moaned, moved, moaned, sat up, moaned, swung my legs down to the floor, and moaned.

"If I so much as suspect you are even thinking about laughing, by Verra's tits and toenails, Loiosh, I will—"

"Never entered my mind, Boss."

Putting on my boots was a test of my manhood; I just barely passed. Then I moaned some more. Eventually, I made my way to the stairs, and then down them, one at a time, slowly.

"Boss, how far can you go?"

"As far as I have to."

Inchay looked up. "Coffee?"

"Brandy," I said. "The foulest you have."

He looked startled, but didn't argue. I took the cup, downed it in one shot, and shook my head. "That's better," I said. "Now I'll have some coffee." I made my way over to a table and sat down.

After about an hour of drinking coffee I started to feel like maybe I could move. I mentally ran through the inventory of witchcraft supplies I had with me. Not many, but they'd do, and I didn't feel like going back to the shop in town and trying to actually purchase anything; I'd either kill the first merchant who looked at me wrong, or, worse, be unable to.

Okay, I had what I needed; I didn't doubt my ability to make the spell work. The only question was: Where should I do it? I didn't want to cast right there at the inn, because I had to take the amulet off, and it was bad enough giving the Jhereg a chance—slim but present—of finding the area where I was; handing them the inn I was staying at was just making their life a little too easy. I could maybe find a place out of town, but being surrounded by people—humans—was part of my protection.

I hated that I had to do this; that I was being forced to take this risk, just because of blisters and stupid body aches that I gotten—

No, no.

Not going to be able to do *any* sort of spell while having dismemberment fantasies. The Art involves channeling and controlling emotion, but the emotion needs to correspond to the spell, and the emotions I was feeling right then didn't have a whole lot to do with healing.

I remembered pleasant days with Cawti, which made me a bit melancholy—okay, maybe more than a bit—but that's always a good cure for rage. I thought about what went wrong, and what went right, and made stupid plans in my head to win her back. Funny, that; they always involved rescuing her, when I knew damned well that rescuing her had been one of the problems. No one likes being rescued. The only thing worse is, well, *not* being rescued.

So, yeah, I played tricks with my own head until I felt like maybe I could do a Working, and by the time I'd done that, I knew where I could do it, too. And, besides, the thought made me chuckle. Loiosh would have a lot to say about it, and that made me chuckle too.

"What are you planning, Boss?"

"Just a spell, Loiosh. You'll see."

I stood up and made my way—still slowly and painfully, but maybe a little better—out of the door, and began walking down the street. Slowly.

"Loiosh, I hurt."

"We can stop for cheese."

"Oh, shut up."

Eventually, I made it to the other end, to the other inn, and went into the stable. The stable-boy was there; he seemed to be in his early twenties, and had deep-set eyes and thin lips. He said, "Greetings, my lord, may I—" He stopped and stared at his hand, into which I had just placed three silver coins. "My lord?"

I gestured to the stable. "I need to use the space there for about an hour."

"My lord?"

"Yes?"

"The stable?"

I nodded.

"You need to use . . ."

"The space. Don't let anyone in. For an hour."

He looked at me, a thousand questions on his lips, then at the coins in his hand, then said, "Ah, the horses—"

"Will not be harmed." He had a sense of responsibility. How about that? "I won't touch them, or even go near them."

He heard the ring of truth in my voice, or the ring of metal in his hand, or something. He nodded abruptly. "Yes, my lord."

I added a fourth coin. "And there's no need to mention this to anyone."

"Of course not, my lord. An hour, you said?"

"An hour."

He bowed clumsily, and I went into the stable and locked it after myself.

"Here?"

"Why not?"

"How can you defend yourself here?"

"I'm hoping I won't need to."

"Um, going to let me in on this?" He was genuinely nervous; I could tell because Rocza seemed jumpy.

"Look, chum, what exactly are we worried about?"

"The Jhereg finding you."

"Right. Now, either they already know where I am, in which case it's pointless to worry about it, or they don't. If they don't, then, if they get lucky, they'll be able to trace me while I have the amulet off doing the witchcraft spell. If they trace me, what will they do?"

"Uh . . . kill you?"

"They'll have to come to Burz to do it."

"Well, yeah."

"Know any Dragaerans liable to have this little Eastern town memorized enough to teleport to it?"

"Probably not, Boss. Going to bet your life that some sorceress from the Left Hand can't work around that?"

"No, but I'll bet my life that if an assassin does show up, I'll be ready. I'm doing a spell, not falling asleep. I'm in the middle of an open space. There's no way he can come at me without you seeing him."

"And if he's invisible?"

"Look around."

"What?"

"Horses, Loiosh. They'll smell him. Keep an eye on the horses during the spell. If the horses suddenly get jumpy, and start looking where there isn't anyone, I'll stop the spell and, ah, kill him." I made a mental note to make up more Nesiffa powder; I didn't mention to Loiosh that I was out of it.

"Boss, sometimes I wonder about you. Okay, and if they track you, but don't come immediately?"

"They'll be across town from where I am, with plenty of time for people to notice that there's an 'elf' in town, and I'll no doubt hear about it."

" 'No doubt'?"

"And they want it Morganti, Loiosh. Morganti. The Jhereg won't be happy with anything less. There is no chance, none, that they can bring a Morganti weapon into a town full of witches without creating an uproar the likes of which this town has never seen."

"And then, sometimes, I don't even wonder."

"Heh."

"Go ahead, then."

"Glad to have your permission."

I cleared an area of hay, because burning the place down would have attracted unnecessary attention to myself as well as disrupting the ritual; not to mention breaking my promise not to harm the horses.

I lit three candles—two white, and one black—then removed the amulet and carefully separated the two parts. The gold I replaced around my neck; the black I set into my pouch. Once I closed that pouch—I'd crafted it myself—the stone might as well have been a hundred miles away.

I laid out what few things I'd need: herbs, a tube of purified water. I didn't have a brazier with me, but I didn't need one for this.

As I combined the salve with purified water—just a drop—I considered the nasty blisters on my fingers, and thought about what my fingers would be like without them, imagined them healing with a chant that came from inside my body painful muscles unknotting working past the resistance because it cannot stand up to me I am Taltos Vladimir and the power is mine and the body is mine it will do as I will keep at as long as my heart continues to drive the blood mixing with the salve and the fingers inside worked them over and understanding the body is the key to opening the doorway of knowledge of all things within and without a pause in the constant drone in the ears full of my own voiceless calling to a place that is here and also not hearing it again and again becoming part of my own fingertips as they clench against the heel of my hand, unwinding and yielding now, flowing faster as they tap the heel and heal and hear and see and smell the damp moldy straw of the stable in the flickering light of the candles as I stopped.

I took a deep breath, and, my hands trembling, removed the piece of the amulet from my pouch, re-attached it, and replaced it around my neck.

"Anything, Loiosh?"

"I'm not sure, Boss. I thought I felt something for a minute, but I can't be sure. It was subtle. Someone good, if it was anything at all."

"You blocked it, then. I didn't feel anything."

"I blocked you from it, Boss, so it wouldn't mess up the ritual. I *don't know if I blocked it from you. I don't know if there was anything to block."*

"All right. If the Jhereg could find a witch at all, I doubt it would be someone good."

As spells go, that one was pretty easy; there isn't much in witchcraft that comes easier than convincing your body to do what it wants to do anyway. By the time my equipment was put away in my pack, the blisters had already started to heal, and the general aches in my body were noticeably improved. I still didn't like the idea of fighting anyone, but I figured I could probably do it if I had to. Of course, I paid a price; I was pretty exhausted and my head was fuzzy, but it was a reasonable trade-off.

Best of all, no assassins showed up to put a nice shine on my epidermis during the process; my remarks to Loiosh notwith-standing, interrupting a spell to fight is neither easy nor fun. I have, a couple of times, actually performed a spell in the middle of a fight, the way sorcerers do. I don't recommend it, and I re-ally hope I'll never have to do it again.

I gave the boy another silver and a smile as I left, shaky but much improved.

"What now, Boss?"

"Hey, I'm up for anything, as long as it doesn't require moving or thinking."

"So, no moving then, but other than that, just as usual."

"After I've worked that out, I'll probably swat you for it."

The walk back across town to the inn seemed very long in-deed. And odd. Things always look different when you've just exhausted yourself with a Working, even a minor one; some-times, I've never figured out exactly when, the effect is ampli-fied: edges are fuzzy, people seem to blur into the background of whatever they're near. Any reflective surface seems shinier, and texturing moves and shifts. There are some witches who believe that in this state you can see profound truths that are normally concealed. Some of them devote themselves, not to the Workings, but to the aftereffects, and reveal hidden secrets of the ages.

I think it's just that your brain is tired and you aren't thinking right.

I made a life-enemy during that walk, too. I think he must have been about six years old, and he was throwing a wooden ball against a house—presumably his—making "thunk-splot" "thunk-splot" sounds as it struck the wall then the street. He missed it, and it rolled across the street right in front of me, and from there down into a gutter and away down the street. I was considerably past it when I realized that I could easily have stopped it, picked it up, and tossed it back to him, and around the time I was finally reaching the Hat it came to me that he had been glaring at me. I actually thought about going back and apologizing, but the explanation would have been beyond my powers so I didn't.

Oddly, I don't remember anything about the smell of the town during the long, long trek; which may indicate something or other. I went to the door and walked through it; the host gave me a sort of look, but I wasn't quite aware of it until I was past him and climbing the long, long, long flight of stairs up to my room, where I collapsed on the bed and stared at the ceiling. The bed felt wonderful, and the ceiling looked remarkably interesting, with all sorts of odd texturing that I could almost see moving if I squinted just a bit.

I wasn't in need of sleep, I was just mentally and physically exhausted. There's a difference, you know. Considering that difference is the last thing I remember for an hour or two.

Naps don't usually do much for me; the few times I've tried napping—when I was with Cawti, who felt about them the way a cat does—they always left me feeling groggy. But that one seemed to do the trick. At any rate, the world wasn't fuzzy anymore when I woke up, and I felt like I could move a bit.

I went back down to the jug-room. Inchay explained that he didn't keep coffee this late in the day. I explained that I wished to drink coffee. Presently coffee appeared.

Inchay had his back to me, and the thought came out of nowhere: What an idiot. He shouldn't have his back to an enemy.

I pondered that for a little while. You know a thought like that comes from somewhere, but that doesn't mean it's reliable. Yes, it could be my subconscious telling me it had noticed something about that guy. It could just as easily be my paranoia at work, combined with some of the nasty looks and remarks he'd given me, starting with his absurd idea, when I'd first walked in, that I take Loiosh and Rocza out.

I mean, I knew I didn't like him much; but that wasn't sufficient to convince me he was working against me. To the left, though, I certainly wasn't about to turn my back on *him*.

When you get a tip like that from your subconscious, there's as much danger in paying it too much heed as too little. You can't ignore it, but you can't let it distract you, either.

When he turned around, naturally, I was no longer looking at him.

Okay, we have a Guild of merchants, unlike any guild Noish-pa told me could exist. No, Noish-pa isn't infallible, but it's enough to make me think there is something very odd going on here.

Then you've got Count Saekeresh Veodric: landowner, and paper factory owner. In the Empire, to have an aristocrat owning a factory wasn't worth a raised eyebrow, but from everything I understood, it was unusual in the East. For one thing, I guess, there were very few factories of any kind, so perhaps I was putting too much weight on that. Still, what was between him and the Guild? Cooperation? Competition? Hostility mitigated by a truce, armed or unarmed? There had to be something.

And then, that strange matter of "light" and "dark" witchcraft. That just made no sense at all. If there was anything to it, I needed to know what; and if there wasn't, I needed to know why it was commonly believed that there was.

How did good old Inchay here fit in, if at all? And Orbahn. He had some part in this too; I was sure of it.

And then, there was the Jhereg; probably not involved in this, but never, ever to be forgotten; I did not want my last sight to be the point of a Morganti dagger. I shuddered.

Someone had brutally killed my mother's family, and at least one of those parties was responsible, or knew who was responsible.

Well, okay, those were the questions I knew about now; efforts to answer them would naturally generate others, but at least I had a place to start.

I sat there and drank my coffee and made plans.

Ha.

You have to understand, looking back on things, that's pretty funny. But it's true, I made plans, just as if I were going to carry them out, just as if no one else could be making plans at the same time. Do you even care what they were? Could it possibly matter, all the things I would have done if . . .

If, if, if.

If the world was what I wanted it to be, instead of what it is.

Pointless. If the world was what I wanted it to be, I'd still be married. I'd never have gotten involved with the Jhereg in the first place, because I'd never have had the need or the desire to. Instead, I'd be . . . what? Count Szurke, safe in my manor near the lake, fishing and having hunting parties, with Cawti on my arm discussing the latest fashions from B'nari Street? No, I couldn't see that either; and, as I said, it's pointless.

When you've been paid to kill a man, you have to learn everything you can about him; there's not a lot of value in learning about what he might be, or you wish he were. Do that, and all you'll get is Fiscom's Honor, which, if you haven't heard the term before, means having your name added to the list cut into the tall, wide marble blocks around the Executioner's Star.

You look at what is, and if you don't know what is, you make it your business to find out. And sometimes that, too, turns out to be just another offering on the altar of the futility deities—the ones who make the crops fail.

So, yeah, I sat there and drank coffee and made plans. Just as if.

Loiosh was still tense; I could feel him watching the door, and Rocza kept shifting and bouncing on my left shoulder.

But I didn't let it bother me; I was working. Turning my anger into decision, decision into intention, intention into plan. I was going to learn who was behind this by going in a neat, orderly way; I had it figured out how to get the information from those who must have it, so I could decide just exactly who was deserving of what I intended to do.

An hour or two must have gone by while I went over it in my mind—or, actually, subvocalized it to Loiosh, who ignored it; just because I think better when I'm talking. Finally I said, "Okay, I've got it."

"Whatever you say."

"Our friend Inchay first, because I don't expect to get anything from him."

"I like your expectations, Boss. Stay with that, and you won't be dis—"

"Orbahn next, if he can be found."

"Which you don't expect."

"Probably not."

"So far, it's perfect."

I took a quick inventory of my body, of the effect of the Working. The blisters were gone, and the muscle aches were manageable. I got up, threw a few coins to Inchay, and said, "I'm looking for a witch."

"There's a shop just down the street where they get their supplies. I'm sure Yulio could direct you to someone."

"Uh huh. Who do you know?"

He spread his hands. I didn't believe him, but I figured I could come back to him later. "Okay," I said. "Any idea where I can find Orbahn?"

"Haven't seen him."

I waited without saying anything, because that makes people uncomfortable. Eventually he added, "I imagine he'll be in later."

"*Good work, Boss. So far, everything's going just as you exp—*"

"Shut up."

"All right," I said. "Where is the Guild hall?"

His eyes narrowed a little. "The Guild hall," he repeated.

I waited.

"Turn right when you leave. On this street about two hundred feet down. Two-story building painted light green."

I nodded a sort of thank-you and went back and sat down.

"*What, not going, Boss?*"

"*Tomorrow. I'm still pretty exhausted, and I need to be at my best to tackle this Guild. I get the feeling they're a bit like the Empire, and a bit like the Jhereg.*"

"*Feeling.*"

"*Yeah. When that's all you've got, that's what you go with. Besides, hitting them early in the morning seems like the right approach.*"

"*I have a suggestion for what to do between now and then, Boss.*"

"*What's that?*"

"*Put as many miles between us and this smelly hole of a town as your feet can manage.*"

"*No,*" I said.

Having made my plans, I let my mind relax, and I hardly moved for the rest of the day. The place filled up again, mostly peasants, no women. Strange. I watched them, and they ignored me, and Orbahn didn't appear.

The next part of the plan involved going to bed early, and I carried it off without a hitch. Loiosh even complimented me on its success. The little punk.

I drank coffee the next morning, and chewed on some poppy-seed rolls, still hot from the oven and with butter and honey. Good stuff. I had the room to myself while I ate, Inchay being in the back taking care of innkeeper things, and I ate slowly, planning how I was going to work things with the Guild.

I should explain: At this point, I was pretty well convinced that it was the Guild that had slaughtered the Merss family. I was ready to change my mind if I had reason to, and I hadn't eliminated the Count or some other person or group I didn't know about; and I wasn't sure enough to act on it. But I was pretty sure they were either responsible, or had a hand in it.

That was going to be the hard part—keeping my temper in check while I dug out the information I needed. I could feel the desire in me to find the Guild Master and watch my stiletto go up under his chin, or into his left eye, whichever was more convenient. I wanted it so bad I almost shook.

"*Boss, this has been happening too much lately. Yesterday—*"

"*I know, Loiosh. I'm working on it.*"

I spent a little extra time calming myself down, reminding myself to treat this like a job. No, it wasn't a job; but if I went at it like an amateur, letting my feelings dictate my methods, I'd end up where all amateurs end up. And maybe I'm going to end up there anyway, but not now; not before I'd finished this.

When I felt like I was ready, I stood up, borrowed a pitcher of water to wash the honey off my hands, took a deep breath, and went back out into the stench.

"We're really going to the Guild, Boss?"

"We really are. I don't know if they're behind this, or just have a big part of it, but either way I need to know what I'm up against, and pull some information out of them."

He sighed.

It was early morning, but the Furnace was hidden by gray clouds, making me feel more at home. I turned right out of the door. It wasn't far; it was before the street that turned off toward the docks. The rain started as I stepped inside.

It was a big room, with about four tables, and various official-looking men—about a dozen all together—sitting behind them, doing official-looking things with papers. No women. Odd. There was a staircase in back leading up. My first reaction was that there was too much activity for a Merchants' Guild in a town this size. But what do I know?

The guy at the table next to the door looked up; a young, serious-looking man who didn't eat enough, and, to judge from his pinched-up face and stiff back, he probably never did anything at all he enjoyed. He probably didn't believe in having fun. I should introduce him to this girl who roams the docks.

He wanted to know if he could be of service to me. I had the feeling it wasn't actually all that important to him one way or the other. I thought about breaking his legs, but that was just because I was in a bad mood.

"Chayoor," I told him. "I want to see him."

He opened his mouth, hesitated, looked me over, closed his mouth, and hesitated again. I can't actually read minds the way Daymar can, but sometimes, you know, you don't need to—the poor guy was trying to decide my status so he'd know whether to address me as "my lord," or "boy" or something in between. He was having trouble, because I looked like a commoner except for the sword at my side. I felt very bad for him.

"Sir," he finally said, "if you will wait here, I will find out if—"

"Save it," I told him. "My name is Merss Vladimir, and there aren't enough of you here to keep me from seeing him. I assume he is up those stairs. Now, do you want to announce me, or shall I just head up?"

His mouth worked for a moment. I guess one of the worst sides of my character is how much I enjoy doing that to poor little bastards who have no defense against it.

"No," he finally said, keeping his voice low but even. "Your name is Vladimir Taltos, and you will see the Guild Master when he is ready to see you. He has been expecting you. I will see if he is free now. Excuse me."

6

About three years later, as I was watching his back disappear up the stairs, Loiosh said, *"Okay, Boss. Now what?"*

Nothing builds confidence in subordinates like a quick decision in the face of unexpected circumstances.

"Um," I told him.

That was as far as I'd gotten when the young man came back down the stairs and gestured for me go up. He sat down and returned to whatever he had been doing without giving me another word. I didn't say anything. When you're licked, you're licked.

I did, however, make a point of flicking my cloak aside so I could get to my rapier in a hurry if I needed to, and checked the surprises I had left about my person to make sure they were ready and accessible.

The upper floor was all one room with a high arched ceiling and decorated, if you will, with a strange assortment of items hanging from the walls: a bunch of plants, a pair of boots, a hat, a shirt, a ladle, a hammer, a bottle of wine, and more. It took me a moment to figure out that these represented some or all of the members of the Guild. It was quaint. Anything that stays trite long enough becomes quaint.

Chayoor was a burly, barrel-chested man with thin black curly hair, a neatly trimmed beard, and dark eyes. He rose as I approached, gave me a perfunctory bow, and seated himself while gesturing me toward one of the chairs in front of his desk. He had a desk, not a table. The benefits of power: You get your own desk. I'm not mocking it; I remember how I felt when I got my own desk.

I sat down.

"Lord Taltos," he said. "I was informed you would be here."

"I should prefer to be known as Merss, if you don't mind."

"Very well," he said.

"Would you mind telling me who it was who informed you?"

"I'm sorry, that I cannot do."

Okay. Well. This conversation just wasn't going at all the way I'd planned it. The whole intimidating him thing had gotten off to a bad start.

"That's unfortunate," I said. "I have enemies, you know. Also friends. If I don't know whether it was a friend or an enemy that alerted you, it puts me in an uncomfortable position."

"It was a friend," he said.

Right. Just so you know, I didn't have any "friends" who knew where I was going. "And if it had been an enemy, you'd have told me?"

"I see your point," he said. "Nevertheless—"

"Yeah. Well, if it was a friend, I assume he asked you to cooperate with me?"

He frowned. "Not as such."

"Uh huh."

He looked uncomfortable, which was at least a little encouraging. "What exactly do you need?"

"I came here looking for my family," I said. "My mother's kin."

"Yes," he said. "I'm sorry about what happened."

I need to explain that Fenarian makes a distinction between, "I apologize for an injury," and, "I express my sympathy." He used the latter formulation. I grunted or something.

"I'm going to find out who did it," I said.

His eyebrow went up. "And then?"

I cocked my head at him. "Why, then I will turn the guilty party over to the duly constituted authority, of course."

It was his turn to grunt. "In Burz," he said, "the duly constituted authority is me."

"Is that the law?" I asked. "Or just how it works?"

"What's the difference?"

"You're a blunt son-of-a-bitch, I'll give you that."

He laughed, throwing his head back and letting his belly shake. I hadn't thought it was that funny.

"Yes, Lord, ah, Merss, I am a blunt son-of-a-bitch. And I'll tell you bluntly that I like how things are here in my town, and if you do anything to interfere with it, we will no longer be friends."

"Yeah," I said. "I guessed that part."

"So," he said. "Now what will you do?"

"Let me assume you had nothing against the Merss family, because if you're responsible, you wouldn't tell me. So, who did?"

"I couldn't tell you," he said.

I rubbed my chin. "You know," I said, "if you interfere with me finding out what I want to find out, you might no longer be my friend."

"Is that a threat?"

"I'm not sure. I guess it'll sort of do for one. As a threat, how does it rate?"

"Hollow," he said.

I fixed him with patented Jhereg stare number six, lowered my voice, and said, "Then you can safely ignore it, I guess."

I had the satisfaction of seeing that go home; he looked uncomfortable.

I stood up abruptly, before he could announce the end of the interview. "I'd appreciate it," I said, "if my name wouldn't go any further."

"It won't," he told me. "Only Shandy and I know it, and he won't say anything."

I nodded, turned, and made my way across the long, long room to the stairway, then down and out. Shandy didn't look up as I walked past him.

It was still raining when I got outside, but not too hard. I made it back to the Hat somewhere between wet and soaked.

"Boss, not to put too fine a point on it, but we need to get out of this place. Now. I mean, without stopping. Pick a direction and start walking."

"Yeah, I know."

"Boss, they know who you are."

"I know."

"That bastard could get rich just by dropping your name in the right ear."

"I know. But, Loiosh, why hasn't he done so already? Why am I still breathing?"

"Boss, can we please talk about this after we're out of town? I'm too old to learn to hunt for myself."

"You don't hunt, you scavenge."

"Boss—"

"Loiosh, have you ever known me to walk into something this strange and just walk away from it without finding out what's going on?"

"This would be a really, really good time to start."

"I'll take it under advisement."

I got inarticulate thoughts that were probably the jhereg equivalent of cursing.

I stamped some of the rain off my clothes and shook my head like a dog.

"Thanks for the shower, Boss."

"Like you were dry before?"

I found a drink and a chair and sat down.

"Loiosh, how in blazes did they learn my name?"

"Huh? You don't know?"

"You do?"

"Of course!"

"All right, how?"

"When you took the amulet off and did the spell, Boss. Remember, I felt something?"

This time it was my turn to curse. "They got it right out of my head."

"There's still the question of who did it."

"Who could it be? It wasn't the Jhereg. If they knew I was here, they'd send someone in to kill me. End of discussion."

"Uh, okay."

"There's Chayoor himself."

"Boss, he didn't tell himself who you are, someone has to have told him."

"Sorry, chum. I'm not just going over who might have told Chayoor, I'm trying to work out all the players in this mess."

"Heh. Good luck with that."

"There's Orbahn, who's either too helpful, or not helpful enough."

"Right."

"There are these witches. There's most likely a Coven. They could have acted on their own behalf, as the Coven. Even if not, one of their members must have done the Working, so either way they could know.

"Then there's the coachman, who's the only guy I've found who has been really helpful, which makes me suspicious."

"Uh . . . all right."

"And then there's Count Saekeresh, however he fits in. Have I left anyone out?"

"Sure. Everyone else in town, and everyone everyone knows."

"I take your point, Loiosh. But let's keep it within reason."

"We're way beyond that, Boss."

"Loiosh."

"All right. The host?"

"Right. The host. Good position to hear things, and knows I've been asking questions."

"Boss, can't we please leave?"

"No."

I accepted the psychic form of a resigned sigh and continued my ruminations.

"What are you thinking about, Boss? You know and I know you're going to march up to the Count and try to intimidate him. Probably work as well as—"

"Shut up."

I hate it when he's right.

Well, if I was going to do it, may as well do it properly. I went over to Inchay. "Can you find someone to run a message to Count Saekeresh for me?"

He looked at me sharply, decided that was a mistake, and washed a cup that didn't need washing while he thought it over. At last he said, "Very well. What is the message?"

"If you have paper and ink."

He nodded, dried his hands, and vanished into a small room behind the bar, then emerged with the necessary equipment. I wrote and handed it to him, unsealed.

"How urgent is it?"

"Today would be good."

"I'll see that it gets there today."

I gave him more of that jingly stuff that keeps tradesmen wanting to be helpful, then settled back to see if Orbahn would show up, and if Loiosh would calm down.

No, and no.

Later I had more lamb stew. Sometimes I get into ruts where I'll eat the same thing for days. I used to do that, long ago, I guess in part out of laziness. Cawti had largely broken me of the habit just because I liked trying new ideas out on her, but now I was falling back into the pattern. But I guess part of it was that the lamb stew was good. I liked the bread, too; having the right kind of bread to mop up stew is its own art.

No, and no.

The place started to fill up, and I moved to a back table. I was getting more covert looks than I had before; I wasn't sure exactly what sort of word was spreading about me, but something was. I reflected that that was part of the problem—I didn't know. I'd gotten spoiled, I suppose, by having Kragar near at hand, and access to Morrolan's spy network (he never used that term, I think he found it distasteful, but that's what it was), and Kiera and her nearly endless knowledge of the arcana of the Underworld. If I wanted to know what was going on, all I had to do was decide who to ask first; eventually I'd find out. Here, I was in the dark, and I didn't care for it. Cawti would have told me to figure out exactly what I wanted to accomplish, and then helped me break it down into steps, and—

I found myself wanting a very strong drink and didn't take it because getting drunk right then would have been a stupid idea, and because I hate being trite. It can lead to being quaint. Instead, I made circles on the table with my finger in the moisture from my glass. I found I'd been doing that a lot lately, and wondered about it. But not very much.

Some hours later, one of the barmaids tapped my shoulder and indicated the host, who was trying to get my attention. I made my way over to him, and he handed me a note. I nodded and returned to my table to read it. I had to shift my chair to a place where my shadow wasn't blocking the light from the nearest lamp; then I broke the seal and unfolded the thick parchment. Good paper, I noticed; they probably made it locally.

"My Lord Merss," it read, "His Lord wishes above all to present His Condolences upon your recent Loss, and to Assure You that all Steps are being Taken to Bring the Perpetrators to Justice. Unfortunately, His Lordship's Health does not Permit Visitors at this Time, but He Hopes you will Know that You are in His Thoughts in the Kindest way. I Remain, my Lord, Your Servant, Tahchay Loiosh, Scribe."

"*Hey, he has the same name as me,*" said Loiosh.

"*He probably doesn't fly as well,*" I said.

I folded the note carefully in half, and put it into an inside pocket of my cloak while I thought about it. It wasn't as if I were surprised; I hadn't expected him to jump at the chance to see me. I'd had a plan for what to do in this case, back a long time ago—

last night—when I'd worked it all out. Only since then everything had come loose, and was now flapping in the breeze.

"*Well, Boss? Going to visit him anyway?*"

"You know damned well I am."

"*Yeah. Boss, are you trying to get killed?*"

"Is that a rhetorical question?"

"*No.*"

"*Okay.*" I gave it some thought. "No, I don't think so."

"*All right. Good.*"

People kept coming into the place, all of them wet and dripping. I didn't feel like going out, and they didn't feel like giving me any more than the occasional hostile glance. I'd somehow built Fenario up in my head into this perfect land, full of happy, smiling people who would greet me like a long-lost brother. It was downright disheartening. I was tempted to just start breaking random arms and legs.

And still no sign of Orbahn. I was beginning to think he was avoiding me. Was that suspicious? Well, sure. What, by Barlan's Sacred Slime Trail, wasn't suspicious at this point? Anything anyone did or didn't do, said or didn't say, might mean he was looking to put a knife in me.

Of course, to some degree, I'd lived with that most of my life. The difference was, I used to know the game and the rules. Yeah, fine, but, okay, Vlad, who broke the rules?

Cawti. She's the one who got herself involved in things we had no business getting involved in.

Well, yeah, but I was the one who had to piss off the whole Jhereg. What was I thinking, anyway? Heroic rescue my ass. Maybe I was just trying to come up with a good excuse to jump off the ship because I didn't want the humiliation of running it into the rocks.

Okay, Vlad. Settle down. This is getting you nowhere. Take a deep breath, another slug of wine, and try to bloody *concen-*

trate. You have a problem. It isn't the first problem you've ever had. Unless you get stupid, it won't be the last. So look at it, analyze it, treat it like the others.

Crap.

When you reach the point of needing to tell yourself how to think, you've already gone beyond the point where you're willing to listen. Or maybe that's just me.

I tried to remember why I'd decided not to get drunk, and I couldn't, so I called over the barmaid and asked for decent brandy. She returned with a bottle of Veeragkasher, which qualifies, I think. After the third glass I didn't care, in any case.

Loiosh tells me I got myself to bed all right. He also tells me I didn't even make it halfway through the bottle. How humiliating.

Sometimes we're treated better than we deserve. I not only woke up feeling fine the next morning, I also woke up. I went down the hall to the cistern, got some hot water, and spent some time getting clean and pretty. Then I walked over to my window and, standing to the side, looked out at the street. It was gray and wet outside, but no longer raining. I continued watching for a couple of minutes, and then the Furnace appeared, making the wet streets glisten. I could have decided it was an omen, the Furnace coming out like that to brighten things, only it was doing the same thing for my enemies.

Well, no doubt it promised good fortune to someone, about something. Omens always prove true if you just allow them enough room to work.

I spent a few more minutes watching the bizarre spectacle of steam rising from the streets, then went downstairs to the jug-room and got some coffee. With enough honey and heavy cream, it was drinkable, but I made a vow that someday I would return here, buy this man a klava press, and teach him how to use it. Or else maybe kill him.

All right, I knew what I was going to do, and I'd already worked out how to do it—I kept that much of my original plan intact. I returned to my room and dressed as well as I could with what I had with me; I've looked better, leave it at that. I took out the Imperial Seal Her Majesty had given me for being an idiot in a good cause—sorry, long story—and folded it up in a square of red silk, which I then sealed with wax and a ring that went with yet another seal, that one in the possession of my grandfather. I put the sealed package, about the size of my palm, in my cloak and went back downstairs to continue waking up.

Eventually the coffee did its work, and my brain started performing in a semblance of its usual manner. I asked the host where the Count's manor was, and was given a scowl, a suspicious look, and directions that were a good ten miles from town. Which meant I could either spend all day walking there and then back, or . . .

I sighed and asked if there was anyone who rented horses. Yes, in fact, he did; there were stables in the back, and a stable-boy who would help me pick one out if I showed him a chit. How much? Okay.

"Quit laughing, Loiosh."

"Boss, sometimes you just ask the impossible."

The muscle aches had completely vanished, so I might as well get new ones. I went back to the table and took my time finishing my coffee, then walked out the back door to the stables, I suppose much the way a man might walk to the Executioner's Star.

This "stable-boy" was somewhat older than I was, balding, tall, and had piercing black eyes as well as enough girth to make me feel sorry for the horses. When he began to take the equipment down I got a look at his right biceps. Maybe part of his job was picking up the horses, I don't know.

He didn't say a lot as he worked, just grunted when I explained I wanted a horse that would let me stay on top of him, and wouldn't do anything to embarrass me. He picked out a rather fat-looking horse that is I think the color horse people call "sorrel" though it looked brown to me. If it's brown, why can't they call it brown?

He led it up to me, helped guide my foot into the stirrup, and held it while I mounted; then he went around and got my other foot placed.

"Her name is Marsi," he said.

"All right."

Marsi seemed indifferent to the proceedings, which pleased me. I felt very, very tall. Too tall. Anything that high up is liable to come down again.

I got going in the right direction, and tried not to let my teeth knock against each other. Marsi, may all the blessings be upon her, walked significantly faster than I did, and felt this meant she had no need to trot, canter, gallop, or turn hand-springs. I made a vow to give a nice tip to the stable-boy for not being one of the practical-joking sort one hears about.

The morning grew warm; I removed my cloak and draped it over Marsi's back—which is much tougher than it sounds on horseback. Thanks to his kindness and Marsi's good nature, as well as the directions from the host, I felt as good as could be expected by the time I saw the double row of trees that had been described as the entrance to the manor.

It was a long ride to the manor itself, during which I rode by gardeners who glanced at me as if uncertain if they were supposed to make an obeisance. It gradually occurred to me that a lot of the doubt came from the horse. I was, perhaps, the only man within a hundred-mile circle who didn't consider himself an expert on horseflesh, and I was probably doing the equivalent of Morrolan riding up to the Ascension Day Ball in a hay wagon.

Well, that's all right, Marsi; I love you anyway.

Some sort of groom, wearing shiny buttons, stood outside the door of the gray stone manor, perfectly positioned at the bottom of the shallow stairway between two white pillars that flanked the red wood doorway. A man-at-arms stood next to each pillar, appearing part of the decoration; they wore red and green and metal hats and each carried some sort of ax-like weapon that was taller than the guy wielding it. It didn't look very practical, but, on the other hand, I'd hate to have one swung at me.

I felt myself come under their gaze. They didn't move, exactly, but they were certainly paying attention. One had the most impressive mustache I think I've ever seen: a massive thing that curled its way well past the sides of his face, held in place by a special sort of waxy-glue that I knew was sold in South Adrilankha. I'd never used it, myself. The other one had a bit of reddish hair peeking out from under his tin hat; I guessed he wasn't a native Fenarian.

If I had to, I could take them both. Enough said.

As I approached, the groom looked at me, frowned, and hesitated. I didn't—I climbed down off the horse, thanking Verra that I managed the trick with a semblance of grace, and kept myself from teetering only by dropping my body weight as my grandfather had taught me to do when fencing. I don't *think* I looked ridiculous. I took the cloak from the back of the horse, then put the reins into the groom's hand before he could decide he didn't want them. I threw my cloak over my shoulder. I can look good doing that because I've practiced, and no, I'm not proud of that. I said, "Baron Vladimir Merss to see His Lordship. See to my horse while I have someone announce me."

If I were going to give myself a new name, why not give myself a new title to go with it?

The groom barely hesitated, then said, "Yes, my lord."

I waited while he led the horse away, watching closely as if I were uncertain he knew his business; in fact, I didn't want to try walking just yet the way my legs were shaking. The guards watched me without appearing to—I know that trick. I have no idea if I fooled them with the watching the groom thing; probably not.

The groom led Marsi down a path and out of sight, and I made my trembling way up the three steps—they seemed much deeper steps when trying to climb them than just looking at them—and leaned against the door for a moment before pulling the rope. I heard a gong echo faintly from inside the house, and not long thereafter the door swung open.

The butler—for so I took him to be, and so he was—looked very much the part. He could very well have been picked for his appearance: tall and well-built, clean-shaven, with a proper fringe of white hair. He gave me a bow and a look of polite, noncommittal inquiry.

I said, "Baron Vladimir Merss to see His Lordship."

"You have a card, my lord?"

"I do not."

His face betrayed nothing. "May I convey to His Lordship the nature of your business?"

"Give him this." I removed the silk package and handed it to him.

"Very good, my lord." He bowed and went away with it.

Ten minutes later he returned with the package; the seal had been broken. I took the package with a small bow and replaced it in my cloak without looking.

The butler cleared his throat and said, "The Count will see you now."

7

He turned and led me into the interior of the manor. I followed, carefully keeping the smirk off my lips.

There was a certain kind of restrained opulence about the manor—its corridors wide and high; its halls hung with pictures of, I presume, ancestors; its furnishings sturdy and elegant without being gaudy. I approved of it a little bit against my will. I saw four men-at-arms during the passage; they seemed to be concentrating on not being bored. They looked like the others, but didn't have metal hats on. I only hoped, for their sakes, that when I was out of sight they got to lean against the wall and scratch themselves.

He led me up a winding set of stairs to a hallway covered in white carpeting with a highly polished tan wooden railing on the side overlooking the central hall. Two more guards stood before it, and they exchanged a look with the butler, then, very quickly, crossed their tall ax-things, barring the door. Rocza almost jumped from my shoulder at the sudden movement, and Loiosh was pretty startled as well. So was I. Before I had time to wonder, the guards snapped back into place, clearing the way again.

At the same time the butler stepped forward and said—how to tell you what he said? It was silly, and it rhymed, but it's hard to translate to get the feel right. The closest I can come is, "Baron Vladimir Merss, on bended knee, requests my lord the Count to see," but it was longer than that, and even stupider. In Fenarian, everything rhymes, so it could have been an accident that this did, but I don't think so. If I hadn't been so surprised, I think I'd have laughed out loud.

The Count was in the room that, I've no doubt, he called his "study." He was old, old, old, old. A big man, though he somehow looked shrunken as he sat. His hands, crossed on the desk in front of him, were lined and wrinkled with veins standing out. His eyes were mild and there were more veins apparent in his nose. His hair and stiff mustaches were iron gray. His complexion was swarthy—about like mine—but had an unhealthy look to it. He wore a sort of red mantle over what looked like blue velvet, which made him look both bigger and more sickly; there was some sort of intricate scrollwork decorating the mantle; very likely it spelled out his lineage or something.

This was my first encounter with the Nobility of my homeland. I was underwhelmed.

His voice, however, was strong. "Baron Merss," he said. "Forgive me if I do not rise."

"My lord Count," I said, bowing deeply. "Thank you on behalf of Her Majesty for seeing me."

"Please, sit. Of course. Wine? Brandy?"

"Wine would be nice."

He rang a bell on his desk. The butler entered, was told to bring in a glass of wine and a snifter of something he called *barparlot*. He left and returned fast enough that I might have suspected he'd had them ready.

"Well," said the Count as he raised his glass and I raised mine. "I trust the Empress wishes for paper?"

I'd half expected it, but I still love it when they hand it to you on a platter; he'd just done ninety percent of my work for me. I did the rest: I nodded.

"No doubt, you will wish to see the facilities?"

"And bring back samples, of course."

"Of course." He hesitated. "May I ask, my lord . . ." He trailed off.

"Why I've been staying in town without letting you or anyone know my business?"

He smiled. He had most of his teeth, though there was one in front on the bottom that was missing.

I shrugged. "I wanted to observe things from an outsider's perspective first. I wanted to see the setting, watch the deliveries go out, speak to some of the workers, that sort of thing."

"Just to buy paper?"

I gave him a smile, and let him interpret it however he wished.

He grunted a little. "I am not involved much in the day-to-day activities of the mill, you know."

"Mill?"

"The paper mill."

"Oh," I said.

"I take it you aren't an expert on paper?"

I laughed. "Hardly. Merely a human with the good fortune

to be trusted by Her Majesty. I am not expected to make informed judgments about the paper, just about the people involved."

"It seems odd," he said, "that the Empire would look to our little kingdom for something like this."

I grinned. "No, it doesn't, my lord. If it had seemed odd, you'd not have known my purpose so quickly. In fact, I would venture to guess that you have been expecting someone like me for some time."

He nodded. "Well, yes. You are aware—or, perhaps, your Empress is, or one of her bureaucrats—that here is made the finest paper anywhere."

"Exactly."

He nodded. "When would be a good time for you to look over the mill?"

"The sooner the better," I said. "How about tomorrow?"

"I'll make the arrangements."

I sat back and looked around. "I like your home."

"Thank you," he said. "It once belonged to the old Baron, before he sold it to my grandfather. It goes back many years. Though perhaps not so many to one who lives among the elfs. Is that difficult?"

"One can get used to anything," I said. "Although, no slur on your, ah, your mill, sir, but the odor in your town is rather noticeable."

He smiled a little. "There is a reason we picked an estate that is ten miles from the mill."

I nodded. "Of course. I should do the same. Other than the odor, it is a pleasant town, though odd."

"Odd?"

"The Guild," I said.

"What of it?" He seemed a bit sharp.

"I didn't mean to give offense," I said. "Indeed, it had been my impression that the Guild had no standing with the county, and hence couldn't reflect on yourself in any way."

His cheek twitched a little; I'm not sure what that meant. "That is true," he said. "I am not offended. But what is unusual about it?"

"Hmmm? I've known of Guilds that had complete control of some local craftsmen, but never of a Guild of merchants, or one that had such complete control of a town."

He blinked. "I have control of the town," he said. He sounded like he meant it.

"Well," I said, "yes. No doubt. But still, the Guild—"

"Fugh," he said, or something like it, and courtesy required me to change the subject. Sometimes in my business you don't know if someone is lying or just plain crazy, and you have to live with that.

Meanwhile, I made a temporary retreat and asked him questions about his furnishings, the pictures in the Great Hall, and so on. He relaxed, and seemed to enjoy the conversation, while I tried to work around to a way to start pumping him again. During a pause between questions about the workings of the Imperial Court (some of which I could answer, the rest of which I could lie about plausibly) I said, "Another oddity is the set of beliefs concerning witchcraft. As a stranger from another country, that is odd to me."

He didn't appear to take the question at any more than face value. "What beliefs?" he asked.

"This notion of 'light' and 'dark' forms of the Art. It is new to me."

"Odd you should bring that up," he said.

"Oh?"

"I had meant to ask you about it."

If he saw some expression of surprise on my face, that was

all right; it was both honest and in character for the role I was playing. He glanced at Loiosh and Rocza, cleared his throat, and said, "It is obvious you're a witch."

"Well, yes," I said.

"I am not. But it would seem that anything may be used for, ah, different purposes."

"Well, yes."

"For good, shall we say, or evil."

"I had never exactly thought of it in those terms," I said honestly, "but I guess I know what you mean."

He nodded. "Well?"

"Uh, well what?"

"How would you describe your own practice?"

I drank some wine, then stared at the glass. It was a very nice glass, hand-blown, thin, delicate. "I have never considered myself evil," I finally said.

"I imagine no one does," he said.

"Maybe you could explain why this is important to you? It seems odd you should ask a stranger that question."

He chuckled. "And impolite? I'm sorry. It has become important."

I sat back a little. "How so?"

He gave one of those looks people give when they imagine they can look into your eyes and see if you're lying. Just for the record, that doesn't work. Well, sometimes it does, if you know what to look for. But don't bet your life on it. And don't try it on me.

After a moment, he said, "There is history there, stretching back for some years. That isn't important right now. More recently, I suspect I have been, ah, harmed by a follower of the darker ways of your craft."

"Recently," I said. "How recently? I only got to town a couple of days ago."

"Last night," he said.

"Indeed? A busy night—I was harmed as well."

"I know. I have simply assumed that it isn't coincidental that, with family in this area, you were sent by your Empress."

"Hardly. And I don't think it coincidental that my kin were murdered after I arrived. Do you?"

"Unlikely," he said laconically.

"I take it you have enemies."

He nodded.

"So, then," I said, "perhaps your enemies are mine."

"Perhaps so," he said. I could see him thinking, *Or perhaps my enemy is you.* Which I guess meant he could be telling the truth, or could be as straightforward as a Yendi—that is to say, not.

"Would you care to tell me what happened to you?"

"Why not?" he said. "It's no secret, or if it is it won't be for long. Last night, my coachman was murdered."

Okay, well, I don't know what I'd expected, but it wasn't that. I couldn't say anything for a moment, while the anger I'd been trying to suppress threatened to erupt right here and now. I don't know what I'd have done—torn apart the room? Thrown his glasses around? Beaten up his butler?

He saw something of what was going on inside of me, I guess, because he flinched.

"Did you know him?" he asked, looking genuinely puzzled.

"Someone," I said, "is going to—"

"Boss!"

Loiosh was right. I stopped and just shook my head. I took a couple of deep breaths. "How was he killed?"

"Witchcraft, I am told. I haven't yet learned the details."

"Who would know them?"

He frowned. "This does not, I think, concern you, my lord."

"My lord, in light of what happened to my family, I beg to disagree with you."

"You think they are connected in some way?"

I knew they were connected in some way. "The timing seems significant," I said. "Unless this sort of thing happens all the time around here."

He nodded. "Yes, you may be right. But I know of no connection between my coachman or the Merss family, or between my coachman and you. Do you?"

"No. Nevertheless—"

"Then, for now, I do not believe I should tell you any more."

It was becoming difficult not to say the things I shouldn't say. I took a moment, then eventually managed, "My lord, I'll not take up any more of your time. I look forward to hearing from your people."

"Of course," he said. "Forgive me if I do not stand. My man will show you out."

I bowed. He leaned back as if exhausted; I guess I'd tired him out a bit. It would be an odd sort of irony if my visit exerted him to the point where he dropped dead.

The butler guided me down the stairs and back toward the front doors.

"Did you know him?" I asked suddenly.

"My lord?"

"Zollie. Did you know him?"

He cleared his throat, started to speak, then just nodded.

"What happened?" I asked him.

We had reached the front door. He stopped with his hand out toward the iron handle and gave me a look of inquiry. "My lord?"

I shrugged and met his gaze. "You must have a theory about who killed him, and why."

"Not at all, my lord."

"Crap."

He hesitated. "Did my lord know him?"

"No, but the matter interests me. I was told he was killed by a witch."

"So it would seem, my lord."

"What was the actual cause of death?"

"Sudden heart failure, my lord."

"Um. And you're sure it was a witch?"

"He had the mark."

"The mark?"

"The witch-mark, my lord."

"What's a witch-mark?"

It's hard to describe the look he gave me. It was a mix of surprise, reserve, disbelief, and courtesy. I'm not certain Teldra could have done it better. I waited him out. He said, "I'm sure I wouldn't know, my lord."

"Who would?"

"My lord?"

"Cut it out. Just don't. I'm in a very bad mood, and you don't want to make it any worse. Where did you hear about it, and who would know?"

I could see him at war with himself for an instant, but training, or fear, or something else won. He said, "My lord, I would have no idea about such things."

"All right," I said. "He had a girl he liked to meet at the inn. What is her name?"

He only hesitated a moment, that time. "Eelie," he said.

"Thanks," I said with a bit of a twist on it.

"I shall have the groom bring your horse." He held the door for me and stood like a statue. I really had no choice but to go through it.

I waited in front, and presently the groom emerged, leading Marsi.

I never did learn the butler's name. Maybe he didn't have one.

I gave the stable-boy back at the Pointy Hat a good tip, which he accepted graciously, and then I said good-bye to Marsi, as good a horse as they get, I think; even Loiosh didn't have anything bad to say about her. Here's an odd thing: The inn was feeling enough like home to me that I found I didn't need to conceal how wobbly I was after dismounting.

I got a glass of coffee from the host and went over to what had become "my table" sometime in the last couple of days. Sitting felt good. The ache in my legs passed quickly; it took longer before I had relaxed enough to think clearly. The coffee helped in that, but klava would have helped more. Dammit.

I noticed I was hungry and thought about getting more lamb stew, but changed my mind. Instead I went back out into the street, where the stench pretty effectively killed my appetite. I walked past the docks and saw the factory—excuse me, the "mill"—churning out smoke and stench. I didn't slow down. I got to the other inn and noticed for the first time that they had incense burners about the room. It must have been fairly subtle incense for me not to have noticed, but it worked. I wondered why the Hat didn't have them. Maybe they did and they were just concealed better.

At this time of the day—it was still early afternoon—I had the place to myself save for a bored-looking middle-aged barmaid, who asked if I wanted anything. My appetite had returned, so I ended up getting some decent bean soup and a loaf of bread served with garlic cloves and a lot of butter. Good butter.

As the barmaid was bringing me a glass of bitter-tasting wine called Enekesner (I got the name to be certain I never accidentally ordered it again), I asked her when Eelie would be showing up.

"Won't be in today," she said.

"Where can I find her?"

She looked me over. She'd done something to darken her

eyebrows, and something else to make her lips shiny. I've always wondered about stuff like that. But not too much.

"Don't waste your time," she said.

"Is she a friend of yours?"

She shrugged. "Not especially. Why?"

I pulled out three silver coins and let them ring on top of the table. "Where can I find her?"

Her eyes widened, and she said, "Upstairs, room at the end of the hall."

I was glad the barmaid hadn't been a friend of hers; it would have cost me another coin. I took my time finishing the meal, then went to the back and up the stairs. I had to hit the door twice before I heard a faint voice say, "What is it?"

"My name is Merss," I said. "I want to talk to you."

"Go away," she suggested.

"Open the door," I suggested back, "or I'll knock the bloody thing down."

There was a pause, and the door opened. She was pretty enough, I guess, except for her eyes. She'd been crying.

"Tell me what you know," I said, continuing with the whole suggestion line.

"What the hell does it matter to you?" She started crying again. I ignored it.

"I'm going to find out who did it, and kill him," I said.

Her red eyes widened a little. "Why?" she said, barely whispering.

"I'm just in that kind of a mood," I said. "Tell me what you know."

She hesitated again, then stood aside, which I took as an invitation to enter her room. I did so, and she shut the door. It was a tiny room, with little enough to show who she was, and that little I paid no attention to. There was the bed and a chair. She didn't suggest I sit, so I just stood there and waited.

"You talked to him last night," she said.

"Yeah."

"He told me about you. He thought you . . ."

"What?"

"He thought you were funny." She started sobbing. I leaned against the door and waited. A moment later she said, "I'm sorry."

"I'm told a witch killed him."

"He had the witch-mark."

"What is the witch-mark?"

Her eyes flicked to Loiosh and Rocza, then back to me; her forehead was creased. "Different lands, different customs, different ways of doing things," I told her. "I've heard of a witch's mark, something that indicates a person is a witch. I don't think you're using the term that way, and, anyway, I don't believe in them. Fill me in. What is a witch-mark?"

"When they found him, his lips were red."

"Um," I said. "Why is that called a witch-mark?"

"You really don't know?"

Patience, Vlad. "I really don't know."

"A witch will send an imp down your throat to your heart. The imp leaves red footprints on the lips."

There were some problems with that—the first being that you can't really get to the heart from the throat (you pick up a bit of anatomy when you kill people for a living), the second being that I don't believe in imps.

To be sure, there is a way to kill someone using the Art that will leave red lips; it involves a simple transformation, replacing the contents of his lungs with the smoke from your brazier. But—

Okay, now wasn't the time. "All right," I said. "Where was he found?"

She looked at me for a long moment, then looked at her bed, then back at me.

"Oh," I said.

"He was going to marry me," she said. "He told me so."

I nodded, choosing not to ask when he had told her and how many times for fear she might take it the right way. Okay, so I'm a bastard; but there are limits. "I'm sorry," I told her. "I'll leave you alone now."

"You'll find out who did it?" she said, and there was something a little scary in her eyes.

"Yes, I will. I'll also find out why."

"And you'll kill him?"

"Yes," I said. "I will."

"Good," she said. "Will you make it slow?"

"I'll make it certain."

She nodded.

Okay, maybe I shouldn't have told her that; I certainly would never have admitted that I was going to kill someone to anyone, ever, back in the Empire. And maybe I was a bit too contemptuous of what this kingdom used for law, and should have been more worried. But I wanted to give her that much, and, in the event, of all the things that turned around and bit me, that wasn't one; so I guess I got away with it, if you like.

I left her and went back down to the main room, and from there back into the stench. It hit me hard that time, I remember; almost like a blow. My stomach turned and I actually gagged there, in the street; the reeking foulness of the whole town was suddenly, just for a moment, too much for me. I made my way back to the Pointy Hat; I can remember my eyes felt glazed and it was all I could do to put one foot in front of another until I'd passed the threshold.

I made it to my table, and, yeah, they had the same subtle incense here they did at the other place, only I couldn't see where it came from. It helped, though. I'd never been fond of incense before; it was another tool of the Art, not something one used just to brighten up one's day. I know that many witches—including my grandfather—live so that there is no clear distinction between practicing the Art and simply living; subtle spells and charms are part of his life. Not me; for me there had always been a sharp line: Here I was doing a spell, here I was done with it. But now, maybe that was changing. I could imagine getting very fond of incense. I could just imagine the look on Cawti's face when I told her I was—

Yeah, shake it off, Vlad.

The thought of brandy repulsed me, and I didn't need coffee, so I did something unusual for me: I had the host draw me a summer ale. It was warmer than I'd have liked, but not too bitter. I nodded my approval to Inchay, who gave me a rare smile. I guess he was proud of his ale.

I sat and drank it slowly while my head stopped turning, and gradually I was able to focus on the problem in front of me. I got up and paced a bit, earning me a look from the host; then I sat down again. It hit me that one thing that was so odd was that there was so much violence going on, and I was pretty sure I was somehow at the center of it, but I wasn't doing any of it, and none of it was directed at me. I wasn't used to that.

Well, but let's think about that, Vlad. If they aren't trying to kill you, there's a reason. The most likely reason is that they know that if they try, you're liable to put a nice pretty shine on a whole lot of them. Which immediately calls up the question: How do they know that? It isn't like I was walking around looking dangerous, or anything. Was the mere fact that I openly carried a blade sufficient to tell them? It didn't seem likely. So either they're good enough to spot me for what I am, or else they have some reason to suspect I'm someone they shouldn't touch.

Or they know who I am.

To be sure, the Guild knew my name, as did whatever witch or witches had pulled it from my mind. But how much more had they gotten? Enough to know to get a message to the Jhereg? And, if so, would they want to? Would they know how?

It was possible. It was possible there was an assassin heading this way, right now, as fast as teleportation and feet could carry him. But why? If they were going to do that, it would be for the money. If they did manage to get hold of the right people in the Jhereg, they wouldn't be told to lay off me; they'd be told they could get a lot of money for delivering my head.

Morganti.

The Jhereg would want it done their way. So, if I assume there is some means of communication between some group here and the Jhereg—dubious, but possible—they could have been told to keep me in town, but not to kill me, and that would account for at least some of what was going on.

Maybe, but it certainly seemed like a stretch. Especially considering that they wouldn't have let me know that my name wasn't a secret; nor would anyone working for them. At least, not if they had any sense.

All in all, it was more likely there was something entirely different going on: something that had to do with the complex politics of a strange Guild, a Count who owned a factory— excuse me, a "mill"—and whatever forces there were that I didn't know about. If so, then whatever was going on, it made them believe I was someone they couldn't touch directly.

"What do you think, chum?"

"I think you're right, Boss. Someone wants you not to find out something, and they don't dare come after you directly."

"Suggestions?"

"You mean, other than leaving?"

"Yeah, other than that."

"No."

I considered the plan I'd come up with, all of—uh, two days ago? The people I'd want to get information from were dead, or had dropped out of sight, or had managed to forestall me one way or another. But I had learned a few things, hadn't I?

Yes.

I'd learned that there were all sorts of talk of witchcraft, and maybe it had been used to kill someone, it had certainly been used to burn a house down, and it was unlike the Art I knew, and there were two sides, one of which involved my family, and they were dead, and the other side—

Had been bloody noticeable by its absence.

Okay.

I needed to find out who those witches were. A Coven? A bunch of individuals who practiced the Art in some particular way that I didn't know about, one of whom happened to be worried about me finding something out? No, there was a Coven of some kind; with all the strange politics in this town, there couldn't not be. How to find it, and learn about it?

Yeah, okay, now at least I had a direction.

Part of the problem is that, at the best of times, witches tend to be secretive. I once asked my grandfather why that was, and he gave me one of those "that's the way it is" kind of answers. I've always hated those. So, how, then, to find a witch?

"Loiosh? You must have a touch of the Sight."

"You're just a laugh a minute, Boss. Okay, what do you want me to do?"

"Nothing special, just stay aware for any castings. If you pick up on one, I want to know where it's coming from."

"Boss, I'd have to be almost on top of it to tell, or else it would have to be an awfully strong Working."

"I know. Just stay aware."

"All right."

I wondered where Orbahn was, and why he'd been making

himself so scarce. It was far from impossible that he was dead by now, like Zollie, and his body concealed.

I wondered where Zollie's body was now, and if I could get permission to look at it, and if I could tell anything if I wanted to risk removing my amulet again, and if I dared do so. The answers were something like "probably not" all the way down the line. But I thought about his red lips and wondered.

8

BORAAN (shrugging): *He is a Jhegaala. We can't know how a Jhegaala will react until we know what stage he is at.*

LEFITT: *Indeed. That is just how one generally finds out.*

BORAAN: *Inefficient, to be sure.*

LEFITT: *Irritating.*

BORAAN: *Frustrating.*

LEFITT: *Enraging.*

BORAAN: *Monstrous.*

LEFITT: *They ought to be required to wear signs.*

—Miersen, *Six Parts Water*
Day Two, Act I, Scene 1

Evening fell, and business picked up a little as it became too dark to work the fields; at the same time, at the other place, workmen would be coming from the mill. All of them, in both places, tired, sweaty, stinking, and determined to forget their dreary lives. Peasants are ignorant and filthy; workmen are smelly and loud. Put 'em together and shake 'em up however you want, and what's the difference? And these were the people Cawti had thrown me over for. How do you make sense of that?

I guess you don't make sense of it, you just deal with it. There's a lot of stuff like that.

I went out into the evening and walked west down the road. A few steps and I was out of the town; I continued about a quarter of a mile the way I'd first come. It was amazing how alone I was. The few lights from Burz did nothing to break up the darkness. There was a breeze in my face and no stench. I looked up. Stars, small lights against the dead black of the sky of these human lands, glittered.

How long I was out there, I don't know, but eventually Loiosh said, *"Someone's coming, Boss."* A moment later I heard footsteps. I probably should have been ready, had a dagger in my hand or something, but I was in a mood. In any case, I wasn't attacked.

The footsteps stopped. Someone had good night vision. "Lord Merss?"

It was a male voice, and not one I recognized. I didn't turn around. "Yes," I said.

"I've been looking for you."

"And you've found me. You must tell me how you do it. I haven't found anything I've been looking for since I set foot in this bloody town."

"You weren't that hard to find. Call me Dahni."

"Good to meet you, Dahni. What's your part in all of this?"

"Ah, there's the question, isn't it?" he said. "Too many factions, and none of them to be trusted."

"I couldn't have said it better myself. There's something about your speech that—"

"No, I'm not a native of this country. I'm from a small kingdom to the east where the women are prettier but the food isn't as good."

"Choose the food," I said. "Can't go wrong that way."

"And so I did."

"Wise."

"Yes, indeed. But, speaking of wisdom, you've put yourself into a bit of what you'd call a situation, haven't you?"

"Have I? And here I thought things were going swimmingly."

"I can help."

"All right, I'm listening."

"First, you're going to want to know why you should listen to me."

"Not at all. I'm listening to you because I like your accent."

He laughed. "You and I could get along, Lord Merss. All right, then, why you should believe me."

"That's going to take some work, yes."

"I'm here as a favor for a friend."

"What's his name?"

He laughed again. "You don't expect me to answer that, do you?"

"Not really, no."

"So then, this friend thinks you might be in a position to do him some good, and that he could do you some good in exchange."

"I'm still listening."

"I'm guessing that what you need more than anything is information."

"Good guess."

"Well, here I am. Ask me things. Preferably things you can check."

Nice idea, that. Only it wasn't so simple: You can learn a lot by what someone wants to know, and I wasn't inclined to let this guy learn a lot. So far, he'd done exactly nothing to convince me I could trust him.

"Anyone else around, Loiosh?"

"No, Boss."

"Okay," I said. "Tell me why this town is so strange."

"Mmmm," he said. "Haven't been in Fenario long, have you?"

"No."

"This town isn't any more strange than any other in this country. Each has its idiosyncrasies."

"Idiosyncrasies."

"The King rarely exerts much control over the counties. They go as they go, and whatever oddities crop up determine the nature of that county. Now, if you want to see a *really* odd place, head all the way east into the mountains, not far from my country. There's a place called Tuz where they train goats to smuggle by getting them to—"

"All right," I said. "I get the idea. Each county is on its own."

"Yes. And this one took a turn, oh, I don't know, a few hundred years ago, maybe, when some peasant turned up an old recipe for making really good paper, and making it in quantity. He sold it to the Count—probably in exchange for a wagon and two horses to get himself out of town—and since then—"

"Tell me what you can about this friend of yours. What does he imagine I can do for him?"

"You have a common enemy, that's always a good basis for an alliance of some sort."

"All right. Who is the enemy?"

"Don't you know?"

"Don't play games with me, Dahni."

"Eh, this is all a big game, Lord Merss. That's why I'm here; I play games well, because I can always find the cracks in the rules."

"And you're careful never to spell out what the rules are to any other players who don't know."

"Exactly."

"Good, then. I'm happy for you. Have your fun. Who is the enemy?"

"I'm sorry, Lord Taltos."

There are any number of ways of dealing with someone who is trying to get information from you, and who you think might be good enough to pull it off. I thought about the simplest one: I almost killed him right then and there. I could have, too. I couldn't see him, but Loiosh knew where he was. I came very close. It would have been a mistake, certainly—I had no real reason to, and if I had, things would have gone, let's say, differently. But I wanted to.

"Turn and walk away," I told him.

I guess he must have picked up something from my tone, because he didn't say another word. I heard his boot-steps receding.

"*Loiosh, keep track of him. I want to make sure he isn't waiting somewhere.*"

He flew off and did so, reporting that he'd gone back to town, and was last seen entering a house. Loiosh marked which house it was, then came back. He also made sure I was walking the right way back to town.

The light from the inn grew quickly, until it was hurting my eyes. I walked more slowly to give my vision time to adjust.

"*Well now. That was certainly interesting. Did we get more information than we gave away?*"

"*You're the expert on that, Boss. I'm just eyes with wings.*"

"*And a good sense of the arcane.*" We had reached the door of the Hat.

"*Is that a question? No, I haven't picked up any witchcraft.*"

"*All right.*"

I muttered. The strange practice of the Art in this strange town was one of the things I needed to know about.

There were only a few people in the inn by this time, and the host was having a quiet conversation with a couple of them.

The barmaid had left, so I interrupted Inchay long enough to get a cup of the summer ale he was so proud of. I was hungry but I didn't feel like eating; I was tired but I knew I wouldn't be able to sleep; I was angry but I didn't have anyone to kill. Random killings, power-hungry guilds, witches with practices—or at least beliefs—that made no sense. It was irritating. There was just too much going on. I didn't know the details of any of them, and I didn't know which ones fit together, or how. I took out a dagger and started flipping it, chewing my lip, trying to make sense of the whole thing.

"Boss. . . ."

The host was staring at me. I gave him a warm smile and put the dagger away. It was either that or carve him with it, and I didn't feel like standing up.

"How many days have we been here, Loiosh?"

"Years, Boss. We've been here years."

"It does sort of feel like that, doesn't it?"

"Does that mean you're thinking about leaving?"

"Not yet."

"Okay."

"How is Rocza doing?"

"Picking up my moods, Boss. Sorry."

"It's all right. This is tough for all of us."

"But why—"

"I need to do this."

"You could always just go poking around and stirring things up with no plan and see what happens," he said, meaning that's just what I'd been doing.

"You're pretty funny," I said, meaning he wasn't.

He was right, though. Stumbling around to stir things up can be effective, up to a point. It can work; you might learn things that way. But sometimes when you do that people get killed, and sometimes it's the wrong people.

Loiosh nuzzled the side of my neck.

"Yeah, I know," I told him.

I got bread and cheese from Inchay and made myself eat some, and fed some to Loiosh and Rocza. The cheese was salty. I don't like salty cheese. I got some more summer ale to wash it down, which was probably why he sold salty cheese. Bastard.

"Tell me something," I said as I picked up the ale. "What sort of witchcraft do they practice around here?"

"Eh." He fixed me with a hard stare. "The clean, decent kind, so far as I know. But I don't practice myself. Ask someone who does."

"Who would that be?"

"Hmmm?"

"Who practices the Art? Point someone out."

"In here?"

"Sure."

There were four people in the place, all by themselves, drinking quietly. Two of them were watching us, the other two were drunk.

"I don't keep track," he said. "And if I did, I wouldn't tell a stranger. All right?"

I shrugged. "Then let me ask you something else."

His eyes narrowed and his jaw set. "What?"

"Do you sell salty cheese on purpose, just to get people to buy more ale?"

After a second, he chuckled, then moved down to the other end of the bar. I went back to my table.

"Well, how about that. You try the direct approach, and it works. I'll have to remember that."

"What do you mean worked, Boss?"

"You weren't watching his eyes."

"He gestured at someone?"

"Not on purpose."

"Who?"

"Middle of the room, long gray coat, curly hair, looks like he's about to pass out."

"Should I follow him when he leaves?"

"Might be a tad obvious for me to follow him out, and then come back in shy one jhereg."

"Window to the roof, and I'll watch the door from there."

"Yeah, sounds good."

I took another swallow of the beer, set the mug down, and went up to my room. I opened the shutters, and Loiosh flew out the window and up. I settled back to wait.

About twenty minutes, that's what it took. He flew back in the window like he didn't have a care in the world.

"Got it, Boss. He was just down the street. I'd have been back sooner if he hadn't fallen on his face a couple of times on the way home."

"Hmm. So, by now, he's probably asleep."

"I thought it was called passed out."

"So if . . . yes. Okay, show me this place."

"You're the boss."

So, down the stairs, and then once more out into the dark and the stench. And if you're getting tired of hearing how much it stank, imagine how tired I was getting of walking through it. Phew.

Loiosh, who has better night vision than I do—which is to say, he has at least some night vision—flew just a bit in front of me, and guided me down the middle of another of the surprisingly wide roads of the town. I quickly had no idea which way we were going, or where we were in relation to the inn, but quite soon Loiosh said, "This is it."

"All right."

I listened and heard snores. I tried the door and found it unlocked; it didn't make too much noise when it opened, and then I was inside.

"One step forward, Boss. Another. Hold out your hand. Right. A little more. There. That's a candle."

There seemed to be a wall between me and the snoring. *"Anyone in this room?"*

"No."

It amazing how bright a single candle can be, and how much it hurts your eyes. There was a simple enchantment to adjust one's eyes to the dark or to the light; but of course I wasn't about to remove my amulet to cast it, so I waited.

The snores stopped, and a drunken voice went, "Huh, what?"

I strained, and there was whispering, followed by the drunk again: "Lemme sleep."

The whisper again, and this time I could make out words: "Lahchi, someone's in the house!"

I considered calling back, "No there isn't," but it didn't seem like that good an idea. I set the candle down.

My eyes had adjusted enough that I was able to position myself next to the door. I turned to the side and pulled up the collar of my cloak. I could hear him fumbling around in the room, and when the door opened I got enough of a glimpse of the bedroom to note the position of people and objects.

I reminded myself that with humans, the throat is more intimidating than the back of the neck; I'm not sure exactly why that is, but it's the sort of thing worth knowing.

This was going to have to be fast. The dagger I carried at my belt had the heaviest pommel, so I picked that; as he walked by me, I gave him a sharp one to the back of the head; I had no idea if he'd lose consciousness, but in his present state it ought to be enough to complete his disorientation. Before he hit the floor I was next to the bed pressing the back of the dagger against the woman's throat. Cold steel against your throat in the dark is going to get your attention, and by using the dull side I could press hard without getting blood everywhere. I spoke in a normal tone of voice.

"Not a sound, not a motion, not a whisper, or you're both dead."

The moment when she might have screamed came and went. I heard him moaning a little.

"Got an eye on him, Loiosh?"

"Got it, Boss."

I said, "I have no intention of killing, hurting, or even stealing from you. Don't do anything to change my mind. I have questions. You'll answer them, then I'll leave. Nod your head."

She nodded once. Her eyes were very wide.

"Your husband is a witch. Are you as well?"

Her eyes widened. I repeated the question.

She nodded again. Good, that saved some trouble.

"Are you a member of the Coven?"

Hesitation, then a nod.

"Who runs it?"

"I, we, I don't know."

"You don't know."

"The heads of the Coven, they appoint each other, secretly. They wear hoods at gatherings. When they invite you, they're all hooded and you never know who they are."

Well, okay; Noish-pa had mentioned that it worked that way sometimes. At least I had confirmed that there *was* a Coven; that was progress.

"I need to know about the two sorts of witchcraft in this town. You'll explain it to me."

From ambient light from the candle in the next room, I could see her just well enough to observe that she looked puzzled. I pulled the knife from her throat, but kept it in my hand. I said, "Take a moment to think. It is important to me to understand, and no one will answer my questions. You will answer my questions. Yes?"

"I don't understand," she whispered.

"You don't need to understand, you just need to tell me what I want to know."

"Who are you?"

"The one with the knife. Someone said something about witches who follow the light, and those who follow the dark. What does that mean?"

I had a certain amount of sympathy for the woman. You wake up in the middle of the night, your husband is dead drunk and then he gets slugged by a stranger who's invaded your home, and the stranger wants to ask you esoteric questions about the nature of the arcane arts. It can't be easy to wrap your head around that well enough to give a coherent answer, no matter how much you want to, so when her mouth had opened and closed a few times, and I saw panic building in her eyes, I said, "All right, let me try something easier. Why did most of the Merss family leave town?"

"The Merss family?"

"Yes. The ones who weren't killed yesterday."

"But they left years ago."

"I know. Why?"

"I don't know. It was years ago. Before I was born. I just heard about it."

"What did you hear?"

"They were the last of the followers of the dark way."

"What do followers of the dark way do that followers of the light way don't?"

"They practiced forbidden magic."

"What magic is forbidden?"

"They summoned demons."

As far as I could tell, she actually believed that. She was a *witch*, and she believed that. How can you practice the Art and yet remain so ignorant of it? It was nonsense, of course. There are such things as demons, and, yes, they can be summoned, but not by witchcraft. To summon a demon requires breaking through the barriers that separate realities—and no, that makes no more sense to me than it does to you, unless you happen to have studied necromancy, in which case you know a lot more about this stuff than I do so why are you asking me? But the point is, the art of the witch is simply to use the energy of the mind to manipulate probabilities, and there are strictly limited ways in which that can be done. Yeah, one time I caused a small object to be transported to me from thousands of miles away using witchcraft, and I know you aren't supposed to be able to do that, either; but that is a lot different from bending the entire shape of reality within a given space to make a rift in something that doesn't exist in the first place.

Besides, I was desperate that time. I don't want to think about it.

What mattered here wasn't whether the "dark" witches had actually done this, what mattered was that this woman thought they could. And this whole "dark" and "light" business had a smell to it that reminded me a lot of the mill—meaning it stank, if that was too subtle for you. The dark way? The light way? Who thinks like that? Who sees the world in those terms? It isn't something to be believed by anyone with any sense, it's something to convince the gullible of.

Which was the answer, wasn't it? Someone was trying to put one over on a lot of people. And, to judge from this woman, it was working.

So, then, why? In whose interest was it to believe that there were a group of people with this sort of power? Someone had gone to a lot of trouble to sell one hell of a big lie, and there had to be a reason for it.

And my family had been the casualty of a big lie; at least, those who hadn't gotten out—

"Wait, you said they left before you were born?"

She nodded.

"I thought they had only left ten or fifteen years ago."

"Oh, them. I don't think they were witches. They just left because, well, because having the name Merss isn't easy around here. I think they went to the City. It wasn't me!" she said suddenly, looking frightened again. "I mean, I didn't do anything to them, or even say anything about them. It was the others, you know."

"What about the ones who were witches?"

"They left the country. Some say they went West to sell their souls to the elfs."

Yeah, some would say that.

"And the ones who were killed—who did it?"

"I don't know!" She sounded close to panic.

"I'm not accusing you. But you must have an idea, a theory. You heard about it, you must have had a thought about who it was."

She shook her head.

Was there any way to get more information out of her? Probably not. I could spend an hour getting her calmed down and she still wouldn't want to name anyone. And if I applied pressure, she'd be much more likely to lie than to point the finger at someone who deserved it. That still might be useful information, though. I was in a sort of mood to apply pressure anyway, just for the satisfaction of seeing someone sweat. But I had something to do, and I'd get more pleasure out of squeezing when I knew it was the right person being squeezed.

Which brought me back to the point that this woman

might well know who that was, if only I could find a way to convince her to tell me. Without spending all night at it. Damn, damn, damn.

"Are you going to kill me?"

I realized that I'd been standing there for quite a while, not saying anything. "No," I said. "The Coven, where does it meet?"

"East of town, in the woods. I don't know exactly. We come to a place near the creek, then they blindfold us and take us one at a time."

Yeah, they would.

"Okay," I said. "I'm done with you. Feel free to tell anyone you want about my visit, and about the questions I asked. No doubt someone will be angry and some people will come after me. When they do, I'll kill them. Then I'll come back and kill you. If you think that's a good argument for keeping your mouth shut, you're probably right, but it's up to you. In any case, I would suggest you remain here and not leave the house or make a sound for at least an hour or so, but that's also up to you. Meanwhile, rest well."

I put my knife away and walked out of the room. The fellow on the floor was now snoring. I gave serious consideration to kicking him, but didn't; I went past him, out the door, and into the star-studded night of Fenario.

"Well, Loiosh?"

"Well, what, Boss? If you want to summon a demon, I'm afraid you're on your own."

"Yeah, I don't think I'm up for that. That was a lot of information. I have to think about it, about what it means. If anything. Loiosh, didn't Sethra once say something about a lie being temporary? How did she put it?"

"I don't remember. But, Boss, I don't think the lie is your problem."

"No, I guess not. It's just another thing to add to the list. It's

*getting to be a pretty long list, Loiosh. And I am going to find out the
name that needs to go at the top of it."*

"Left here. There, that light on your right is the inn."

I made it back without mishap. I had to bang on the door to
convince the host to let me in. I could have picked the lock in
the dark, but I had no interest in letting it be known that I could
do that. He glowered at me as he opened the door; I gave him a
warm smile and went past him up to my room, where I stripped
off my outer garments, and threw myself onto the bed. The last
thing I remember was Loiosh and Rocza, perched next to each
other on the chair, twining their necks around each other. It reminded me of something painful, but I fell asleep before I could
remember exactly what it was.

9

BORAAN: *Nothing is confusing once the facts are assembled and the proper conclusions drawn.*

LEFITT: *Nonsense, darling. All the facts and conclusions about a confusing situation simply confirm the confusion.*

BORAAN: *You think so?*

LEFITT: *I'm afraid I do, though I do hate to dispute your lovely epigram.*

BORAAN: *Your lovely epigram, my dear. I was quoting you during the affair of the Fisherman's Lamp.*

LEFITT: *Yes, my love, only I said it after we had solved the crime.*

—Miersen, *Six Parts Water*
Day Two, Act II, Scene 3

I'd forgotten to close the shutters again, and so woke with the Furnace burning painfully into my eyes. I cursed for a little while, then got up and closed them, because it is better to close the shutters than curse the light, or however that goes. I tried to sleep some more but it didn't take.

I dressed and went downstairs for coffee. The host's wife was behind the bar, and she gave me a look that indicated she wouldn't have been there if her husband hadn't been woken up in the middle of the night to let me into the inn. But she didn't say anything, so I kept my thoughts on the subject to myself and just drank my coffee: bitter on the tongue, but it works just as well as good klava when it hits the belly. That's the difference, I guess: klava is a pleasure, coffee is merely physic.

Pretty effective physic, though. As it started working, my attitude got a little better—or, rather, less bad—and when I got some toasted bread and cheese from her I tipped her well. This cheese, unlike what I'd had last night, turned out to be sharp and musky and neither crumbly nor salty, which I could have considered a reward from the gods for my generosity. I fed some to Loiosh and Rocza, who seemed to agree with my preference.

"Got a plan for today, Boss?"

"Part of one. I'm going to sit here and find out if our friend from last night kept her mouth shut."

"What if she didn't?"

"Then I will engage in acts of violence and mayhem."

"Oh, good. I've been missing those."

A little later the host came down and walked up to me. For a minute, I thought I was going to be evicted, and wondered how I'd respond, but he put a folded and sealed paper in front of me, saying, "This arrived for you from His Lordship," and stalked off with no other remarks.

I opened it. In four times as many words as it should have taken, it told the "Daylord" (whatever that might mean) to see that I was given full access to the mill and treated with all courtesy due to an honored friend of &c &c and to the boat crew to provide, to and from, transportation such as was available and befitting &c &c.

"Well, there it is, Boss. We going to visit it today?"

"*Maybe. Not right away.*" I folded up the paper and put it away for later consideration.

I drank enough coffee to convince myself that no group of enraged citizens or dour law-enforcement officials were going to charge into the inn with the intention of pulling me out to face justice for my criminal actions of the night before. I think I was relieved.

"*Okay,*" I said. "*That's enough. Let's take a walk.*"

"*Anywhere in particular?*"

"*I'll tell you when we get there.*"

"*That means no, which means we're going to the dock.*"

"*Shut up.*"

I headed for the dock, and stood looking out at the mill, churning away, smoke rising and dissipating and meandering off to the northeast. The smell wasn't quite as bad today. I wondered if there were people living to the northeast, and how they were liking the breeze about now.

"*What is, Boss?*"

"*Hmm?*"

"*You muttered 'trap.'*"

"*Oh, did I?*"

The mill across the river was squat and long and built of stone, and I didn't see one single Verra-be-damned window in the place.

"*Yeah, well, I don't know if it is, but it looks like one.*"

"*I see what you mean. Let's not go there.*"

"*Not until we know more, anyway.*"

It was well before noon, and the Furnace cast long shadows of the houses to my left. My grandfather had once mentioned something called "Shadowreading," which involved somehow seeing portents and omens in the shape of shadows of various objects at certain times. I never learned much about it, because he thought it was nonsense.

I wondered what he'd tell me about this. He approved of the idea of me finding out something about my mother; I know because he said so, and because he gave me that note. But I'd dearly love to hear his thoughts on "light" and "dark" forms of the Art, and all of the strange politics of this place.

He'd tell me not to be distracted by the shadows, but to concentrate on the target. And I'd tell him that all I could see were the shadows. And he'd point out that shadows need a light source, and a real object to define the shape.

Well, okay, Noish-pa. I'll describe the shadows, and you tell me what object has a shape like that, eh? We have a Count who owns a paper mill. We have a family killed because I was asking questions about them. We have a coachman killed because he answered the questions. We have Dahni, who carries on conversations in the dark and wants to recruit me to his side, but won't say which side is his, or even what the sides are. We have Orbahn, in the bright blue vest, who gives me vague hints and warnings and then vanishes. We have a Merchants' Guild that runs the entire town, and the rest of the county too, for all I know, and may or may not be tied into bizarre customs of witchcraft, one of which forbids the summoning of demons, which, in turn, is impossible to begin with. Which parts are shadow, and what is casting them, Noish-pa?

I paced, and stared at the mill across the river, and listened to water lap against the dock. As I stood there, the Furnace rose, and the shadows became shorter. It was becoming warm, and I thought about going back to the inn and getting a lighter cloak, but transferring even those few surprises I still carried with me seemed like too much work. I really wanted someone to attack me, so I could hit something and watch it bleed. The sight of the Merss farm, burned and smoking, fixed itself in my mind's eye, superimposed over the river and the smoking mill.

A sort of boat—long and ungainly—set out from the mill

and began to work its way downriver, mostly drifting with the current. There were two or three figures on it, though what they were doing I couldn't say. I watched it until it was out of sight, then turned my back on the river.

A few women, some with babes, went into shops along the street; a few children played here and there. Everything looked innocent. Whatever was going on, it was well concealed.

Damn this town. Damn this country.

All right, then.

I could allow myself a certain amount of moaning and complaining and wishing the world were something other than it is, but enough is enough. Besides, I had to tell myself to stop feeling sorry for myself before Loiosh got around to it.

Sometimes if you can find a thread, you can take it and start following it to see where it leads. When I thought about it, I realized that the trouble wasn't lack of threads, but rather too many. So: Pick one, grab hold, see where it goes, and hope someone tries to stop me because that will give me someone to take my frustrations out on.

Dahni.

He'd come out of nowhere, in the middle of the night, talking in all sorts of vague circumlocutions. He wanted me to do something but wouldn't say what it was: therefore, he knew something, and I needed to know it.

"*Loiosh.*"

"*Dahni's house, Boss? Keep a watch on it?*"

"*Yep.*"

"*On my way.*"

I could have gone back to the inn and waited there, but I was getting tired of the bloody place; and besides, I had the feeling that the host and I were reaching the point where something would happen, and unless he turned out to be a key player in all of this (after all, anyone might be), that would just be a waste of perfectly good violence. So I went over to the west side of a warehouse a few steps from where I'd been watching the mill, squatted down in its shade, and waited.

After about half an hour, Loiosh said, *"Either he isn't here, or he's asleep. I haven't heard a sound."*

"All right. Stay with it."

That's how I spent the morning and the afternoon. Well, how Loiosh spent it; I was able to run off and get some bread and sausage, whereas he was stuck there. I mention this because Loiosh did. Repeatedly. I gave Rocza some sausage and sent her to Loiosh, but this just barely diminished the remarks I was getting. When Rocza returned she seemed amused, which meant that either I was finally beginning to get some level of rapport with her, or I was imagining things. I'd call it fifty-fifty.

But for the most part, I just sat there, under the shade, watching nothing happen in several directions. This time, there wasn't a friendly tag showing up to offer me her services and sell me information. Information aside, I'd have welcomed the distraction.

As it got toward evening the wind shifted, now coming directly at me from the mill. You can imagine how pleased I was about that. But then half an hour or so later it shifted again, now blowing back toward the mountains, which doesn't make sense, but I've never claimed to understand weather.

Loiosh wanted to know how long he was going to have to sit there. So did I, which answer pleased him about as much as you'd expect. We were getting on each other's nerves, I guess; which is surprising only when you consider how rarely it had happened over the years. I was aware of it, and tried not to push things, for his part, he did his job.

There was still plenty of light left in the day when he said, *"Here he is, Boss. Just coming home."*

"Walking?"

"Nope. A small coach and two, Boss. Unmarked."

"Hmm. Means nothing."

"Boss? I think I recognize the guy driving it."

"Give me a look. Ah. Good one, chum."

"Who—?"

"Can't really see the red hair in this light, but he was one of the Count's men-at-arms outside the manor."

"Okay, Boss. Now what?"

"Now I get to say 'ah ha.'"

"Good. Say it. Then you can explain what it means."

"I haven't gotten that far yet. One ah-ha at a time."

"I'm just saying, it doesn't prove he's working for the Count. He might have been on an errand to—"

"I know. But it's something to start with."

"Sure, Boss. Do I watch for Dahni to leave again, or are you visiting him at home?"

"I'll be right there."

"Boss, you might want to wait until full dark; it's awfully exposed here. Lots of shacks in the same place, all looking at each other, and people coming and going."

"You know that leaves you stuck there watching until I can make it?"

He sighed into my mind, which I took as a yes, so I settled back to wait some more. Presently, as the darkness came, the docks across the river began to come to life as the boatmen prepared to bring the mill workers back to this side of the river. I wondered why none of them seemed to have built houses on that side, and saved themselves the trip twice a day. Maybe because of the stench, or because the Count forbade it. The latter was more likely.

They poured out of the place like small insects with a predator in the nest—emerging from all the holes, desperate to reach the boats and get away from the place. From what I could see, there was pushing and shoving and maybe a few fights as some were left behind until the return trip. And now there were a few more people—women showing off their ankles—out on the street, walking past me and some of them giving me quick speculative glances. The boats began to arrive, and there were the sounds of talking and laughing and cursing and the tramping of feet. Twenty minutes later, the second boatloads arrived, and this was repeated on a slightly smaller scale, finally falling to silence as the darkness thickened.

Sometime, watch it get dark in a lightless city—preferably somewhere like the East where the Furnace blazes in such plain sight that you can't bear to look at it. It's different than in a place with Enclouding, and also different from the country. The shadows of the buildings and the occasional lonely tree gradually get longer and longer until they blend in with other buildings, with other shadows, and with the night itself, and you realize that dark has quite fallen, and you are in a new place, in a town in the night.

Loiosh guided me there, using Rocza's eyes and giving me directions. Occasionally a bit of light spilled from a house, so I could see my way for a few steps, or sometimes someone would come along swinging a lamp, used by everyone in town with any sense—that is to say, everyone but me. But for the most part Loiosh guided me. The greater part of my effort went into staying quiet; you'd be surprised how much harder it is to stay quiet when you can't see anything. Or maybe you wouldn't.

When I reached the house, Loiosh gave his wings a quick flap so I could identify where he was. He usually flies as quietly as an owl, but can make noise if he wants. I asked him about that once and he said owls are stupid, which hadn't been what I was asking about at all, so I dropped the subject.

He landed on my shoulder. There was a tiny bit of light leaking from a shuttered window.

"What's the play, Boss?"

"I bash in the door, you and Rocza get in his face, and we improvise from there. You're pretty sure he's the only one in the place?"

"No sounds from in there for hours, Boss."

"All right. Ready?"

"Yeah. I didn't hear the door lock, by the way."

"You mean I don't get to break it down? Damn."

He was right, the latch lifted easily, and I flung it open. The damned light assaulted my eyes, and I was mostly blind. Loiosh and Rocza flew in and I followed, hoping for the best.

There was a flurry of movement, some cursing, and I squinted hard and got my hands on him; then I had a dagger out and was holding it at the back of his neck. He lashed out and caught me one in the face, then kicked, but I saw that well enough to dodge it. I grabbed him harder and remembered I was dealing with a human, so I shifted the knife to his throat and he obligingly stopped moving. The loudest sound in the room was his breathing. I had the feeling he wasn't happy.

"Well met, friend Dahni. How are you on this fine evening, with the stars shining and all crickets chirping merrily and night-finches cooing so sweetly?"

He just kept breathing.

My eyes were starting to adjust. I pushed him backward and onto a stuffed chair, keeping pressure on the knife at his throat. He brought his chin up. I could now see that he was glaring, which failed to startle me.

"I will ask questions," I said. "And you will answer them. If you don't answer them, I'll decide you have no value to me. If you do answer them, I'll let you live. If I later find out you've lied to me, I will return. Are we clear on the basics?"

"It was the jhereg," he said. "They followed me."

"My familiar has skills which aren't exactly traditional," I said.

"It isn't too late," he told me. "Walk out the door, and I'll just forget this happened."

"Kind of you," I said. "Now, first of all, who do you work for?"

"You have no idea what you're—"

I slapped him, hard. "Don't even start."

He just sat there, glaring at me.

"No," I said. "That won't do. I need an answer. If you don't answer me, I will kill you. Has your employer earned that kind of loyalty?"

Somewhere, behind his eyes, he was thinking. I gave him some time.

"I work for Count Saekeresh," he said at last.

I released the pressure on his throat just a little—call it a reward of sorts. "What do you for him?"

"I, ah, handle problems, I'd guess you'd say."

"I guess I would. What did he want to recruit me for?"

"I don't know," he said. "He never told me."

I considered whether I believed that. While considering, I said, "Then I suppose you have no idea why he didn't just ask me himself when we spoke?"

There was a little flicker there as I watched him; a hint of confusion, as if the question puzzled him. That deserved some consideration.

About two seconds' worth.

"When were you given the job?"

"What job?"

"Of recruiting me."

He blinked. "I don't know. Two, three days ago, I guess?"

"And what, exactly, were you told?"

"To recruit you."

I quickly pulled the dagger from his throat, turned it in my hand, and smacked the side of his face with the hilt; not too hard, but hard enough to leave a little cut on his cheekbone. Before he could react, the blade was back at his throat, pressing almost hard enough to cut. "You've been doing so well. Why mess it up?"

He glowered. I waited. He said, "I was told to find out what you were up to."

I nodded and once more relieved the pressure a bit. "It's much better when you tell the truth."

His eyes glinted. "My ma always told me that," he said. "But when I told the truth, I'd get a whupping."

I decided I liked him. I hoped I wouldn't have to kill him.

"And what did you find out that I'm up to?"

"I haven't come to any conclusions."

"You'll let me know when you do?"

"I'll send it by the post."

"Is there a good post system in this country?"

"So-so. The county system is good, though. The Guild runs it."

"Is there anything they don't run?"

"The Count. Me. Perhaps you."

"Perhaps?"

His eyes flicked down to my wrist, still holding the knife at his throat, then back to my face. "I shouldn't presume. Isn't your arm getting tired?"

"No, I'm fine. What happened to Orbahn?"

"Who? Oh. Him. I've no idea. He might be traveling. He travels a lot."

"Does he work for the Guild?"

"Everyone either works for the Guild, or works for the Count. Everyone."

"Including the witches?"

"Hmm. I don't know. I think you need to have lived here all your life to understand how that works. And maybe you still wouldn't."

That agreed with my assessment too, but I didn't say so. "And this business of 'light' and 'dark' witches?"

"I've heard of dark witches. I'm told the Merss family practiced the darker sort. I don't know if it's true. And I don't know what it means. It sounds odd to me. Am I going to get a turn asking questions?"

"Sure, when you're holding the knife."

"Speaking of, would you mind taking that thing away from my throat? I get the feeling that if say something that annoys you it might slip."

"I have to admire your instincts. Keep talking."

He looked unhappy. He evidently didn't want to tell me. People seem never to want to tell me the things I want to know. It could get on my nerves, if I let it. I increased the pressure on his neck.

"You must know," he said, "you made quite, um, an impression when you arrived."

"Go on," I said.

"I mean, you immediately found the representative of the Guild and, as I understand it, as much as told him to his face you were going to break up the Guild."

"Orbahn," I said.

He nodded. "And then, of course, the Guild put word out to keep an eye on you."

"Uh huh."

"And then you started looking for Black Witches."

Of course I did. Yeah, it even made sense. Sometimes I just assume people are lying, and I try to figure out the motive behind the lie. That's not that bad, really; only I forget that other people might be doing the same thing to me.

"Right," I said. "Keep talking."

"This wasn't what His Lordship told me, this was just stuff I've heard."

"Yes, I understand. You hear things. Go on."

"So His Lordship called me in, and said I was to approach you about working with him, but wasn't to say who he was. I was just to see if you had any interest in working with, ah, an unnamed party in finding out who had killed those witches. He told me—"

"Witches," I repeated. "It was a family. There were kids. One of them couldn't have been more than . . . okay, go on."

He swallowed and nodded. "He told me that you had been representing them as your family, and were using their name, so that I was to stick with that."

"Did you ask him what he thought my real name might be?"

He shook his head. "I don't ask him things. He just—"

"Yeah, yeah. I got it. Would you say he had an idea of what my name might be?"

He spread his hands. "I have no way of guessing, Lord M . . . my lord. I'm sorry."

"Keep calling me Merss. You might as well."

"Yes, Lord Merss."

"What else did he tell you? Anything to imply that I might be dangerous?"

He frowned. "Not in so many words, but, well, there was something about the way he talked about you that made me nervous."

"You know, friend Dahni, this is the strangest town I have ever been in."

"You need to get out more."

"Thanks. I'll keep that in mind. Who killed them?"

"Who?"

"You know who."

"The Merss family? I don't know. The Count doesn't know. He doesn't think you did."

"Yeah, I don't I think did either."

"But he isn't sure."

"Who is supposed to be finding out?"

"I'm sorry?"

"When something like this happens, when someone is killed, who is supposed to be finding out who did it? Who is responsible?"

"Oh. Ah, the Count, I imagine. Or maybe the King. I'm not sure."

"And the Count, who would he assign it to?"

"Well, I guess that would be me."

"You?"

"I guess."

"And instead, he has you following me around and proposing alliances in the dark."

"You have to admit, it was dramatic."

"Not good enough, Dahni. Why there and then?"

"Well, I saw you heading out there. I thought it might give me an edge. I didn't know about your familiars."

"Yeah. How long had you been following me, waiting for an opportunity?"

"Not long. A couple of days."

"A couple of days?"

He nodded.

"Well. Now you've hurt my pride."

"*And mine, Boss. I think he may be lying.*"

"*I always think that, Loiosh. And looks where it's gotten me.*"

"*You're still breathing.*"

"You really followed me for two days?"

He nodded.

"Mind if I test you on it?"

"Go ahead."

I asked some questions about where I'd gone and who I'd seen, and he knew most of the answers. I'd rather not dwell on it. It was humiliating.

"All right," I said when I'd heard enough. "And what conclusions did you come to?"

"My lord?"

"You spent two days following me. What do you think I'm up to?"

He shrugged. "You're good. I haven't been able to come to any conclusions."

"And you told the Count that?"

He nodded.

"And that," I said, "would have relieved any suspicions he might have had."

Dahni looked uncomfortable.

"What if I'd accepted?"

"It was a legitimate offer."

"Was it?"

"Yes."

"Is it still on the table?"

"Not if you slit my throat. That's a deal-breaker."

"Yeah? Tough bargainer."

"Not me. It's the Count. He's pretty hard-nosed about that sort of thing."

I put the knife away. "All right," I said. "If he wants to find and—to find whoever killed the Merss family, I'll help. You know where to find me."

He rubbed his throat. "In the middle of a field in the dark?"

"I was thinking of the inn, myself."

"That'll work."

"Good. Don't get up. I'll let myself out."

I turned my back on him with complete confidence. And I did have complete confidence—complete confidence that Loiosh was watching.

"Well, well. We've learned something, I think."

"Seems like, Boss. I'm surprised."

"I'm slightly stunned myself."

We made it back to the inn without undue incident. It was busy enough that my entrance wasn't remarked. My table was occupied, so I got another, feeling unreasonably resentful about it. The lamb stew hadn't changed, however, and I felt better with a good bowl of it inside of me.

As I scraped up the last bits of stew with good, warm bread (one of my favorite parts of eating stew, and yours too if you have any sense), I ignored the hum of conversation around me and tried to consider what I'd just learned.

A fair bit, really, depending on whether and how much Dahni was telling the truth. I was inclined to believe him on at least a number of points. At any rate, I now understood more of what he was up to. Was he acting on his own? Of course he was; working for Saekeresh, and running a little free-lance business on the side. On a certain level, I couldn't blame him. The question was, what to do about it.

Could I make a good guess on timing? No, not really. At least a day, no matter what. Probably not more than a week. Could be anywhere in that range. Damn, damn, damn.

Yeah, no question, I was going to hurt someone very badly. And I was beginning to get a pretty good idea who it was going to be. In any case, it was best not to mention my latest conclusions to Loiosh, who was already upset at sticking around this place.

He picked up a bit of that thought, I guess. He said, *"We should be getting out of here, Boss."*

"I know."

"We aren't going to, are we?"

"No. You'll just have to stay alert."

"Can we at least get out of this inn?"

"Where would you suggest we go?"

"The other inn?"

"I just told Dahni he could get a message to me here."

"Boss."

"Yeah, all right. I'll see if there are any rooms at the other inn."

Presently I did. Either the wind was blowing the stench elsewhere, or I really was getting used to it, because it was a pleasant walk, from one end of the little town to the other. The place wasn't too crowded, and the hostess, a delightfully rotund woman of middle years, was pleased to let me a room at reasonable cost. After some consideration, I decided not to tell the host at the Hat that I'd checked out. Loiosh was annoyed because I'd had to consider it. Money changed hands, and a drab little man wearing clothes that were too big for him showed me upstairs.

I got a room with a window that looked out onto the street, and was assured that the Furnace (actually, the "nawp," but I figured out what she meant) wouldn't wake me in the morning, even if I forgot to close the shutter. The bed was narrow and too short, but soft and free of wildlife. There was also a washbasin and a chamber pot right in the room, and I was told that if I opened my door and rang that little bell there, someone would come up and bring me hot water in the morning. Could the person also bring me klava? No, but there was coffee, and it would be cheerfully delivered. Yes, coffee would do, with heavy cream and honey, although I said it with a sigh I couldn't quite repress.

10

FIRST STUDENT (whispering): *I believe our hosts are drunk.*
SECOND STUDENT (whispering): *What should we do?*
NURSE: *In the first place, stop whispering. It annoys them when they're passed out.*

—Miersen, *Six Parts Water*
Day One, Act III, Scene 2

I have to give this one to Loiosh: Even if no one was going to hit me in the head if I'd stayed at the Hat, I must have been worried about it, because I relaxed that night and I slept hard and long and until nearly noon. The same drab little guy in almost the same clothing brought me hot water and coffee klava and made no comments about the hours I kept.

Having a kettle of coffee brought up to me was so pleasant it almost made up for it being coffee. I drank it all, staring out at the street watching a couple of dogs chase each other. Eventually I dressed, then went down, and the hostess was there, chatting with a couple of middle-aged gentlemen who had that indefinable something that told you they were from somewhere else. She gave me a gap-toothed smile and said, "Good morning, Lord Merss."

"Good morning," I said. I sniffed. Hickory. "Something smells good. Lunch?"

She nodded. "Pig eatin's. We make 'em like nowhere else."

"I'll be back to try them, then." I touched my forehead with the tips of four fingers and went out and into the day. First thing was to visit the Hat and see if any messages had come in. No, no messages, unless the speculative look from the host was a message about the propriety of spending the night away. If so, I chose to disregard it. The lamb stew smelled good, but my loyalty had shifted. I'm just fickle, I guess.

I went back to the Mouse and had lunch. It was good, though I wouldn't have used quite so much hickory, myself. But I took my time with it, letting what I'd learned the night before bounce around in my head, trying to decide how much of whom I should believe. I actually felt pretty good. The anger was still there, but I knew that sooner or later—probably sooner—I was going to track down whoever it was that had caused that anger. Things hadn't come together, but I had enough pieces that eventually I'd see how they fit.

I got another glass of wine—it was a particularly harsh and acidic red that tasted better than it should have—and nursed it while I considered things.

An hour or so of that got me nowhere, so I went back to the Hat, and as I walked through the door, the host looked at me, frowning.

"Message for you," he said. Obviously, to him there was something very suspicious about me having asked if there were any messages this morning, and then had one delivered in the afternoon. Obviously, I was up to something.

I returned to the Mouse, found an ugly brown chair, and sat. Then I broke the seal, unfolded the heavy pink parchment, and read. It was, unlike the last missive, very simple and straightforward, with no excess words. It suggested I visit His Lordship tomorrow early in the afternoon.

"Looks like we have a deal, Loiosh."

"Or a trap."

"Or a trap. Right now, I'll be happy with a trap. It'll give me something to break out of. There's nothing worse than wanting to push and not having anything to push against."

He started naming things that were worse until I told him to shut up. There's nothing worse than a smartass who pretends not to understand hyperbole.

The more important question was: Were there any ways to protect myself in case it *was* a trap? Were there any arrangements worth making?

"Go armed, Boss."

"Good thinking."

After a while, I noticed the place had pretty much emptied out. The hostess, whose name was Mahri, came over and poured me another glass of wine and asked if something was troubling me.

"No," I said. "Just making plans for an errand I need to run tomorrow."

"Plans?"

I nodded. "So far, I've picked the horse I'm going to ride."

"Well, may it prosper you," she said.

"Indeed." I passed a coin across the table. "Drink with me to that sentiment."

She smiled big and nodded, and went behind the bar and poured something golden into a small glass and lifted it to me, drank. I did too. She said, "Well, you think about your plans, then. I won't disturb you."

"I appreciate that," I said.

Usually when people say that, it's a prelude to an ongoing stream of disturbance, but she was as good as her word, and said nothing while I sat there beating into a headwind, as the Orca say. I wondered if she was the only one in town as good as her word. Which brought up the question of whether she was In On It Too. I didn't really think so (and, just for the record, no she wasn't), but it gives you an idea of how my mind was working.

Eventually I sighed and raised my glass for more wine. I couldn't think of any steps to make this safer; I was just going to have to do it. As she brought the wine, I said, "Do you know a light-haired, freckle-faced foreigner named Dahni?"

She nodded. "He's been in a few times."

"Do you trust him?"

She frowned. I had the feeling she was one of those people who trusted everyone, and didn't understand why one wouldn't. "I don't understand."

I smiled. "He's made a business proposition to me, and I'm wondering if he's the sort who can be depended on to be honest in his dealings."

The question seemed to make her unhappy, like she didn't want to consider that the answer might be no. "I'm afraid I don't know him that well," she said.

"What have you heard?"

"Heard?"

"Gossip? Rumors?"

She looked even more uncomfortable.

"I don't know as I should say anything."

"I'd take it as a kindness."

"It isn't a kindness to pass on ill-tongue."

"It would be this time."

She studied me, squinting through troubled dark brown

eyes. "Well," she said at last, "some say he works for His Lordship, the Count."

I had the feeling that that, in itself, wasn't necessarily something she might be reluctant to say about someone, so I just nodded and waited.

"Well some say . . . you know the Count is an old man."

I nodded, having not only heard but seen it.

"Well, he . . ." She coughed, and I noticed she was turning red, and I was suddenly convinced that whatever I was about to hear would be of no interest to me at all. "Well, I'm not saying there's anything wrong, mind, but they say he has girls who, you know, who do things for him. And Dahni, they say he's the one who finds them for him."

She finished quickly, blushing furiously, and I was pleased to know my instincts were still intact. I put forth all of my effort, all of my power, all of my will that had been hardened in the fires of death and crime—and I didn't laugh.

"Thank you," I said. "That is of great importance to me, and you have done me great good. I assure you, no one will hear of this through me."

She nodded and returned to the bar. I said, "Pardon me, good hostess."

"My lord?" she said, looking worried.

I held up my glass.

"Oh," she said, blushing even more, if that were possible, and quickly filled it. "This is on me," she said, with a sheepish grin.

"Thank you," I said, passing over a coin. "Then call this a gratuity." She accepted it gratefully and found something to do in the back room while she recovered from her embarrassment.

"Damn good thing I'm so skilled at investigation, Loiosh. Someone else might never have uncovered that vital scrap of information."

"You're just saying that because if you don't you know I will, aren't you, Boss?"

"See there? You have the makings of a skilled investigator your-self."

If you can imagine the mental equivalent of the sound a horse makes when it exhales loudly through its nose, that's what I received then.

I drank my wine and thought many thoughts, none of them having anything to do with the Count's love life. Eventually I made my way back to the Hat, spoke with the stable-boy, and said I wanted to make sure Marsi would be available tomorrow. He agreed Marsi would be ready, and I almost thought I saw a flicker of something like amusement in his eyes. If I'd been sure, I'd have hit him. Not for mocking me, but for the implied insult to Marsi, that fine, fine beast.

"So, that's it, Boss? That's all we're going to do?"

"I'm open to suggestions."

He made muttering sounds.

I left the place and found another merchant, this one a bookseller, hoping to find something entertaining to kill the time until tomorrow afternoon. I'd left all my books with Cawti. I missed them. I missed sitting around with her, reading; listening to her giggle while indulging her weakness for light verse; reading favorite passages to each other.

They didn't have anything good in the place, so I left and walked around the town until I felt tired; then I went back to the Mouse and went to bed. I'd now been almost a week in the village of Burz, paper-making center of Fenario, if not the world. I'd come here looking for family, and I guess I'd found them, after a fashion.

My thoughts on waking were not excessively cheerful. But I still liked the part where hot water and coffee were brought to me at the pull of a bell; that was something I decided I could get used to. I wondered why Cawti and I had never hired a servant. We could have afforded one, and I'd obliquely brought up the subject now and then. I tried to remember her reaction on those occasions, and how the subject had been put aside, but I couldn't.

As I drank that harsh, bitter stuff, I removed the daggers and throwing knives I carried about my person, and took out my whetstone (practically new, I'd bought it on the way out of Adrilankha), and carefully sharpened and honed each one, then my rapier. It felt like it might turn into that sort of day. Dragons don't seem so concerned with getting a fine edge on a weapon; I guess because the way they fight they'll bludgeon you to death as much as cut you. My approach is more elegant and precise. And elegance and precision are important because, uh, because they're important.

Yeah.

Coffeed, cleaned, dressed, and armed, I went down the stairs, ready to face anything the world threw at me. That's more hyperbole, just in case you were wondering. Loiosh was on my left shoulder, Rocza on my right, and they both scanned the room, fully alert for assassins, hostile citizens, or pieces of sausage that had been left on the floor. It was a reasonably dramatic entrance; too bad the room was empty.

I went straight out onto the street, walking past a pair of dogs that looked like hornless lyorns, and turned left toward the Hat. There were lots of people around today, many of them looking like they worked at the mill, which was strange because it wasn't Endweek. Seems they had a different Endweek here. Well, why not? Everything else about the place was strange.

I stopped near the docks and looked across the river. Yeah, there was no smoke coming from the thing, and the boats were all pulled up on this side All of the shops were busy, even the bookseller's. The Guild, whatever it was, was prospering today. It was odd how I seemed to fit right in among all the passersby; I wasn't used to that.

"*About how long do I have until I should leave for the Count's?*"

"*Boss, you have better time sense than I do. How should I know if you don't?*"

Noish-pa had told me he used to be able to look at the position of the Furnace and judge the time to within five minutes. I glanced up at it, and looked at the shadows. Yeah, it was definitely daytime.

I thought about asking someone, but I had the feeling I'd sound like an idiot, and feeling like an idiot is bad enough. Muttering to myself, I went back to the Mouse, and found the hostess at her station. She greeted me with a warm smile; she apparently held no ill-will over my coercing her into revealing deep, dark, and vital secrets about one of her patrons. I said, "Pardon me, good hostess, but do you happen to know what time it is?"

She glanced quickly out the window. "Almost half past the twelfth hour," she said.

I thanked her, got more coffee, and sat down to drink it.

"It never used to matter, they tell me."

I looked up. Her hands were out of sight below the bar; I guessed she was cleaning something.

"The time of day never used to be so important, they tell me."

"Oh?"

"I mean, before the mill."

I said, "I'm told that was a long, long time ago."

She nodded. "Yes, it was a whole different world then. But they say time only started mattering when the mill opened, and you had to be somewhere at a certain time, and coordinate with a lot of other people. There are peasants around here, and free farmers as well, who still don't much care what time it is. Some mill worker will agree to meet a peasant at a certain time, and the peasant will be an hour or two late, and the mill worker will take offense on account of being kept waiting, and the peasant won't understand. It causes fights. I've seen it."

I nodded, wondering if this was going somewhere, or if she just wanted to talk. She moved down the bar a little and continued whatever she'd been doing.

"They say it mucks up the river, too. Count Noijlahb, down-river, he complains all the time about his people's stock dying. There have been skirmishes over that, too. And it stinks. They named the town Burz, you know, after the mill was built."

"Sounds like a bad thing all around."

"Yes and no," she said. "People eat better now, and the free farmers and even the peasants get better prices. It's good and bad."

"But it's been there for hundreds of years."

"Oh, not hundreds," she said. "About eighty, I think. It was in my grandmother's day."

"Oh," I said. "I was misinformed. And is that when there got to be all that talk of strange forms of witchcraft, and one sort not liking the other?"

"I wouldn't know anything about that," she said.

"And the Guild?"

She sniffed. "Them."

"What about them?"

"Well, I'm a member, like everyone else. But I can't say as I care for them much."

"Why is that?"

"Oh, you know how they are."

"No, actually I don't. But I'm curious."

"Well, you have to do everything their way. And turn in accounts, and all that nonsense. And they'll tell you who you have to buy from, and who you can't sell to. It's all such silliness."

Actually, it was starting to sound familiar. I smiled and

nodded. She asked if I'd care for any pig eatin's. I declined, but accepted some bread fresh from a Guild-approved baker down the street, who did good work. Too bad the stench of the town overwhelmed his shop, or I'd have found him myself. I had the bread with lots of butter and honey from bees that had been raised on something I'd never tasted before, but had a very faint nutty flavor that I liked. I had one more cup of coffee, then stopped because I didn't want to spend the entire ride out to the manor stopping to relieve myself.

People started drifting in, and she started paying attention to them, so I got up and walked down the street to the Hat.

It was pretty busy, but the host found time to accept payment for another week's lodging, and to ask, in a carefully studious tone, where I'd been. That stopped me a little. He was being surprisingly open about it. Had something changed? Was the blade finally coming free? Did my concealed enemy now suddenly not care about being concealed?

I said, "Why do you want to know?"

"Eh? No reason. Just making conversation."

"Just making conversation. I see."

He went down to the other end of the bar to open a bottle of wine for someone. I watched him. The list of people in this town I didn't trust was too long to have any actual use. A little while later he came back. I said, "Have you seen Orbahn lately?"

"You keep asking about him."

"And you keep not telling me where he is."

"Why do you want to know?"

"No reason, just making conversation."

He gave me a look. "Haven't seen him in days," he said. "Probably off making a delivery."

"Probably," I said.

"So," he said with a sniff. "How'd you like the undercooked pork at the Rodent?"

I looked at him carefully. "You've been paid. What's your problem?"

"No problem," he said, scowling only a little. "Just wondered."

"The pig eatin's were fine."

"And did the bedbugs give you good company?"

"Not as much as I'd hoped. Just when the party was starting to get good they had to go off and study for exams the next day."

He sniffed. "Why the hell you'd want to—"

"A stranger needs to spread his business around, don't you think? Especially if he plans to set up shop, as it were. Create good-will everywhere: that's my motto."

"Set up shop?"

"Yep."

"Here?"

"I'm thinking about it. Nice town. I like it."

"What sort of . . . excuse me." He returned a moment later. "What sort of shop? You thinking of opening another inn?"

"Now, do I look like an innkeeper to you?"

He shrugged. "How would I know?"

"No, no," I said. "I'm in another line of work entirely."

He frowned. "What would that be, exactly?"

I smiled. "I'd rather surprise you."

"Well, surprising me is all well and good. But we have a Guild here, and they're pretty particular about who they let in."

"Really? I hadn't thought they were."

It sailed right past him. "Oh, they are, all right. Trust me. Can I get you something?"

"Do you have any pig eatin's?"

He scowled and didn't answer, so I got another one of his summer ales to make him feel better, then returned to my table and drank it slowly.

In fact, you know, it wasn't bad, for beer.

When I decided enough time had passed, I made my way slowly toward the stables, still thinking about everything. Things were happening quickly now—too quickly for me to take the time I needed to think them through. If someone was orchestrating this, I could be in severe trouble. I'd been in trouble before. I didn't care for it.

The stable-boy nodded to me and brought out Marsi, saddled her. He worked quickly and efficiently, like he'd done this a thousand times. He probably had. What a life. Marsi was able to contain her enthusiasm on seeing me again. Or maybe not—she did lift her head for a moment, and for her that might have been enthusiasm. The stable-boy looked things over carefully, tightened this and that, then nodded and put the reins in my hand.

I led dear Marsi out of the stable, and, with the assistance of the stable-boy, got mounted. Once again, I was struck by the sense of height—looking at a horse, you don't think you should feel as high up as you do. I wondered if this explained the attitude of the Mounted Guard—always the most obnoxious of the Phoenix Guard to deal with.

For her part, Marsi seemed bored with the whole thing. I took the reins in both hands, touched her flanks with my heels, and sort of urged her forward with my hips. I couldn't see her face well enough to know if she rolled her eyes, but she started moving forward.

"Boss!"

"What is it, Loi—"

"Behind you!"

I turned in the saddle, which wasn't as easy as it should have been. Marsi stopped. I looked. There were a few people in the street, but none close to me.

"What? Where?"

"About forty yards down, north side of the street, under the awning, walking away from you. Blue vest."

And there he was, easily recognizable even from the back. Now was a fine time for him to show up. I started to turn Marsi around. I guess I did something wrong, because she seemed confused. But then I thought about it. What was I going to do? Could I stop now and have a long conversation with him, and just ignore the invitation that was supposed to actually tell me what was going on? Make an appointment to meet him later? What if he didn't want to talk to me?

Damn and blast.

"Loiosh, stay with him."

"I don't like leaving you right now, Boss."

"I'm not crazy about it either, but I need to see the Count, and I do not want to lose that slippery bastard again. Go."

There were mutterings into my mind, but he flew off. I got Marsi headed in the right direction and started out of town.

"Where is he going, Loiosh?"

"Looks like back to the Hat, Boss, just as carefree as you please."

"I don't suppose you can go in there. I want to see if he's meeting with someone. Dammit."

"If there's a window open I can stick my snakey little head through it."

"Yeah, I guess that's the best we can do."

I continued my leisurely pace out of town.

"Whoops, guess I was wrong, Boss. He's not going into the inn, he's going behind it."

"Oh, that's interesting."

"To the stables."

"Good place to find a horse."

"He's talking to the stable-boy."

"Can you get close enough to listen?"

"I'll try . . . yes. Boss, he's asking about you. Where you went and how long ago."

"Is he getting answers?"

"No. Wait. Money is changing hands. Yes, he's getting answers."

I thought hard about turning around right then, but it seemed that as long as I was getting information, this was working and I should stay with it. And the visit to the Count was too important to throw over.

"Okay, he's done talking to the stable-boy. He's heading away from the inn and . . . he seems to be going across town."

It was a pleasant day for a ride, I have to say. And Marsi was as delightful as ever. Rocza seemed to consider herself fully on duty; she kept looking around, and sometimes leaving my shoulder to fly in a wide circle overhead.

Then, "There's a warehouse near the docks with an overhanging doorway. He's in the doorway, looks like he's waiting for someone."

"All right."

More countryside went by. A few birds sang, and I passed a flock of sheep grazing on a low hill with no shepherd in sight. It was calm and peaceful and pastoral and I loosened my rapier in its sheath because I don't trust calm and peaceful and pastoral.

"Oh my, Boss! You'll never guess who just showed up to meet him."

"The Empress?"

"Funny."

"Tell."

"Remember that tag who told you about the coachman? Well, she hasn't left town."

Well. Well.

Now, just how was I going to fit that into my calculations?

"Well, Boss? Just how are you going to fit that into your calculations?"

"I'm just working on that, Loiosh. Can you get close enough to hear what they're saying?"

"No way, Boss. I'm right above them, and they're talking too low to hear."

"*Damn. Okay, can you instruct Rocza to follow one of them, while you follow the other? I really want to know where they both go.*"

"*And leave you unprotected?*"

"*I'm armed. Can she do it?*"

He hesitated, and I got the feeling he didn't want to answer. But he finally said, "*If the conversation continues long enough. It's going to take her half an hour at least to get back here.*"

"*Let's try for it, Loiosh.*"

"*Boss. . . .*"

"*Do it.*"

Rocza flew from my shoulder, heading back toward town.

I almost chewed my nails. I very much wanted Rocza to get there in time. I very much wanted to know what they were talking about. Marsi picked up my nervousness and got a bit skittish, so I patted her neck and tried to calm down.

"*You sure there's no way you can hear what they're saying?*"

"*Sorry, Boss. There's just no place I can slide my snakey head without them seeing it.*"

I had a suggestion about where he could slide his snakey head, but I kept it to myself.

Just about the time I was arriving at the Count's estate, Loiosh said, "*Rocza is here, Boss, and they're still talking about whatever they're talking about.*"

"*Good,*" I said. "*Stay with them.*"

"*Will do, Boss. Be careful.*"

"*I always am.*"

As I approached the entry area, the groom seemed to recognize me, or, at any rate, Marsi. He came forward with his hand out to assist me down. I gave him a cool nod. Once I was on the ground again, he took the reins and said, "You are expected, my lord."

I stood there, waiting until I felt like my legs would start working again, which took a couple of minutes. I spent it looking around the grounds as if I were just sort of vaguely curious.

When I could move without embarrassing myself, I climbed the low stairway up to the door. I pulled on the rope, the low gong sounded within, and presently the door swung open.

The same butler as before made the same bow as before. "Welcome, Lord Merss. His Lordship is expecting you."

We met in the same room, and I was offered the same chair. I took a different one, partly to be contrary, and partly because I was a little jumpy. The butler pretended not to noice. The Count gave me a sort of look, but let it pass.

"Thank you for agreeing to see me," he said.

"On the contrary," I told him. "Thank *you*."

He smiled. "Brandy? Ale? Wine?"

"Wine," I said.

He nodded at the butler, who went off to fetch the necessities.

"So then," said the Count, sitting back a little and folding his hands over his belly. "We have something in common."

"An enemy, it would seem."

He nodded, and the butler gave me my wine, and gave the Count a glass of the same amber liquid he'd had before. He lifted his, I did the same, we sipped. It was slightly sweeter than the last one had been, and agreeably spicy.

"*Okay, Boss. They've split up. I'm staying with him.*"

"*All right.*"

"What I propose," said the Count, "is simply this: that we share information. I suspect you know things that will help me track down who is behind the murders, and I am certain that I could give you information that would be of use to you."

I nodded. "That makes sense, and I'm inclined to agree."

"Inclined?"

"There some things I'd like to understand first, my lord, before I make any agreements."

"Such as?"

I had some more wine and tried to figure out how to approach it. This was the tricky part.

"Just what sort of information do you imagine I have, my lord?"

"Eh? Well, it's obvious you've been investigating on your own. Haven't you found out anything?"

"As to that," I said. "Maybe. But, you know, I have no special skills in that field; I've simply been asking questions as anyone might."

"Indeed?" he said. From the expression in his voice, I couldn't tell if he was just skeptical, or knew I was lying, and that is exactly what I needed to know.

"Yes," I said. "That's what puzzles me about this. To be blunt: What help could I possibly give you?"

"Well," he said, and had another sip. He licked his lips. "That is a difficult question to answer."

I nodded and gave him some time, sipping wine and putting on my innocent inquiring look.

"I guess," he said, "that will require some background explanation."

"All right," I said. "I'm listening."

"The mill was first founded by my grandfather, some eighty-three years ago." He went on from there, but I wasn't really paying attention.

"*Boss?*"

I wanted more wine because my mouth was dry, but the glass wasn't in my hand, which was odd.

"*Boss?*"

And I couldn't move my arm, either, and the Count's voice was a buzzing in my ears, and the floor was very hard against my cheek.

Part Four

NOTONIDE

While there remains some question because of its short duration, most natural philosophers now agree that the notonide should be considered an actual stage; yet it is a stage of constant transformation. It is here, accompanied by a ninety percent loss in mass, that the wings are formed, the venom glands develop, and the eggs are fertilized. This all happens in an astonishingly brief time: a few days at the most. Needless to say, during this entire stage the jhegaala is exceptionally vulnerable. . . .

Two interesting and contradictory phenomena occur during this stage: To the right, the intense pressure of the constant transformation overwhelms the individual characteristics of the notonide, each reacting for the most part identically. And yet, as is the case with all organisms, it is never so much itself as when under intense pressure. Thus the future nature of this particular levidopt becomes apparent from the present notonide if one knows what to look for. . . .

—Oscaani: *Fauna of the Middle South: A Brief Survey,*
Volume 6, Chapter 18

11

BORAAN: *My dear, have you ever wondered why it seems to go on so terribly long?*

LEFITT: *It would hardly be punishment if it were short.*

BORAAN (glances at audience): *Quite so.*

———Miersen, Six Parts Water
Day Two, Act III, Scene 4

Movement is meaningless without *time*. Movement, as an Athyra once explained to me, means that you're either in two places at once, or to put it another way, at a certain instant, you both are and are not in one place. In that sense, I wasn't moving, because there was no time, and I wasn't anywhere at all. The odd part is that there was the sensation of movement; a rattling, jolting, rocking thing. But sometimes we cannot trust our perceptions.

There was a damnable itch in the middle of my back, and a droning in my ears that wouldn't go away. I wanted to scratch my back, but I couldn't reach it.

My hips and my back hurt.

Horse, I thought. *Been riding a damned horse. No wonder I hurt.* I opened my eyes, but the droning kept going in my ears. I couldn't figure out why the droning didn't stop when I opened my eyes. After what seemed the longest time, I realized it was because my eyes weren't really open. That made sense. I tried to work out if I were feeling sick to my stomach, but it required too much concentration and didn't seem important anyway.

The humming got louder, and someone was calling my name, and the humming got softer, and several someones were calling my name, in different tones, in different ways, and I felt not the least urge to answer any of them; all I wanted to do was open my eyes, because I knew that would make the humming stop. It isn't that the humming was painful, it just wouldn't stop, and I was getting annoyed.

Then someone in a soft, almost melodious voice I didn't recognize was asking me questions, and whoever it was seemed very friendly, and I'd have answered if the questions had made any sense. Then there was silence again except for the humming in my ears, and then more nonsense questions. It was only later—hours or days—that I was able to remember the questions and make some sort of sense out of them. "Who are you working for?" was the most frequent. And then there were lists of names that sounded like Fenarian noblemen, but I didn't recognize any of them. And once he asked, "How had you planned to open the vault?," which was enough for me to figure it out, later, when I could figure.

You can learn a lot from the questions someone asks; it seems like I had made that observation not long before. In this case, it was easy to put together, once my mind was clear. Not that it helped, especially. At the time, I only realized that I couldn't answer them because they made no sense and that I should try to explain that. I wanted to explain it. It was terribly frustrating that I couldn't seem to find the right words.

I know I threw up sometime in there, and I remember being

pleased that my stomach felt better, although something about it seemed odd. And that damned humming in my ears wouldn't go away, which was the worst of it. I mean, it wasn't, but it was.

Something grabbed my head, not especially gently, and there was water poured into my mouth. I drank it, and noticed I was shivering. I wasn't sick, I was just cold. Well, no problem. I'd cover myself up just as soon as I could find a blanket. Cawti'd probably stolen the damned blanket again. Well, no, because then she'd be warming me up, and if she were warming me up, the humming in my ears would stop, wouldn't it? So where was she, anyway? Why wasn't she here? She should be here to warm me up and stop the buzzing in my ears. I'd stop the buzzing in *her* ears if she needed me to.

A child's voice whispered, "I'm sorry," and I have no idea what makes me think it was a child's voice—how can you tell from a whisper? But I thought so at the time, and I wondered what she'd done. But the voice seemed to warm me, somehow, and I stopped shivering.

"Boss?"

"What the—"

"Boss, *don't let them know you're yourself!*"

"Let—"

"*Play dead!*"

Loiosh doesn't sound peremptory very often, so when he does, I listen, and right then, when I was just becoming aware that I was just becoming aware, and had no idea how or what or where or like that, it seemed a good idea to listen to him, so I remained still.

"What—?"

"Boss, Rocza is hurt."

"How bad?"

"I don't know. She won't tell me. She's afraid if I think she's hurt bad I'll find a new mate."

"Is that what jhereg do?"

"In the wild."

"Did you explain that you're civilized?"

"She doesn't believe me."

"She doesn't know you very well, does she?"

"It's sort of instinct."

"All right. Do what you can for her. Any idea what happened?"

"That woman. She used a dart of some kind. Orbahn tried to get me, but I was expecting it."

"Expecting it."

"When they grabbed you, Boss. As soon as they grabbed you—"

"Who grabbed me?"

Fortunately, I had some time right then. Loiosh explained as best he could what had been going on, and gradually my memory kicked in, bringing me up to the point I've already brought you. After that, I hope you're confused about what happened, because if not I haven't explained it well.

By that time, I knew that I was naked, on my back, blindfolded, and couldn't move my arms or my legs. It seemed very likely that, whoever had me, they were planning to do unpleasant things to me. That had happened once before, and I hadn't done well with it, during or after. It was something, even now, my memory shied away from. Had I learned anything last time that might be useful this time? Not really, no. I knew that the anticipation was part of it—they wanted me to be afraid, to work on myself; and my memory of what had happened before was making it easier on them. I knew that.

It was astonishing how little it helped that I knew that.

Loiosh and I continued talking; he filled me in on the details of the attack, and said hopefully that he thought Rocza wasn't hurt too badly, and we talked about how thoroughly we had been set up, and I made some amusing—in intent, anyway—remarks about how they could have done it better. In short, he kept me occupied while I waited for something to happen.

Loiosh, still being hopeful, suggested that, if they hadn't done anything terrible to me by now, maybe they weren't going to.

By now?

"Loiosh, how long has it been?"

"Three days, Boss."

"Three—Loiosh, what have I been doing for three days?"

"I don't know, Boss! I couldn't tell!" If he were human, it would have sounded like he was on the verge of tears.

"All right, chum. Take it easy. We'll get out of this. The drugs have worn off. I can think now." Loiosh kept whatever wisecrack that might have generated to himself.

I was beginning to be able to see, and more important, my mind was clear enough to realize that I'd been drugged. My inquisitor wore a gray hood over his face; I couldn't help but wonder if he was trying to conceal his features or if he was just doing it for effect. Other than that, I had the impression that the room I was in was something like a larder, or small storage room of some kind. In any case it was small, not too much bigger than it had to be to hold the table I was strapped to. I was strapped in pretty well, by the way, and the table was solid.

The man peered out at me from under his hood and said, "As you no doubt are aware by now, your familiars are no more."

"Hear that, Loiosh? You are no more."

"True, Boss. I'm no less, either."

"Funny guy."

"I have been asked to get information from you. You will tell me what I want to know. How much screaming you do before you give the information is up to you."

I cleared my throat, wondering if I could talk. "You could just ask. I've been known to be cooperative."

"Oh, I'll try that first. But if I don't like the answers I get, I will hurt you. I will cause you pain. If that doesn't work, then let me remind you that you have ten fingers, ten toes, two eyes, two ears, and various other bits and pieces that can be treated individually. Also remember that I don't much care what condition you're in when I'm done."

"If you're trying to scare me," I said, "it's working."

"I can do a great deal more than scare you."

Where do they get this stuff? "Um, if I thought all you could do was scare me, you couldn't scare me, if you see what I mean."

"We'll see how funny you are in a little while."

I was mildly curious about that myself.

Then and then and now.

Then, it was all about the moment; each instant a transition from terror to its realization, almost as a relief; and then back. But each isolated, unique, individual.

Then it was sharp as a knife, clear as the sky in the East, distinct as the face of a loved one. Each event was pure and moments flowed together like a river, where no droplet has meaning save as part of those around it, and the entirety moving according to its own logic, regardless of what pieces of driftwood may be caught in a momentary eddy.

Now it is what memory has left. A single strip of cloth implies the garment from which it was torn, but yet I cannot, from a few dirty pieces, give you the cut and the fit and the blend of colors. The implication must remain implication, because memory preserves, and it protects, and in doing so picks for its own reasons, so if now I give you tattered rags, it is because they are what remain to me. You may regret this; I do not.

"Who are you working for?"

Blinding, impossible brilliance washing over me.

"What was your mission?"

High in an upper corner of the room was a spider, too small for me to see clearly, but her web grew as I watched, lines forming in patterns that reminded me of something I'd seen once, something associated with vast quantities of water. I tried to remember what it was. Spiders are by nature very patient. The flow of moments means nothing to them.

"Who do you report to?"

The room fading in and out, in and out, trying to focus on the spiderweb, annoyed that it kept vanishing into a pale haze.

"*How is Rocza?*"

"*Snappy and bad-tempered, Boss.*"

"*Is that a good sign?*"

"*I wish I knew.*"

"Are you working for the Empire?"

"No," I said. I remember that. I said, "No."

"Very well. I will accept that provisionally, though I don't really believe you. But I'll give you a chance. Who are you working for?"

"I'm not working for anyone," I said. "I came here looking for my family."

"No, no," he said. "That won't do at all."

"Sorry," I said; and honestly, I was.

And fractured pieces of the spiderweb fluttered about inside my head, and I know it is impossible to grind your teeth when your mouth is wide open; why is it that I remember doing so?

Islands of calm in a sea of pain, a sky of fear covering all.

I know there were times when I was myself. I don't know who I was the rest of the time, and I'm glad of that.

"We know what you are doing here, we just aren't certain who you're doing it for."

"Well, all right. I'll be happy to say whatever you'd like, you know. If you give me a name—"

"Don't play with us, Lord Merss, or whoever you are."

I didn't answer that.

"Would you like some water, Lord Merss?"

"I don't know. Drugged, or undrugged?"

"Oh, undrugged. I wish your mental faculties to be at their sharpest."

"Then I'd be delighted."

He held my head carefully as I drank; his eyes were brown, and actually seemed rather friendly, even kind. Shows how reliable eyes are, I guess. He put ice on the inside of my forearms; I'm not sure what that was supposed to do. It felt nice, though.

He gave me a few minutes, I guess to think things over.

"All right," he said. "Now, let us consider this. You are working either for the Empire, or for a private entrepreneur. In the latter case, it is a question of money. In the former, it could be loyalty. If it is money, how much pain is the money worth, not to mention being unable to spend it? In the latter, would the Empress truly wish you to endure great pain for what must be a minor project for her?"

He had a point. Well, if I said it was an individual, he'd want a name, and I didn't have a good name to give him. "All right," I said. "It's the Empire."

He smiled. "Good," he said. "Who do you report to?"

I don't remember what I said, then, or the next questions, but eventually he must have tripped me up, because I remember him saying, "Why would you lie about something like that? I admit it, you are puzzling me."

"I'll take my satisfaction in that, I guess."

And—days? Hours? Years?

What's time to a kethna? Sorry, private joke. In any case, call it a blank space of some duration.

I leaned against the back wall of a little room, massaging my wrists and studying the chain on my ankles, and where it was connected to the floor. It was a wooden floor; there ought to be a way to pry that connection out, if they'd leave me alone for a while. I felt weak—most likely lack of food—but I thought I could still do it.

Thinking about that, how to do it, focusing on—

The spiderweb was bigger now, more elaborate.

"Be reasonable," he said. "It isn't that I want to hurt you; I don't. It's just that there are things we need to know. You are forcing me to do things I find distasteful."

"I hope that doesn't make me a bad person," I said. My voice, in my own ears, lacked the jaunty quality I'd been trying for.

My sweat stank.

"*Boss?*"

"*How is Rocza?*"

"*I think she's going to be fine.*"

"*Good!*"

"*I don't know what to do, Boss.*"

"*Take care of Rocza, and stay out of sight.*"

He was running a cool cloth over my forehead; I have to admit it felt good. "You're stubborn," he said. "That's an impressive quality."

"If you're leading up to courting me," I said, "I sort of have my eye on someone already. But thanks."

What did he want me to tell him, anyway? His questions weren't making sense. I'd even tried to explain that once or twice, but he'd just gotten this idea firmly in his head, and it wasn't budging. That's a problem a lot of people have, I've noticed: they get a notion locked in, and then refuse to examine it in the light of new evidence.

"*Boss!*"

"*Loiosh, can't you see I'm trying to talk to this nice man?*"

"*What nice man?*"

"*The one asking the questions.*"

"You're all alone, Boss."

"Oh, so I am. I must have dozed off. He's a boring fellow, really, though well-intentioned."

"I hope that's sarcasm."

"I prefer to think of it as gentle irony, but close enough."

"If a way opens up, Boss, will you be able to walk out of there?"

"Why wouldn't I?"

"Boss."

"Mmmm?"

"See if you can walk."

"All right, if it makes you happy."

I tried to stand up.

"Okay, I guess you were right to check. I need to complain about the meals in this place; evidently I'm not getting enough of something in my diet."

"Boss, do you know where they put your things?"

He sounded like he was fighting to stay calm. I wished I could think of a way to reassure him I was all right.

"No, 'fraid not," I said. "I'm not that concerned about it, frankly. Most of it is replaceable, and I don't know how much good Spellbreaker would do under these circumstances."

"I'm thinking of the amulet, Boss. The Jhereg can trace you."

"Oh, the amulet I have. It's sort of attached to me. They must have figured out that if it weren't on me I could do sorcery, and they'd have trouble keeping me here."

"Can you remove it?"

"Uh, no."

"We'll have to come up with something, Boss. I don't know how much longer you can survive there."

"How long has it been?"

"You've been in there for a week now."

"Oh, have I?" That seemed odd, but not terribly important. "How is Rocza?"

"Boss, she's fine! Just . . ."

"What?"

"Nothing, Boss."

"Lord Taltos," he said slowly, "I'm having trouble under-standing why you took the name Merss when you came here. Even if I were to believe your story of why you are under an assumed name, why *that* name? No, no. I'm sorry, that is preposterous. What I would like you to say is the truth. Yes, I am convinced the Count was wrong in his initial idea about you. But you really shouldn't be so stubborn—I told you what I want."

"He found out my name, Loiosh."

"You told him, Boss."

"I told him? Why would I do that?"

"We need to get you out of there, Boss."

"Yeah, well, mark me down in favor. Do you even know where I am?"

"No. Do you?"

"Basement of the paper mill."

"How long have you known that?"

"Just put it together now. I don't know. The smell. And the sounds. Didn't even know I was aware of the sounds. Isn't it odd that—"

"Okay, Boss. But how do I get you out? There's no one I can talk to."

"It's just funny that I knew that. It's funny how the mind works—"

"How do I get you out, Boss?"

"Find Dahni, of course."

"Boss?"

"Find him."

"But how do I talk to him?"

"You won't have to."

"How does that work?"

"He's smart, and he knows you. He'll see you, ask about me, you won't answer, he'll figure it out. It might take him a while. I'm sorry I won't be there to watch."

"You think he'll help?"

"He'll help."

"Why?"

"He'll help."

I didn't feel like telling Loiosh how I knew; he'd raise all sorts of objections, and I couldn't deal with those right now.

"My dear Lord Taltos, all you need to do is tell me a few, simple things, and all of this will stop: What is the name of the traitor, what does the King plan, and when will he be making his move?"

King? Now there were kings involved in this? Where was I, anyway? The East? Oh, yeah, I was. So, okay, I guess it made sense that there were kings involved. I just shook my head. There wasn't anything I could say by this time.

"I'm afraid," he told me, "that I'm going to have to get serious."

"Well, all right, though I've been enjoying the frivolous part."

"No doubt."

"One thing, before you get too serious."

"Yes?"

"Mind telling me your name, so I can remember you in my prayers?"

He just shook his head. I suddenly remembered the child's whisper I'd heard, and it occurred to me that the child hadn't been apologizing, she'd been expressing sympathy. I felt very pleased that I now understood that.

"Boss? We're coming. Can you hang on just a little longer?"

"No problem, Loiosh. I'm trying to get him to tell me his name. I'll see if I can get it out of him before you show up."

The spiderweb was finished; that made me sad, though I imagine the spider took some satisfaction from it.

My questioner continued, and it got to be something of a running joke between us; he'd ask me questions I couldn't answer, and I'd ask him his name.

He never did tell me, though; he continued not wanting to tell me right up to the moment when the point of a knife suddenly emerged through the front of his throat.

12

BORAAN: *And, I suppose, you will want the explanation, my lord?*

LEFITT: *Oh, let's skip that part.*

BORAAN: *My dear, you know we'd be killed.*

LEFITT: *Of course. But it might be worth it, just for novelty.*

—Miersen, *Six Parts Water*
Day Two, Act VI, Scene 5

He gagged and choked and clawed the floor and took a long time dying. I watched him carefully. I'm not sure why; I didn't feel any special malice toward him. But I just had the feeling that someday I would want to have been watching while he died. People were talking to me as it was going on, but I ignored them; I guess it was really important to watch. I don't know. I noted the details with a sort of professional detached interest—the terror in his eyes, the helplessness on his face. He wrapped his hands around his throat as if he could stop the bleeding, looking like he was choking himself—an effect increased by the blueish color that crept over him. I kept watching. I didn't miss an instant.

After a while, his mouth open, his hands tried to grip the floor, wet and sticky with his blood, as was the front of his clothing. There was a lot of blood. A whole lot. His eyes took on a glassy look, open-eyed, and he became mostly still except for some twitching, jerking motions for some time.

Eventually, he stopped twitching.

"Lord Merss?"

Still watching the body, I nodded. I think I nodded; I tried to nod. Hands I didn't know took me and unstrapped me and moved me from the table. I know I screamed then as they moved me, which is very odd, when you stop and think about it.

I saw a face I recognized. "Well, hello there, Dahni. What with one thing and another, I prefer your method of interrogation."

His face was like iron. He seemed not to hear me, which was possible. I didn't seem able to generate much volume. I tried again, but this time said, "Can you find my things?"

His expression became, if anything, sterner. "I"m sorry, we can't take the time," he said.

"Gold chain," I said.

"What?" He leaned closer. I repeated it.

He shook his head. "No, I'm taking you out of here."

"Bad move," I said.

For the first time, a bit of humor returned to his expression. "This time, Lord Merss, you're in no condition to be threatening anyone."

"Wrong," I said.

"Wait," he told those carrying me; four men I didn't recognize, but who had that same quality as people I'd known during my brief stint in the army. Odd situation, and not worth going into now. But I was convinced they were soldiers of some kind, which fit in nicely with my conclusions. Of course, the fact that Dahni had shown up at all pretty much confirmed my conclusions. Which, like so many things, was good and bad.

"Okay, let's hear it. I'll be curious about what you're going to threaten me with when you're so weak you can't even speak above a whisp—"

Their timing was perfect. Right in the middle of his sentence, they leaped up and flew at him. He ducked. They circled his head like they'd planned it, then perched next to me and hissed at him.

He stood back up, eying them warily. In his hand was a big, curved, clunky-looking sword with a wide blade, narrowing near the hilt. He seemed hesitant to use it—with good reason.

"The venom is very fast-acting," I said, as loudly as I could—which wasn't very. "You'll feel chest constrictions first, then be unable to breathe. Heart palpitations, sweat, and your body will shake as you become incontinent. The last minute or so you'll be entirely unable to move. You'll die by suffocation. The entire process will take about four minutes. There's no known antidote."

Just for the record, almost none of that was true; but few people actually know about the bites of poisonous reptiles; they know they're poisonous and that's enough, so you can tell them anything and have a good chance of being believed.

Dahni studied me carefully, then glanced at the four men holding me. "Set him down," he said. "Gently. I'll go look for your gear."

"Loiosh will keep you company," I whispered.

"Yeah," he said.

"*You know, Boss, that was fun.*"

"*Why am I not surprised?*"

"*Someday, you're going to have to explain how you knew he'd rescue you.*"

"*Someday,*" I agreed.

"*Tomorrow would be good.*"

"*If there is a tomorrow, I'll consider the matter.*"

After what seemed a long time, Loiosh flew back into the room, accompanied by Dahni, who was carrying a large box that had arcane writing on it that I guess described some sort of paper product. "Got it all," he said. "Want to look it over and see if everything's there?"

"Yes," I said, and I think I half fainted there. I'm not sure what happened next—maybe they just stood around the place waiting for my senses to return, or maybe it was only a second or two. But Dahni held the box while I looked inside, and then moved things around so I could see everything. My purses and my money belt seemed intact, and, more important, Spellbreaker was there. I tried to reach for it and I guess I passed out again.

The next thing I remember is a breeze in my face that felt so good I didn't even mind the stench. It was night, and the mill wasn't working. I saw a bit of wall, some sky, and the backs of those who were carrying me; evidently they had found a blanket somewhere and were toting me on that, though I had no memory of how or when they'd worked that.

"All right, the boat's waiting down there," said Dahni. "After that, I know a safe place—"

"No," I said, almost killing myself to make sure I was loud enough to be heard.

"Eh?"

"No," I repeated. "Bring me to the manor. The Count."

He shook his head as if he hadn't heard me. He probably hadn't. He leaned closer and I repeated it.

"*Boss! You aren't thinking! He's the one who—*"

"*I know.*"

"*Think, Boss. I know you've—*"

"*Back me on this, Loiosh. Make sure he brings me to the Count. If he doesn't, I'm dead.*"

"What makes you think—"

"The same thing that made me think he'd rescue me."

There was a pause, then, *"All right, Boss."* He sounded worried. Yeah, me too.

Meanwhile, Dahni had been saying things I'd missed while talking with Loiosh. I shook my head. "The manor," I told him. "I must insist."

Loiosh and Rocza hissed. Dahni looked at those who were carrying me, and I could see his thought process. The soldiers, or, if you will, Vlad-bearers, were giving the jhereg nervous looks. Thinking back, I have to admire them. Those fangs were inches from the hands of a couple of the guys; if it had been me, I'd have dropped me and bolted. But I was concentrating on Dahni. This was the crucial moment of the whole thing. I wondered if I was going to have to tell Loiosh and Rocza to attack. I hoped not. For one thing, there really is no way to predict how jhereg venom will affect any given individual; it could be anything from dropping helpless in seconds and dying within minutes to only becoming mildly ill, and I didn't like to chance it. For another, however it ended it was liable to leave me flat on my back, unable to move, at the mercy of someone who made a career of being merciless.

I told Dahni, "You can't make it."

After a moment, he said, "And what happens to me?"

"Once I'm at the Count's, you can go. The jhereg won't hurt you."

"Why should I trust you?"

"I trusted you to rescue me, didn't I?"

He gave a short, bitter laugh.

"Think it over," I said. "You were my best shot so I took it. Right now, doing what I want is your best shot."

He hesitated another second or two, then nodded to the

men holding my blanket. "Get him to the wagon, then take him back home. On my authority."

One of them said, "Yes, lord," and they started moving with me again. I think I might have passed out somewhere in there, because I don't remember the boat trip across the river.

I remember the wagon ride, however. It wasn't as much fun as you might imagine. I'm sure I can't have been awake and aware for the entire journey, but it sure seems like it. Days. It took days. And it's funny how a wagon catches even the tiniest rut or pothole in the road. The worst part was when we stopped, and I thought we'd finally arrived; but it turned out the Count's guards were having words with a patrol. When the jolting and bouncing started up again I bit my lip because I didn't want them to hear me cry out.

At last it really stopped. They came around, and opened the back, and then I was slipping in and out of consciousness again for a while. It wasn't pain, it was just exhaustion. I remember the butler, looking down at me, and saying, "The east room," and thinking how appropriate it was, what with me being an Easterner. I tried to say something about that but it didn't get far. As I stared into his face, I wondered what he was thinking: How much of that bland indifference was hiding his emotions, and how much was training himself not to have any? He wasn't like an Issola; it wasn't a desire to make someone feel comfortable. It was something else. A natural or cultivated distancing of himself from anything beyond what he ought to display.

The more I thought about him, the less I thought about anything else, which was the point of the exercise, in case I need to spell it out for you.

The butler's face turned into that of the Count himself, and I couldn't read his expression, but he didn't give the appearance of someone about to kill me. I saw him walk away with Dahni, the two of them speaking in low tones. I don't think it was paranoia to conclude that my name might have come up in that conversation. I asked Loiosh if he could listen in, but they were being careful. Still, I was pretty sure he wasn't planning to kill me.

Not that I could have done anything about it at that point anyway. I'd pitched all my flat stones and now I was going to see where the round stones stopped rolling.

They carried me up a flight of stairs, which wasn't as bad as the wagon, and put me on a soft bed. Loiosh curled up by my ear with Rocza next to him. I could feel his head moving back and forth, watching everything. I could almost hear him thinking, *Try something; let anyone just try something.* That's my last memory for a while.

Later—I have no idea how much later—there was a bearded, gray-eyed older man bending over me, looking at me with great concern and speaking—I couldn't see to whom—to a low voice in an uncouth language I'd never heard before.

I tried to take an inventory of how I felt, but all I felt was numb—not that I was complaining about that. I also felt too weak to move, but I didn't mind so much. Then I became aware that my left arm wouldn't move at all and I started to panic. The old man said, "Shhhh," and held his palm out. "It's all right," he said in a strange accent, with a sort of singsong quality to the end of his phrases. "It was me. I have tied down your hand so you can't injure it more."

I tried to ask if something was wrong with my hand, but talking seemed like a lot of work.

Confused flashes of faces and lights in my face and concerned looks, soothing voices, worried voices, one fading into the other and the smell of herbs steaming reminding me of Noish-pa while I floated there, still, things happening to me as if they were happening around me and all the time my familiar's voice in mind, saying I know not what, but soothing and warming. I slept and dreamt and I woke and, I don't know how to say it, at some point the world stopped slipping in and out of the dreamland and I started to know what was real. I think it was getting toward morning when I finally fell into a real sleep that lasted more than an hour.

I remember Loiosh asking me if I was able to carry on a coherent conversation yet. I told him I was, but I preferred not to. He didn't seem happy about it, but let me alone for another timeless time.

I won't swear to it, but I'm pretty sure everything I've mentioned was the same night, that first night I was there, all before dawn. It was an event-filled time when nothing happened, and I wouldn't care to repeat it.

Sometime later, I think it was the next day, Loiosh said, "*Is it time for you to tell me how you figured out Dahni would rescue you?*"

"No."

"*That's because when I hear, I'm going to panic, aren't I?*"

"Yes."

A servant I didn't recognize poked his head in while I was awake. Loiosh and Rocza instantly became fully alert, but I decided he really was just a servant. He asked if I needed anything and I couldn't speak to answer. He went out, but returned later with another. They gave me thin soup and brandy—good brandy. I refrained from asking if it had been drugged.

The next several hours went that way. They seemed to think I needed to eat every five minutes or so, but that I couldn't be permitted much when I did. I was most often served by the butler, who never let a human remark pass his lips. If I'd had more energy, I'd have worked on him. After the first time, they didn't give me any more brandy, which was a shame. If the soup had any effect I didn't notice it.

"How much time do you think we have, Boss?"

"Before what?"

"Before whatever you haven't told me about happens."

"Oh. Maybe a day, maybe two. Hard to say."

Later, the old man made me sniff something pungent and peppery to knock me out, and the amulet was removed from my chest. I know this because he told me about it when I was awake again; I have no memory of any of it. He also put some sort of powder where it had been so that the wound wouldn't mortify.

When I woke up, it was lying by my pillow, and there were fresh bandages around my chest to add to the collection. He hadn't told me what he was going to do; if he had, I might have wanted to keep it there. Think how much trouble it would save. Then again, maybe not.

I spent a day there doing nothing except being fed and looked at by the old man, and nothing bad happened that day or that night, except that I didn't sleep particularly well. The next day, two men and one woman came, introduced themselves as witches, and tried to do what they could.

They worked, and had whispered conversations, and worked some more, and, at last, tried the measure of desperation: they talked to me.

"Our spells seem unable to aid you."

"Yes," I said. "The Art has no direct effect on me. I don't know why, it's been like that all my life. My maternal grandfather was the same way."

This seemed to throw them, but they didn't question it. One said, "You say, 'direct' effect?"

"Herbs, infusions, and things of that nature, prepared with the Art, appear to work normally, it is just that they cannot be prepared by me or close to me, and a glamour cast upon me will have no effect, and my aura is invisible. I have no idea why this might be."

I lay on my pillow next to the amulet of black Phoenix Stone and looked sincerely puzzled at them.

They ended by making poultices and infusions and such. They concealed what they were doing, or I might have been able to offer suggestions, but they did seem to know what they were about except for making infusions that looked and smelled like poultices.

I drank soup and infusions, and tried to decide if the poultices smelled worse than the paper mill, and let them tend me. The Count owed me that much, by Verra's tits! I dozed off, woke up, dodged Loiosh's questions, stared at the ceiling. Meanwhile, I was trying to figure out a way to keep all of their work from being wasted.

I didn't come up with anything.

Loiosh was getting jumpier by the moment. He finally said, "Boss, if I know what I'm scared of, it can't be worse than this."

"Yes it can."

"And I have been known to come up with an idea once in a while."

"Okay, that much I'll agree with."

"Well?"

I sighed. "All right. Dahni said that talking to me in the dark like that would give him an edge."

"And?"

"And why would it give him an edge?"

"Because you have—oh."

"Right. How could he know that?"

"Uh, how could he know that?"

"Only one way I can think of. He'd been in touch with the Jhereg. You know how we work. You know how I work. When I'm planning to take someone down, I find out everything about him. Everything. I learn what color hose he prefers, and how hot he likes his bathwater, and—"

"The Jhereg would have learned that you have bad night vision."

"Yes."

"And told Dahni, because it might give him an edge in—"

"In taking me and hauling me out to them, so they don't have to make a stir by coming into town as Dragaerans, excuse me, 'elfs.' Much less as elfs with a Morganti weapon."

"You say 'them.'"

"Probably just one."

"You're telling me that there is a Jhereg assassin here?"

"Not here, exactly. But nearby, probably within an hour or so of town."

"Boss! We—wait, I still don't see—Dahni is working for the Jhereg?"

"Not working, exactly. I'm guessing they just found a local willing to do some things for them. You know, 'Deliver this guy to me, and I will make you a wealthy man indeed.' That sort of thing."

"But then, you must have—oh. He'd be willing to rescue you because if he didn't, he wouldn't get paid."

"Right."

"So, he was going to bring you—"

"Right to the assassin, yes. I had to count on you, chum."

"When did you put this together, Boss?"

"When Dahni made the remark about talking to me in the dark giving him an edge."

"Pretty clever."

"That's why you work for me, instead of the other way around."

"It thought it was the opposable thumbs."

"That too."

"You might have told me."

"It wasn't the time for long explanations and recriminations. And hearing about how I should have gotten out of town when you said, and about how—"

"—you shouldn't have taken the amulet off just because your muscles were tired?"

"That, too."

"So you think that's how they found you?"

"Probably. If they'd trailed me they'd have taken me before I got to a town. A day to teleport into the mountains to somewhere someone has memorized, and, with a good horse, maybe another day or two to get here. Yeah, it's about right."

"So here you are, flat on your back, can hardly stand up, with your left hand . . ."

He trailed off. "What's wrong with my left hand?"

"We'll know when the physicker is done. Maybe nothing."

A chill went through me.

"Two words, Boss: Castle Black."

"You know I won't do that to Morrolan. Besides, we'll never make it there."

After a moment's thought, he agreed with the second.

"What will they do now, Boss? Sneak in here and put a shine on you?"

"They know about you and Rocza. They'll need to come up with a way to disable you."

"Which is why they tried to—no, that doesn't make sense."

"No, that was the Count."

"But then, I still don't understand why the Count is protecting you, if he's the one who first took you."

I sighed. "Let me rest for a bit, Loiosh. That's going to take more explanation than I can deal with right now."

"Okay, Boss. Get some rest. I'll try to get us out of this mess, since it's obvious that you can't."

"You just always pick the right thing to say to cheer me up."

I did get some rest, though the dreams were ugly and woke me up repeatedly, as did the witches and the physicker. Why is it that when you most need rest and healing, those in charge of healing you never let you rest?

Later that day, the Count stopped by to see me. "My lord Merss," he said. "I'm sorry. If there's anything I can do—"

"You're doing it," I said, trying to speak loud enough for him to hear me. "And it isn't done."

His pure white brows came together. "How—?"

"I imagine someone will be sneaking in here to kill me. Probably tonight or tomorrow. No, I shouldn't say that. He'll be trying to kill me, I have no way of knowing if it will involve sneaking in here or some other approach entirely."

He shook his head. "No. I've, ah, spoken to those responsible. They'll make no effort—"

"They aren't the ones who will be coming."

"Then who?"

"I can't tell you."

"Can't tell me?"

"That is, I don't choose to."

He opened his mouth and closed it. "Very well," he said. "Can you tell me how best to guard you?"

Now he was asking the hard questions.

Well, if it were me, how would I do it? I wouldn't bribe a guard; too risky if he said no. Pure stealth would be an option, but how to deal with guards in the actual room, which is an obvious step, not to mention Loiosh and Rocza? If it were me, I'd never have a plan that involved fighting. Fighting is dangerous, even if you have an edge because, say, you're invis—

"Sorcery," I said. "The attack will come using sorcery."

"Witchcraft?"

"No, the, ah, the Art of the elfs. It's different."

He rubbed the back of his hand over his lips. "I've heard of such things. I know nothing about how it works, or how to defend against it."

"Yeah," I said. "I know something about it, but defending against it, when you don't know what form the attack will take, well, that's rough. He can't come at me directly because, ah, he can't. But he could blow up your manor, or make a chunk of roof fall on my head, or, well, I don't know. There are many possibilities."

"Perhaps I should I hide you."

I thought about another ride on a wagon and moaned to myself. "Perhaps you should," I said.

"Aybrahmis says you shouldn't be moved, but—"

"Who?"

"The physicker."

"Oh."

"But if it's between that, and permitting you to be, to be taken from under my roof—"

"What about you?"

"Me? Once I have you safe, I shall retire to the City. I shall be having the servants pack what I need directly we finish our talk."

"What a coward, Boss!"

"I knew there was something I admired about him."

"I'll never get tired of handing you set-ups."

"Someday I may ignore one, just to watch you twitch."

He sort of hissed a disbelieving laugh into my head.

"I don't suppose you know of a convenient cave?"

"Cave? No, I know of no caves. Why?"

"I don't know, hiding in caves is supposed to be traditional."

He looked dubious. I hadn't been serious anyway.

The trouble was, the assassin could do anything, especially if he were a sorcerer. Well, okay, he couldn't do anything to me directly; the gold Phoenix Stone prevented that. But he didn't need to, either. He could blow up the entire manor. Sure, assassins don't like to do things that will call attention to ourselves—

that is, themselves—but out here in the East, who cared? And I had no idea how skilled he was. When you're after someone, you know who he is—as I told Loiosh, you know everything there is to know about him before you make a move. When someone is coming after you, you don't know anything.

Well, no, there was one thing we knew: that there was an assassin after me. And there was another thing that we could find out, if we went about it right.

"*What do you think, Loiosh?*"

"*He might have bolted.*"

"Yeah, I know. But if he hasn't?"

"*I can't think of anything better, Boss. But we'd best do it fast. It would be embarrassing if the Jhereg put a shine on you right before we were about to go into action.*"

"You're sounding like me."

"*Easterners are short. Jhereg are reptiles. Water is wet. I sound like you.*"

I let him have that one and turned my attention—what there was of it—back to His Lordship. "Okay, here's what we're going to do."

"Eh?" He put his ear next to my mouth so I wouldn't have to shout.

"Get Dahni," I told him.

He looked like he was about to ask why but thought better of it, and just nodded. He went out to give the orders, and Aybrahmis came back in and fiddled with my left hand while I studied a painting on the wall to my right. It showed a waterfall. I like waterfalls. This one had a sort of dreamy quality, which is neither here nor there, but it did have the sense of motion, which is what a painting of a waterfall ought to have. There were also some effects where the droplets of water blended into the mist; a sort of fool-the-eye kind of effect that I liked. In my next life, I'll be an art critic. I wondered which House an art critic was likely to be found in. I hadn't read enough of them to know.

Unlikely to be any of the six (or five, or seven) Houses of the true aristocracy, unless perhaps an errant Tiassa wanted to go that way for a little while if he felt he could inspire better work; but eventually he'd get tired of it and want to do the painting himself.

An Issola might, if he could find a way to be critical without ever wounding the artist's feelings; and if anyone could do that, an Issola could, but, really I didn't think so. I had trouble imagining a Teckla getting the education and drive necessary to understand art and how to write out his thoughts and feelings well enough. An Orca wouldn't do it because there wasn't enough money in it. At least, I'd never heard of anyone becoming wealthy on the proceeds from writing art columns for the local rags. Jhereg? Please. It is to laugh. Vallista? Yeah, I could see that. Maybe a Vallista. When he isn't making something, perhaps he'd enjoy ripping apart the efforts of those who are. Those things sort of go together. Or maybe a Jhegaala at a certain stage in his life, when he's tired of one thing but hasn't yet gone on to the next. I'd known a few; young Jhegaala flock to games of chance. Older ones generally avoid them, but pay up promptly if they play. They're unpredictable bastards, though; just when you think you have a guy figured as a dull, boring clerk in a leather-goods store, he'll suddenly turn into an art critic on you. Hard to pin a Jhegaala down; you never know what one will be up to next. And that could trap you—thinking you understood a guy, only to find out you only understood what he used to be like. That's the thing about them, though: they're always moving. A moving target, like moving water: You can't pick it up, can't keep hold of it if you have it. You try, and find your hand doesn't work anymore. Because your hand is going from one thing to another, all the time, changing, moving, shifting. Everything shifts

like that. As soon as you've figured out what something is, it becomes something different. Try to slap a label on it and you've
just confused yourself. There's more to understanding than finding the right label, just like there's more to torture than causing
pain. You have to keep the guy in the here-and-now; let his mind
drift, and he's beat you, because whatever you're doing to his
body, it's his mind you want. Just like trying to fix a label on
someone, you have to stay on top of it as it changes. You have to
ride it, keep with it, turn when it turns, let it carry you, let it
change you. It's no fun, but what else can you do?

"Your legs are splinted, and I've treated the burns as best I
can and, ah, made certain you didn't move in such a way as to
hurt yourself further. There's nothing more I can do for you
right now, Lord Merss."

I nodded, still studying the waterfall, and tried not to shake.
I heard his footsteps receding, and relaxed a little. Then I very
softly, under my breath, got caught up on all the cursing I might
have missed in the last quarter century or so.

A servant I didn't recognize came in with more soup. Have
I mentioned that they had to hold the spoon up to my lips? After they were done feeding me, I shook for a while, which probably took more energy than I'd gotten from the soup. It didn't
taste very good either. Barley, I think, with not enough garlic
and too much brownroot powder.

I guess I slept for a while after that, until His Lordship returned, with Dahni in tow. Dahni looked like he wanted to look
confident and poised.

I managed to lift my right arm enough to beckon him. He
tried to look jaunty as he walked. The Count gestured to the
two men-at-arms—one of whom I think I recognized—to leave.
I said, "No, my lord."

"Eh?"

"You'll want them here."

Part Five

LEVIDOPT

The female lays the eggs, the male protects them; yet, like the jhereg (and hence the common etymology of the names, see Appendix B, this volume), both sexes develop venom, as well as wings. No suitable explanation for this peculiarity has been postulated. . . .

The most important and most often overlooked aspect of the levidopt is that, in a sense recapitulating the entire development of the Jhegaala, it, too, is in a constant state of change.

—Oscaani: *Fauna of the Middle South: A Brief Survey,* Volume 6, Chapter 19

13

LEFITT: *Can't anyone tell me anything?*
    [Enter Tadmar]
TADMAR: *I can.*
LEFITT: *Thank all the gods! Well then, please do!*
TADMAR: *There's a merchant at the door.*
LEFITT (aside): *I asked for that, didn't I?*

—Miersen, *Six Parts Water*
Day One, Act IV, Scene 3

The guards hesitated—I guess my voice was a little stronger—and looked at the Count. He frowned. Dahni tried not to look uncomfortable.

"Where is he?" I said.

"And of whom might you be speaking?" Dahni asked.

I shook my head wearily. "I'm too tired for this, and there's no time. Unless you want His Lordship hunting you down wherever you go—and me, if I happen to live through it—just answer the bloody question. The Jhereg. The elf. The assassin. The Dragaeran. The man you've been paid to deliver me to. Where is he?

Oh, and don't try to pretend to be carefree and calm unless you can pull it off, it just leaves you looking ridiculous."

He looked at His Lordship, who, to his credit, had picked up my play immediately and put on a stone face.

Dahni sighed. "Yes, well. If I tell you, do I get out of this alive?" He was looking at His Lordship.

"As far as I'm concerned," he said. "I can't speak for him."

I said, "Not much I could do to you if I wanted to right now." He glanced significantly at Loiosh and Rocza.

"Oh," I said. "Yeah, we'll leave you alone."

"We're not really letting him go, Boss, are we?"

"I haven't decided yet."

He nodded. "About two miles northeast of town by the Lumber Camp Trail there is a row of old shacks. Right behind the third one is a trail that leads over a hill. At the bottom of the hill is a sort of office area the camp leader used to use. He's in there."

"I know it," said the Count.

Dahni nodded, and looked like he was about to leave.

"Not quite yet," I said. "Did he give you a name?"

"Mahket." He stumbled a little saying the name, I guess because the stress was on the last syllable, and Fenarian never does that.

I laughed a little. "Mahket" means "peace-lover." He had a sense of humor, did this assassin. And no more desire to give his real name than I would have had. "When did he first make contact with you?"

"It would have been, ah, two weeks ago."

I made the adjustment from the Eastern "week" to the Dragaeran, and nodded. "How did he find you?"

"I don't know. It was after His Lordship gave me the assignment to follow you. Perhaps a servant?"

"Probably. Finding the local lord and pumping one of his servants for information would have been a natural first step."

The Count said, "I will discover who it was."

"If you wish," I said. "I don't think it matters much. If you paid your servants enough so they weren't susceptible to bribes, they'd no longer be servants." I turned back to Dahni. "When does he expect to hear from you again?"

"Today, an hour before dusk."

"And?"

He winced.

"Relax," I said. "You've been given your life, and it's much too late for any of us to start liking you. Now let's hear it."

He nodded. "I'm to deliver a layout of the manor, precisely where you are within it, the position of the guards, and how closely you are guarded."

"And then?"

"When he returns, I am to be paid. If he really plans to pay me, of course, and not to either just leave, or kill me."

"Don't worry," I said. "He'll carry out his bargain. Or, well, he would."

"You know him?"

"I know his kind. I presume you were paid something up front?"

He nodded.

"Then not only do you get to live, but, ah, one moment."

"*Loiosh, how much gold am I carrying with me?*"

"*I don't know, Boss. A lot. Five pounds or so?*"

I said, "You can also pick up ten gold coins of the Empire. Pure gold. Interested?"

"Ten coins," he said. "Each coin is, ah, what?"

"An ounce," I said. "A seventeenth of an Imperial pound."

"That's what you call an ounce?"

"Yes."

"That's strange."

"It's an Imperial measure. What do you call an ounce?"

"A sixteenth of a standard pound."

"And that isn't strange?"

"Good point."

"Well?"

"What do I have to do?"

"Dissemble."

"I think I see where this is going."

"I suspect you do. Well?"

He thought it over, but I knew which way it would go—I could see the greed dancing in his eyes. I knew that look well; I'd made my living on it, directly or indirectly, for many years.

"All right," he said.

"Good. Give him the information, just as agreed. Only leave out this conversation, and anything else that might give him the idea he's expected. As far as he's concerned, everything's fine. Understand?"

He nodded.

"Tell him things get quiet here about four hours after sunset."

He nodded again.

"Do you think you can pull it off?"

"Dissembling? What do you think?"

"Good point. Look at me, Dahni."

"I am looking at you."

"No, look at what's been done to me." My voice sounded hoarse to my ears.

He swallowed and nodded.

"Keep it in mind, Dahni. Because I don't trust you. And if you turn on me, I'm going to have you delivered to me, and this is what I'm going to do to you."

I looked at His Lordship, who looked back at me, hesitated, then nodded once.

"I understand," said Dahni.

"Good. Go keep your appointment. You'll be paid when—when matters have been attended to."

"Aren't you going to ask how much I was to be paid for delivering you?"

"I never indulge in morbid curiosity," I lied.

After he'd gone, and before I could make the suggestion, His Lordship turned to one of the guards and said, "Do we have anyone who can follow him without making it obvious?"

"Yes, my lord."

"Then do so."

He dismissed the other guard as well, and we were alone.

"Well?" he said. "Now what?"

Now I wanted to sleep.

"Send a troop. Good men, who can move in close before doing anything. Don't give him time to get a spell off, assuming he can—"

"Just kill him? With no warning, no capture, no trial, on your say-so alone?"

"Yes," I said, and waited.

I figured I didn't need to draw it out for him, and I didn't; he finally nodded. "All right."

"Find a witch and tell him you need Nesiffa powder. A lot of it. A sackful."

"What is it?"

"It's the base of an infusion for curing migraines, but that isn't what you want it for. It's a powder, but each grain will stick to skin or cloth. You have everyone in the attack group carry some in his left hand, and throw it at the guy first thing."

"Because?"

"He won't teleport; that takes too long. When he realizes

he's being attacked—which ought to be no more than a second before the attack starts or we're out of luck—the first thing he's likely to try is to disappear, if he can. And he probably can; it's a simple enough spell. Covered with that stuff, your men can still see him. It's an old trick, but a good one."

"All right. What was it called?"

"Nesiffa powder. Find good people, who can stay quiet. I mean, dead quiet. Hide outside of the cabin and wait for him to come out, and then just take him. No warning, or you'll lose him."

He nodded. He didn't like it. Me, the only part I didn't like was the chance for a screw-up.

"You'll find a money belt in the box they brought in with me. Take—"

"No," he said. "I'll see that he's paid."

"All right," I said.

Once His Lordship was clear on everything, he wished me well and let himself out. The witches came in right away and changed my poultices and made me drink more disgusting messes; then the physicker's assistant, whom I hadn't seen before, came in and muttered various well-meant meaningless sounds and changed my dressings, after which I was finally left alone.

I was exhausted.

"If this works, we'll be—"

"In the same situation we're in now, Boss. The Jhereg knows where you are."

"We'll have bought some time."

"A day? Two days? A week?"

"They'll still have the same problem, Loiosh. I'll have to be moved back into town is all." I tried not to think of another ride in the back of a wagon. *"One thing at a time, right, chum?"*

"Right, Boss." He didn't seem happy.

As far as I could tell, Rocza was fine. I asked Loiosh and he agreed. *"I think she was just trying to get my sympathy, Boss."*

Sometimes, it's best for Loiosh that Rocza can't hear what he's telling me.

The next thing I did was sleep.

I think I slept three or four hours, which was the longest uninterrupted sleep I could remember in a long time. The witches had returned, and they consulted each other in low voices while mixing things at the opposite end of the room so I couldn't see. I guess they didn't value my opinions. They came back and made me drink things, and put wet things on me. I had to admit, the wet things felt pretty good. Then I guess I slept some more.

I awoke to Loiosh's voice in my head, saying, *"Boss, they're back."*

"Who? What?"

I opened my eyes as His Lordship came into the room, flanked by a pair of guards, one looking bright and shiny, the other dusty and dirty and, yes indeed, bloodstained.

I looked my question at the Count.

"They did it," he said. "He's dead."

I felt a tension drain out of me, and I nodded.

He gestured to the bloodstained guard. "Show him."

The guard came forward and for a second I thought he was going to show me the guy's head, but the bundle in his hand was too small and the wrong shape. He unwrapped it and showed it to me. A dagger, about nine inches of blade, almost all point. Just the sort of thing I'd have picked. The metal was grayish black and didn't reflect the light. I couldn't feel it, but I shuddered anyway.

"What is it?" asked the old man, harshly.

"A special sort of weapon. It is—" I broke off. I didn't want to say "evil" because it sounded silly. But no other word quite described that thing. "It is something you should keep. Set it aside, put it in your vault, make—"

"I don't have a vault," he said too quickly.

"—it an heirloom. Never use it. You probably don't even want to touch it."

The guard looked even more nervous than he had before. Saekeresh nodded to him and said, "Set it over there, I'll see to it later." Then he turned back to me. "So, is it over, then?"

"Over?" I said. "Not even close. But if you get me out of your house, and into town, it should be over for you. In any case, we can hope we have some time."

"There won't be more of these, whatever they are, after you?"

"There will, but they won't have come together. At least, most likely. They generally work alone."

"But, these others, they'll know where you are?"

"I imagine whoever sent Mahket will know."

"So, then, when he doesn't report back—"

"Yes."

He rubbed the back of his hand over his mouth again. "You'll be safe in the inn?"

"I'll be safer somewhere that isn't here. And, yes, if he has to come into town to get me, he'll be more likely to be noticed. In particular, because he'll have one of those with him." I gestured toward the counter. "There are enough witches in town that it'll be noticed. And why is that, anyway? The place is lousy with witches. Can't cross the street without tripping over one. Is this whole country like that?"

His mouth worked. "Actually, we have fewer here than in many places."

Which reminded me that the number had been reduced by an entire family not long ago. Whatever shape I was in, I was better off than they were. Or Mahket, for that matter.

I said, "Well, can you get word to them?"

"Some of them. A fair number."

"Good. Let them stay alert for an ugly sort of foulness they haven't encountered before. If they relax and let themselves, they can feel it a long way away. It will be a weapon of the same sort that you took from Mahket. When they feel it, another elf is here to kill me."

"What did you do to them?"

"Eh, I made enemies."

He let it go.

Aybrahmis came in with two guards and a servant, and they lifted me up and turned me over and changed the bedding. He asked if I needed to use the chamber pot, and I did, and the less said about that experience the better. The guards politely looked away. When I was back on the bed I was shaking. Then I was fed again, and after that I slept some more. I had dreams and woke up several times. During one of those half-awake, half-asleep times, I noticed Rocza suddenly being very affectionate—rubbing her head against my face, and licking the corner of my mouth—which was a new development. I asked Loiosh about it and he said, *"She likes you, Boss,"* which was oddly warming in my present state. Things between Rocza and me were always odd. I had acquired her, I guess you could say, by magic that shouldn't have worked. I had summoned her the way you summon a familiar, but as an adult. She had taken up with Loiosh, and so stayed with me, but communication between us was vague at best and generally filtered through Loiosh. To discover that she had some affection for me was agreeably disappointing.

The night passed, somehow. I didn't feel noticeably better the next morning, but I suppose Aybrahmis must have thought I was because he let me eat some dry bread in addition to the soup. He looked at what the witches had done for the burns and nodded his approval; then he looked at my hand again while

I studied the painting some more. Wherever I end up living, if I ever end up living somewhere (or, in fact, if I end up living), I don't think I will ever have a painting of a waterfall there. And forget that art critic idea, too.

I was left alone at last.

"We need to plan our next move, Boss."

"It's planned. We're going back to the inn. The Mouse."

"After that?"

"I don't know. I need to recover, I guess."

"Boss, you have two choices. One is to take months to recover"— he didn't add "if you ever do"—"and the other is to take that amulet off, which is liable to get you killed fast."

"Maybe there's another choice."

"What?"

"I don't know."

"We need to figure out the safest way for us to be gone from here before—"

"No. I have things left to do in this place."

"Boss, tell me you're just teasing your old buddy."

"No."

I shocked him into a silence that lasted the two or three minutes until they came to move me to the inn. They picked me up, mattress and all, and carried me down the stairs and out to the wagon. My box came with me.

This trip, also at night, wasn't as bad as the other had been; I didn't have to concentrate all of my energy on not screaming. I could look at the stars, and wonder and speculate and pick out imaginary patterns as does anyone else who has seen them.

We stopped just outside of town. I called over one of the guards and asked why. He shrugged and said, "Orders."

I was about to tell Loiosh to find out what was up, but he flew off before I could formulate it; Rocza stood over me, wings spread, chest out, neck arched, opening and closing her mouth the way jhereg do when they want you to remember that they have really sharp fangs. The guards who had remained behind kept giving her nervous glances.

"It's all right, Boss."

"What? What's going on?"

"We should have thought of it ourselves. They're arranging for you to be brought in a back way."

"Oh. Yeah, we should have thought of it ourselves."

We started up again, and they finally had to take me off the mattress to make it up the back stairway of the Mouse, which had been built narrow for no possibly good reason, and if I ever meet whoever designed it I'll break both his legs. It took years to get up those stairs, with one guy holding my legs and another my arms.

When I was finally deposited in a bed—different room, but the bed felt the same—I could only lie there and contemplate the sweet sounds of my moaning. I'll let you in on a secret: I don't sound all that good.

My entourage—the physicker and the witches—arrived within the hour and Aybrahmis made a clicking sound with his tongue as he looked me over. "With these people coming in to see me every day, Loiosh, it isn't going to be much of a secret where I am."

"Being secret wasn't part of the plan, was it?"

"No, but it would have been nice."

"It would have been nice if . . ."

He didn't say it.

"I think," said Aybrahmis, "that you will, for the most part, recover full use of your hand."

"For the most part?"

"There should be no loss of strength or flexibility, I believe."

"All right."

"Are you cold?"

"Yes."

He went out and came back about ten minutes later with another blanket. "I have arranged for meals to be brought up to you. I will need to have someone come in and help you with, ah, other things. The Count will pay for it."

"Good of him," I said dryly.

About half an hour after he and the witch had left (just one this time—the fat one with the long sideburns), someone struck the door. Loiosh, Rocza, and I all jumped, then remembered. "Come in," I said.

The door opened and a light-haired, beardless face appeared, followed by a pair of shoulders that looked like they wouldn't fit through the door. He was big. He wasn't exceptionally tall, just very, very big. It looked like he could have crushed my head in one of his hands. Maybe he could have. He smiled—he was missing a few teeth and the others didn't look so good—and said, "You are Lord Merss? I am Meehayi. His Lordship"—he made a quick gesture here that I didn't catch—"sent me to assist you."

I still had to concentrate on speaking so he could hear me. "I am Merss Vladimir," I told him.

He looked me over and shook his head. "What happened?"

"I fell down the stairs," I said.

He nodded, as if he'd seen the same result from a stair fall many times.

He seemed to be harmless and stupid. If he wasn't here to kill me (there's always that possibility, after all) then chances were I'd get him killed in less than a week. But he'd be useful to have around until then.

Am I getting cynical?

Heh. That fruit's already picked.

"So, you tell me what you need done," he said, "and old Meehayi will do it."

"Old Meehayi" was maybe sixteen. I moaned to myself.

But he was careful when he picked me up. I guess he could be; he could have lifted three of me. I told him what I needed, and he did it without comment or, as far as I could tell, any re-action at all. A bit like the butler, I suppose, only from a different source and in a different way.

When he was done, he ran a thin rope out of my window and, as he explained, into his room next door, where it was at-tached to a bell. "Just ring if you need anything," he said, grin-ning his ugly grin. I nodded and shut my eyes.

When he had gone I cried for a long time without making a sound. Loiosh and Rocza remained perfectly still.

I slept for a little, and Meehayi brought soup and bread from downstairs. This was better soup, oily and peppery with some substance, not to mention meat. Aybrahmis probably wouldn't have approved, but it made me feel as if it just might be worth staying alive. I mean, after doing what I meant to do; before I dealt with that, nothing was going to take me down.

You hear about guys messing themselves up because they wanted revenge and didn't care about anything else. Then you hear about guys who will tell you that revenge is "wrong," what-ever that means. Well, they can all go "plunk" at the bottom of Deathgate for all of me. I had come into town to learn what I could about my mother's family, and now they were dead, and if I didn't do anything about it then the bastards who did it would just go on doing things that way because it worked so well. And as for getting messed up: well, you do things and there are con-sequences; I ought to know. I can live with consequences. Be-sides, how much more messed up could I get?

But that's all justification, and I knew it even as I lay there, more dead than alive, and told it to myself. The real issue was just that the idea of letting them get away with it was unthinkable. I didn't have any more justification than that, and I didn't need any.

I put my mind to planning how I was going to pull it off. If I couldn't do anything else, at least I could lie there and think. You don't come up with a plan by thinking, "What's the best way to do this?" You start with what you know, assembling it in your head (I prefer to talk it over with Loiosh, actually, because I formulate my thoughts better when I say them), and make special note of oddities—things that stick out as not fitting in some way. You get as clear a picture of the situation as you can, and then—usually—openings start presenting themselves. At least, that was how I approached it when I made my living by making others stop living, and I couldn't see a good reason to change it.

Once, many years ago, I had talked about this with a colleague. It was the only time I had ever discussed the methods of assassination with anyone, including Cawti, because, well, there are things you just don't talk about. But this guy and I were both drunk that night, and talked about how we approached it, and it turned out he did things the same way I did. He called it "the process of elimination." I wish I could claim credit for that line. I thought it was funny.

He eventually got to thinking he was too tough to have to pay off his gambling debts and he got shined. I can't remember his name.

On this occasion, I didn't want to go through it with Loiosh yet, so I just ran things over in my head, organizing what I knew and noting things I still needed to learn. The more I thought about it, the more I realized my picture wasn't complete. To be sure, I had the broad outlines; I now knew who was behind the thing, and who had done what and why. But the holes in the picture could be troublesome when I got around to doing something about it.

"Boss, is this when you finally get around to telling me what's been going on?"

"It's all been a big misunderstanding."

"Why do I get the feeling you aren't kidding about that?"

"I'm not."

"Uh, okay, Boss. You talk, I'll listen."

I shook my head and stared at the ceiling, feeling suddenly empty: empty of ambition, empty of anger, empty of energy. Does this always happen when you're seriously hurt, you feel full of desire to make plans one minute, the next minute you just want to soak in self-pity, and the minute after that you don't feel anything? If this pattern was going to continue, it would get very old. I didn't have time for it. I needed to do things.

But not right now.

I slept some, I think.

Later, Meehayi came in and fed me soup.

"What is this?" I asked.

"Soup," he said.

"Hardly. There's nothing in it."

"The physicker had them make this specially for you."

I'd have knocked the bowl into his face if I could have moved.

"Eat it, Boss. Please."

I ate it; every tasteless, disagreeable spoonful of it. Then I shook some more, though I can't say why; I wasn't cold. I slept some, and the next time Meehayi brought soup I was able to feed myself. If I told you how much of a sense of triumph that brought me you'd think I was an idiot, or else just pitiful.

As I was recovering from the exertion, Loiosh said, "How much of this was the assassin, Boss?"

"What do you mean?"

"How much of, of what happened to you was his doing?"

"Oh. You think the invisible hand of the assassin was behind it? No chance. For one thing, it started before he got here. For another, the last thing he wanted was for me to be taken. It put me out of his reach. In fact, it . . ."

I let that thought trail off, and Loiosh didn't pick it up. Yeah, it might have saved my life. Eventually I'd decide if it was a good trade-off. Meanwhile, he was one problem solved, one complication gone. Not that I was in danger of running out of those anytime soon.

"There are things I need to know, Loiosh, and I can't move, so you're going to have to find out for me."

"Sure, Boss. Just give me the list of questions and the people to ask."

"Now isn't the time to be funny."

"Now isn't the time for me to be anywhere but here."

"There are things I need to know."

"How bad do you need to know them if you're dead?"

That conversation consumed a considerable amount of time, and became rather passionate. In the end, however, he agreed to do what I wanted, because the alternative would have been to say that Rocza was incompetent. Sometimes you have to fight dirty.

"Okay," he said grudgingly. "What do you need to know?"

"Do you think you could follow Orbahn without him seeing you?"

"Don't make me laugh. The question is, can I see Orbahn without finding out how far into him I can sink my fangs."

"Um. Well, can you?"

"Maybe. What do you need to know?"

"I need him followed."

"Any guess where I can find him?"

"Try the Hat."

"Okay. Now? Or is there more?"

"There will be more eventually."

"Of that, Boss, I have no doubt at all."

"But this will do for now."

"Just one thing before I go flying off on this errand."

"What?"

"How do I get out of here?"

"Huh? Through the . . . oh." I scowled and rang the bell for Meehayi to open the window. It was about time for me to have more of the wonderful soup anyway.

14

MAGISTRATE: *This is what comes of everyone acting in his own self-interest.*
BORAAN: *In whose interest ought everyone to act, my lord?*
MAGISTRATE: *Why, mine, of course.*
LEFITT: *Some people are so self-centered.*

—Miersen, *Six Parts Water*
Day Two, Act IV, Scene 5

Meehayi seemed unduly impressed that I was able to feed myself again, given that I'd already done so once. I should have felt insulted, but for whatever reason I wasn't. He did things for me and I hated feeling grateful to him and to the Count. In an effort to direct his and my attention away from what was going on (I swear to you, that's all I was doing) I said, "Are you from a large family?"

"Large enough," he said. "Three sisters, four brothers. Who lived, I mean," he added matter-of-factly.

"Farm?"

He nodded. "For the Count, now."

I almost let that go, but I was desperate to talk about something, anything. "Now?" I said.

"Well, all my life."

"Who was it before that?"

"The old Baron, of course." He dropped his voice. "He was an evil man. He used to bathe in the blood of young virgins." He nodded seriously.

"Yes, well," I said. "That certainly qualifies as evil, though I'm having some trouble imagining he'd have found it pleasant."

That seemed to puzzle him and he fell silent.

"What became of him?" I asked.

"There was a great battle between the Count and the Baron, and in the end the Count dragged him down to Hell."

"Where is Hell, exactly? I've often wondered."

He looked at me to see if I were mocking him, which I was, but I felt bad about it so I kept my face straight and looked sincere.

"Under the ground," he finally said.

"It must have been some battle."

He nodded eagerly, as if he'd been there. "The Baron summoned demons and devils, and all the witches of light gathered together to banish them."

I made a noncommittal sound, wondering if there were any shades of truth anywhere in it. "This must have been a long time ago."

"Oh, yes. It was in my great-great-grandfather's time."

Of course it was.

"I see. That must have been about the time the paper mill was opening."

He nodded. "I think so. It was the Count who opened the mill, you know. My brother and my uncle work there."

"The old Count. Back then. Not the same man."

"Oh, no! He'd be over a hundred years old."

I nodded. "His grandson, then?"

He frowned. "I think so." I guess he wasn't used to keeping track of progressions of his overlords.

"So then, there was a great battle of good magic and evil magic and the brave Count banished the foul Baron and took over his holdings and opened a paper mill and all was well."

"Um, I guess so."

By this time I was back on the bed, but my mind was working so hard I hardly noticed my body. "Who would know the details about this?"

"Details, Lord Merss?"

"Yes. Your story interests me. I'd like to learn more. The names of everyone involved on both sides, and how the battle was fought, all of it. Perhaps I'll write a history."

He looked awestruck. "A history? You'll really write a history?"

"I might. But to do that, I need to know someone who knows all about it. Who would that be?"

"Father Noij."

"Right. Of course. Father Noij. Would you be good enough to ask Father Noij to come and visit me when he gets the chance?"

"All right, I will!" he said. I think he was excited to be part of someone writing a history.

"Don't tell him what it's about. I'd rather introduce the subject myself."

He nodded enthusiastically and dashed off, leaving me to my contemplations. I didn't have time for a lot of them before he returned, somewhat breathless and beaming. "He said he'll stop by this evening."

"Good," I said, and realized that I was now, without effort, speaking in an almost normal tone of voice. I was getting better. Perhaps in a year or two I'd even be able to walk.

I'm going to stop mentioning being hit with waves of frustration, or misery, or anger. You can just figure that they happened, one after the other, quicker or longer, weaker or stronger, and plug them in where you want to. They don't matter. When you have to do something, it doesn't matter how you feel when doing it, it matters that you do it.

"So, Meehayi, how is it you were picked for this?"

"For what, Lord Merss?"

"For taking care of me. Why you?"

"Oh. I don't know. I'm strong, I guess that's why."

"You are that."

"And I think he wanted someone stupid, too."

"Stupid," I repeated stupidly.

"Well, I'm strong, so they think I must be stupid."

"Ah," I said. "I see. Yes."

He flashed me a grin. "Oh, I know. You think I'm stupid too. That's all right, I don't mind." He frowned suddenly. "Maybe not minding is why I was picked, come to think of it."

I didn't know what to say to that, so I didn't say anything. He gave me a little bow and said, "Ring the bell if you need anything, Lord Merss."

"Call me Vlad," I said. When he was gone, I watched the ceiling for a while to see if it would do anything interesting. It didn't.

Loiosh reported in that he had nothing to report, and then I slept some, and then ate some more bread and broth; this time I was given more brandy with it, for which I was disgustingly grateful. There came a sort of tap at the door, and evidently I said "Come in" loud enough, because the door opened and there was Father Noij. He came in, and lost his smile when he saw me.

"Oh," he said. "I didn't know." For no reason I can place, he suddenly reminded me of Noish-pa. I told myself sternly not to rely on that feeling.

"Sit down," I told him. He did, looking at me. I couldn't identify all the emotions that passed over his face, but he was, at least, upset. That could mean anything.

He sat down and folded his hands in his lap. "What is it you wish of me, Lord Merss?"

"You talk, I listen."

"Talk about . . ."

"History, Father. Not so ancient history."

"History of—?"

"When a Count and a Baron went to war over whether peasants would be working land, or working in a paper mill."

His eyebrows went up. "You would seem to know a great deal about it already."

"You mean, more than those who believe stories of demons being summoned, and the ultimate war of good and evil, and barons who bathe in the blood of virgins?"

"Well, yes." He smiled a little. "Didn't quite buy that, eh?"

"I don't believe in virgins."

"Yes, I guess that is a bit hard to take, isn't it?"

"So, what really happened?"

"You have most of it."

"What's the rest, Father Noij?"

"Well, no demons were summoned."

"Yes, I'd suspected that."

"It's pretty simple. Old Saekeresh—the grandfather of the current Count Saekeresh—found a process for making paper and wanted to open a mill."

"Go on."

"In order to work, it needed to be run on a large scale. That meant he had to find workers for it, not to mention loggers. Lots and lots of loggers. We call them *favagoti*."

"All right."

"So he moved to this area, because—"

"Wait. Moved here? From where?"

"I'm not sure exactly. Back East somewhere."

"All right."

"He moved because there was the river right here, and the forest."

"Yes. Though I'm surprised the forest is still left."

"Old Saekeresh was something of a witch, and, as I understand it, very concerned about preserving nature. He made sure new trees were planted as he cut the old ones down."

"I see. How noble of him."

He shrugged. "So he came here, and, well, made his preparations, then in the course of a week he had slaughtered Baron Neeyali and all of his people."

"All of them?"

"Nearly."

I said, "A few witches who were loyal to the old Baron escaped."

He nodded.

"Most of the survivors left," I said. "Why not the others?"

"Your family."

"Yes."

"I don't know exactly. I know old Saabo was—"

"Saabo?"

"That was what the family was called, then. I know he had a small piece of land that he wanted to keep. I think he looked at it as one, ah, one . . ."

"Bastard?"

Nodded. ". . . had replaced another, and so three of his sons went to work in the mill. The oldest agreed with him enough to change his name. I guess he was thinking to leave the past behind."

"So, the old Baron, as you call him, was no one especially deserving of loyalty?"

He spread his hands. "I've heard nothing about him to say he was better or worse than any others of his kind."

I nodded. "What of the other sons? Are there more Saabos in the area?"

"There is one family, yes."

"And I imagine they'd just as soon I stayed far away from them."

He looked down. "I don't think they are aware of you, Lord Merss. It has been several generations. They know they are related in some way to the family who was, that is, to those who were, ah—"

"Slaughtered," I said.

"Yes. Miki mentioned it to me. He said, 'Father, did you know we were related to the Merss family? A terrible thing, that was.'" He spread his hands. It seemed to be a favorite gesture. "They do not understand."

"And you didn't enlighten them, of course."

"No. They are simple people."

"Yes. Like Meehayi."

He nodded. I guess he wasn't good with irony.

"So then," I said, "it was less a war than, what was the word you used? A slaughter."

He cleared his throat. "You must understand, I have the journals of my predecessor, and his, and his, as my successor will have mine. I read them because I wished to understand how this town—"

"Speaking of, when was the name of the town changed? It has to have been after the mill opened."

"Yes. The son of old Saekeresh changed the name when he inherited the property. He inherited it, changed the name, and moved back East. That was a hard time for people here. There was no law, there was no—"

"The Guild," I said. "That's when the Guild began to run things, isn't it?"

He nodded. "Someone had to."

"Speaking of running things, what of the King?"

"Excuse me?"

"Back in the day of the great slaughter. The King did nothing?"

"No. I don't know why. I've heard it said that the King was weak then, and old, and concerned with his own troubles."

I nodded. There have been Emperors like that too, I've been told.

"And all of this talk about witches of the dark and the light, that's just—what?"

"Nonsense, really."

"Yeah, I knew that much. But where did it come from?"

"I'm not sure. There were some witches who were killed by old Saekeresh. I guess, in part, there had to be a story about it, and in part it just grew on its own."

I shook my head. "There's more to it than that," I said.

"You mean the Guild?"

"Yes."

"I don't think they invented it; I doubt they even deliberately encourage it."

"But?"

"It suits their purposes to have the foolish and ignorant believe such things."

His talk about the foolish and ignorant was beginning to annoy me. He was sounding like me, and only Loiosh gets to sound like me. No, it wasn't that—there was an air about him as if he and I were in some sort of elite club that was above the commoner. And he wasn't elite enough to be in my club.

"What purpose is that?"

"The Guild—the leaders of the Guild, I mean, Chayoor and his lieutenants—they like to keep things, I don't know, peaceful. They don't like to see conflict."

"What conflict in particular are they trying to avoid?"

"Well, with Count Saekeresh, of course."

"I'm missing something here," I said. "Why would there be conflict with Saekeresh?" He seemed a little uncomfortable with my referring to the Count without honorific. That pleased me and I resolved to do it more.

"The interests of the Guild and those of His Lordship don't always line up, you know. The Guild likes prices high, the Count likes them low. The Guild wants easy trade with the rest of the country, the Count wants things kept locally. It is in everyone's interest for the conflict to be contained. You see—" He paused a moment, looking for the right words, I guess. "We have a kind of balance here. There is the Guild and His Lordship, of course. And the mill workers and *favagoti*, and the peasants who work the land."

"Feeding the others."

"Exactly. And the others provide the peasants with a sort of income. But if one faction becomes restless, or discontent, it throws everything off, do you see?"

"Yes, I see. So, that's why the story?"

"What story?"

"The stuff about virgins and demons and—"

"That does happen, you know. There is evil—pure evil—in the world. And sick people, who may act evil."

"All right. But you didn't answer my question."

"I'm not—"

"Why make up all that nonsense?"

"It wasn't made up, exactly. And, to be sure, I didn't have any hand in it. I am a priest of Verra, not a storyteller. It's just that some parts of what happened have been emphasized over the years, de-emphasizing others. The peasants themselves make up or add to the stories."

"And you do nothing to discourage them, or to set them straight."

He shrugged. "I suppose that's true."

"Why don't you?"

"You know peasants."

I remembered a Teckla I'd recently met and said, "Not as much as I'd thought. What about them?"

"You just don't want them knowing, understanding how things work. It doesn't make them any happier, you know."

"Um. Okay. Does that work? Making up wild yarns just to keep them confused?"

"For a while."

"And after that?"

"With any luck, it'll be after I'm gone."

"Um. So, why?"

"Mmm?"

"What do you get out of it?"

"It permits me to take care of my people, to see to their needs."

"Lying to them?"

"Sometimes, yes. If I didn't, I'd be gone, and there would be someone here who wouldn't care about them."

"All right."

"Do not presume to judge me, Merss Vladimir."

I let that go. It was pointless. Talking to him any more was pointless, for that matter; I had things to do that were more important, like eating watery broth. Although, as he was leaving, I couldn't resist asking if he had ever actually had contact with the Demon Goddess.

He hesitated, frowned, and said, "Not that I've ever been certain of."

"She's a bitch," I told him.

He hurried away and I thought over what I'd learned. Not about him—that wasn't worth considering. But about the background to this place, and how it fit into the things I knew and the things I still didn't. I realized that it had gotten late and told Loiosh he may as well give it up for the night. When he got back, I filled him in on my conversation with Father Noij. He had a few choice comments about the character of those who chose to serve my Demon Goddess. I could have pointed out that I was in no position to talk, but I agreed with him so I didn't.

"Does it give us anything, Boss?"

"Not instantly. Maybe after I've got the rest of the picture."

The next time Meehayi came in he was wearing a big smile and had a steaming bowl of something that wasn't broth. In fact, it was the Mouse's version of lamb stew, only for me they prepared it without meat, potatoes, or much of anything else, but it was stew rather than broth and it came with bread and a small glass of wine and it was one of the best meals I've ever had.

While I ate, he asked about my conversation with Father Noij. I tried to answer in grunts, but he wasn't having any. He was so excited about the whole thing it was as painful as—no it wasn't, but it was painful. I finally said, "Look, a lot of what you've thought was wrong, all right? It wasn't an evil Baron and a noble Count, there was no bathing in the blood of virgins or demon summoning or heroic battles. It was two bastards who wanted the same thing and went for each other's throats. Everything after that was made up to justify how it came out. Ask Father Noij. And tell me what he says, because I'm curious about whether he'll give you the same answers he gave me."

That last was unkind and Meehayi looked unhappy so I asked him if there were any girls he had his eye on, and yeah there was and when he got over blushing that took over the conversation and he left feeling better.

See, I'm not such a bad guy. Really.

That night, I slept better than I had since I'd gotten out, only waking up three or four times and then falling asleep again right away; and the worst dream was the old one of being pursued by something I couldn't define. Big improvement. I was ready to take on the world, as long as the world was a bit of lamb stew.

Aybrahmis was back with one witch—the youngest of the lot—in the morning, and we went through what was becoming a ritual. He tsked and shook his head and looked generally worried and unhappy and told me I was doing fine. The witch removed my dressings and had a whispered conversation with the physicker; nice to see they were working together. Then he replaced my dressings and announced that the burns seemed to be "responding to treatment," which made it sound like they were getting better, only if they were why didn't he say so? The physicker was pleased that I'd been able to feed myself, though he cautioned me against over-exertion, which for some reason I found funny.

I asked if I could try walking soon and he looked at me like I had brain fever. I didn't think that was funny.

When they'd gone, Loiosh continued the cheerful conversation. *"By now, the Jhereg has to know Mahket is dead, and someone else has to be on the way. If they use one of those professional teleport places, that knows everywhere, he could be here in a day or two."*

"Yeah, okay. Does this information come with a suggestion?"

"The Count would probably arrange for you to be moved somewhere safe."

"Does it come with another suggestion?"

"Boss, I wanted to get out of here before. I was right, wasn't I?"

"Yes."

"Well, I want to get out of here again."

"Good thing you've used up your yearly allotment of being right."

"Boss—"

"Otherwise, I might be a bit concerned."

"Boss—"

"Leave it be."

"All right, then." He said it the way I'd say, "I'll take the brown ones, then," if they were out of the black ones. And I'd really had my heart set on the black ones.

I sighed. It wasn't as if I could blame him.

"This has been tough for us both, Loiosh. And we have a long way to go. Accept that I'm in this, and you're in it with me, and let's do the best we can from there."

There was a bit of a pause, and then he said, "All right, Boss. One way or another, we see it through."

"Thanks."

"Back to trying to pick up Orbahn?"

"Yes. This time with Rocza so you can watch his house at the same time."

"Boss—okay."

Meehayi came and went, taking care of things, none of which are worth talking about. I ate a little more, and maybe wasn't quite as tired afterward; or maybe I just didn't want to be and convinced myself I wasn't. It's hard to judge these things.

I was just finishing lunch when Loiosh said, "Found him, Boss! Leaving the Guild hall."

"Good. Now, let's see what happens."

"Can I send Rocza back to you?"

"All right."

A few minutes later she came back through the window and landed on the bed. She twisted her neck around as if to look into my eyes, then, very gently, bit the bridge of my nose. Then she curled up by my ear. When Loiosh wasn't busy, I'd have to ask him what that meant.

"He's heading out of town to the east, Boss. Strolling, really. It's odd. Like he's taking a walk to enjoy the day. I suppose he might be."

I glanced out the window to see what sort of day it was. Seemed bright, and the breeze through my window wasn't excessively hot or cold.

"Any chance he's spotted you?"

"No."

"Anyone around?"

"Not so far. He's near where you and Dahni had that talk."

"Doesn't the wood come bumping up against the road right about there?"

"Just ahead."

"Two dead Teckla against one sincere compliment he turns off into the woods."

"No bet. I couldn't afford to lose. And . . . yes, there he goes, off to the left. It's harder to stay with him here, but less chance he'll see me."

"Okay. I just need to know."

"To know? Boss, is he going to meet an assassin?"

"Eh? I hope not! For one thing, I don't want there to be an assassin this close yet. More important, it would mean everything I've figured is wrong. There's no way he ought to be able to get in touch with the Jhereg."

"Then, Boss, what is he going to do?"

"Wait and see."

"Is this any way to treat your familiar and best friend?"

"Evidently."

He used a few adjectives he's known for a long time and some nouns I hadn't realized he'd picked up. I found that I was smiling for the first time in longer than I could remember.

"Okay now he's looking around and I'm being all secretive and stuff so he won't see me so I can carry out your orders which is more than you deserve."

"But you're so good at it."

"You're going to find out how good I can be at—hey! He's gone!"

"Look carefully. There should be a cave, or a, I don't know, a concealed something."

"I don't know, Boss. He's just gone."

"Keep looking."

Then, "Found it. It's a cave, lots of shrubs around it. I can't fly in, but I can slither."

"I didn't know you slithered."

"I save it for special occasions."

"Be careful."

A little later he said, "This would be a bad place for someone with poor night vision."

"Can you see anything?"

"A little bit leaks in from the outside. After that I'm not sure."

"Can you smell anything?"

"Dammit, Boss, I'm a jhereg, not a bloodhound."

"Sorry."

"I can see a box of torches, but, you know, there's the whole opposable thumb problem. Not to mention lighting them. I—wait. Something just . . . okay, there's a doorway at the far end. Just a curtain over it. People moving."

"Careful, careful."

"No worries, Boss. There's a place right above it where I can perch and listen, if there's anything to listen to."

A little later I said, "Anything going on, Loiosh?"

"Voices, Boss. Can't make out what they're saying."

"Anything from the tones?"

"It sounds just like conversation, Boss. At least six or seven voices, and they're, well, gabbing."

"They won't be for much longer. Stay with it."

"Boss, what—"

"Just wait. I need to be sure."

"All right, I'll . . . they're quiet now."

"Yeah."

"Okay, now I'm hearing . . . Boss! It's a Coven!"

"Had to be."

"And Orbahn—"

"Yeah. And Orbahn."

"How did you know?"

"I didn't."

"Does that mean he—"

"No, he isn't behind all of this. No one is behind all of this. There are too many different interests working for any one person to be behind all of this. I know most of them, and so do you. The only question is how they fit together. We just got a piece of that."

"Okay, Boss. Whatever you say. What do I do now?"

"It's almost suppertime. Come on back and share it with me."

"What if they've started letting you eat good food?"

"Then you won't get quite so much."

15

BORAAN: *Gracious! Could there be two different plots at work here?*
LEFITT: *Impossible.*
BORAAN: *You're certain?*
LEFITT: *Quite certain. I can see four at the least.*
> —Miersen, *Six Parts Water*
> Day Two, Act III, Scene 2

He won, I lost.

Supper was the same lamb stew as before, but it included everything this time, and I was allowed an entire glass of wine. I enjoyed it very much.

"Boss, how did you know Orbahn was going to a Coven? And that there was a Coven? And—"

"Not now, Loiosh."

"You're really enjoying this, aren't you?"

"Parts of it, yes. Other parts, not so much."

"I didn't mean that, I meant showing off how clever you are."

"If I were clever, Loiosh, I wouldn't be in this position."

"You couldn't have known—"

"Of course I could. I'm an idiot not to have seen it."

"How, Boss?"

"Just exactly what was a tag doing on the street at that time of day, when all the workmen were at the mill? She was there to see me, to find me, which means someone had set her on me. I should have figured it out and followed her and been ready when they made the move on me. But then, at that point, I had no idea what any of it meant. There's just one question left about her. Hmmm."

"What's that, Boss?"

I didn't respond; I was thinking about Tereza, trying to figure exactly how she fit into this.

"Another thing, Boss. If you didn't know then, when did you figure it out?"

"The questions they asked me," I said. *"Now let me concentrate on this."*

This whole thing should be a lesson to me, and it would have been if I'd known what the lesson was. Come to think of it, I still don't know.

"I don't see what you're hesitating about, Boss. You know you want me to find her and see where she goes and who she talks to."

"Uh, yeah."

"See you soon," he said, and flew out the window, startling poor Meehayi, who happened to be there seeing to it I didn't stab myself in the mouth with my fork.

Meehayi said, "Where is he going?"

"I'm tired of lamb. He's going to bring me back a cow."

He shook his head. "No one raises cattle nearby. He'd have to go—"

"I was kidding, Meehayi."

"I know," he said.

I sighed. If I kept underestimating people, I'd never make it out of this bed. "Meehayi, do you know a family called Saabo?"

"Huh? Sure. A town this size, you know everyone."

"Tell me about them."

"What do you want to know?"

"For starters, how big is it?"

"Four. Er, six, I mean. Three boys, one girl. The oldest is Yanosh. He's a year younger than me."

"Does he farm?"

"Oh, no, no. They work in the mill. All of them."

"All of them?"

"Except the baby, Chilla. She's only four."

"How old is the youngest who works in the mill?"

"That would be Foolop. He's nine."

"Nine."

He nodded.

"And the father?"

He frowned. "I don't know. Forty? Forty-five?"

"No, I mean, what is his name?"

"Oh. Venchel. I don't know his wife's name, everyone calls her Sis. Vlad?"

"Hmmm?"

"You aren't going to get them, get them, involved in this, are you?"

I studied him. "Just what do you know about what 'this' is?"

The blood rushed to his face and his mouth opened and closed. If he was planning to conceal something, he could give it up right away. I've known Dzurlords who could dissemble better than this guy.

I waited him out. He finally said, "I guess I know what everybody knows. I hear what they say."

"Uh huh," I said. "Let's hear it."

"Well, you wanted to see your—to see the Mersses, and they're dead. And you talked to Zollie, and he's dead."

"And why did I come to town, Meehayi? What are 'they' saying about that?"

"No one seems to know."

"But there are theories. There are always theories."

"That you came to kill His Lordship. That's one."

"Heh. If I had, he'd be dead. What else?"

"That you are a spirit of the Evil Baron, returned for revenge."

"Oh, I like that. Whose opinion is that?"

He looked uncomfortable. "It was Inchay who said it."

"The host at the Pointy Hat?"

"The what?"

"The inn."

"Oh, why do you call it the Pointy Hat?"

"I don't know. What do you call it?"

"Inchay's."

"I see."

"Anyway, yeah, him."

"He thinks I'm going to kill Count Saekeresh. Well. Yeah, that answers a lot of nagging questions. And asks a few more. And what's your opinion?"

"I don't know. But—" He shrugged. "His Lordship likes you, and wants to protect you. So I guess maybe you're working with him against the Guild?"

"Yeah, he loves me," I said. "He'll do anything for me."

He frowned at that.

I said, trying to sound casual, "I understand about the Guild and Sae—and His Lordship. But how does the Coven fit into it?"

"I don't know," he said. "I've never even been certain that, you know, there *was* a Coven."

I nodded.

"Is there?" he said.

"I think so," I told him.

"How do you know?"

"I'll tell you what, Meehayi. I like you. On the off chance that we're both alive when this is all over, I'll explain it all to you."

"Both alive?"

"Yeah, well, not to scare you, but right now I don't like either of our chances much."

"Don't worry," he said. "His Lordship is protecting you. And he's let people know that—"

"Yeah, yeah. He's put the word out not to kill me. I'm now under the same protection Zollie was."

He looked down. I guess I'd hurt his feelings again. It's a damned good thing Cawti and I never had kids; I'm just no good with them.

After a few minutes, he said, "Do you want me to ask Mr. Saabo to come see you?"

"Yes, please," I said.

"I don't know if he will."

"If he won't, he won't. I wonder which rumors about me he believes."

Meehayi shrugged.

Loiosh returned several hours later, not having found Tereza. Each day that passed made me a little stronger. It also brought the next assassin that much closer. It occurred to me that I should be grateful the Dagger of the Jhereg was no longer in business, she'd have been perfect for this job. If you see the irony in that thought you can enjoy it with me. If not, sorry; I don't feel like explaining.

The next morning, Loiosh resumed his search of the city, while I waited to hear if I'd have company. The physicker and the witch returned shortly after the noon hour, and once more I was poked, prodded, and muttered over as they changed my dressings and inspected the damage. "There shouldn't be much scarring," he said at one point.

I informed him, through clenched teeth, just how little I cared one way or the other about scars. He appeared not to care about whether I cared about scars; I guess it was a question of professional pride with him. I cared just about as much about his professional pride as my own "patients" cared about mine.

When the examination was finally over he and the witch fussed over me a little longer, and had a few more murmured conversations, then went off to speak to Meehayi about the care and feeding of maltreated itinerant assassins.

"I think you're out of danger," said Aybrahmis, which almost made me burst out into laughter.

Then it hit me, and I said, "Wait, you thought I might have been about to die?"

"Your body has been through a lot."

"I don't die that easy," I said.

He grunted, as if to say bravado is cheap. Yeah, I guess it is; that was a stupid thing to say. But then, he's a physicker; he's probably heard a lot of stupid things said. That's one advantage of my profession, or my ex-profession I should say: If you do it right, the "patient" doesn't have a chance to say anything stupid.

Loiosh didn't find Tereza, and talked me out of sending Rocza to help him. She stayed with me, curled up by my ear. The entire day passed that way—little happened that I care to talk about, or to think about, come to that—until the evening, when I was hearing the faint echoes of laughter and conversation from the inn below, and there came a hesitant tap at the door.

Rocza was instantly alert, like a koovash scenting a wolf. Anyone coming to kill me wouldn't have tapped at the door, and it wouldn't matter if I said to go away, so I called out for the person to enter freely.

He was a small man, dressed in some sort of brown tunic and loose pantaloons that I think had been black once. He had a sharply angled jaw, and a beard that he obviously took great pride in: It was a little chin growth that continued the jaw angle to a sharp point about an inch and a half below his chin. He half looked at me, and half looked down, and in his hand was a faded blue cap.

"Come in," I said again, and he did. Deferentially. He didn't look like a peasant—a peasant would never shape his beard—but he acted like one.

"Greetings, my lord," he said. He oozed deference. It was revolting.

"Find a place to sit," I told him. "I'd stand and bow, only I'm not quite able to manage."

He didn't know quite what to say to that, so he sat down and stared at his cap.

"I am Merss Vladimir," I told him.

"Yes, my lord."

"I understand that we're related."

He nodded, suddenly looking a little afraid. Of me? Or what being related to me might mean? Probably not the latter; apparently not many people believed that my name was really Merss. Which it wasn't, so I guess they were right.

"You know, of course, about what happened? To the family?"

He nodded tersely, still looking at his cap. If I hadn't been unable to move, I'd have slapped him.

"That was your family once, you know. You are related to them."

He nodded, and it was obvious he didn't like where this was going.

I said, "It doesn't bother you, what happened to them?"

He looked up at me for the first time, and I caught a flash of something in his eyes, very quickly, that I hadn't suspected would be there. Then he looked down at his cap again and said, "It does, my lord."

"Well, it's my intention to do something about it."

"My lord?" He looked like I had just announced plans to grow another head.

"It is not my intention to permit someone to feel my family may be slaughtered with impunity. Do you think this should be permitted?"

His mouth opened and closed a few times, then he said, "No, my lord, but—"

"But what?"

"What can I—?"

"If you're willing, you can help me."

He very badly wanted to ask, "What if I say no?" but he didn't dare. I don't mind cowardice. I can respect cowardice. I practice it whenever possible. But craven I have no use for. No, I mean, I don't like it; quite often I find I have use for it.

"What can I do?" he finally asked; asking it with the tone of, "What use could I possibly be?" rather than, "I am offering to help."

I said, "Well, I'm not going to ask you to kill anyone."

Once again, he lifted his head briefly, and I saw that look; but it didn't last.

"What do you want of me?"

"I've told you what I'm doing. Are you willing to help me, or not?"

He clamped his jaws shut. Finally, still staring at his cap, he said, "Not without knowing what you want me to do."

Well! Good on him. I was impressed in spite of myself. "Fair enough," I told him. "I want answers to some questions."

He nodded. "That I will do."

"We'll see," I told him. "How much of your family history do you know?"

"My lord? I already said we were related to—"

"Yes. But why was your name changed?"

"M'lord? It wasn't."

"Eh?"

"No, sir. Old Matyawsh changed the name. My great-grandfather, Matyawsh's brother, kept the name he was born with."

"All right," I said. That much, at least, agreed with what I'd been told by Father Noij. I like having things confirmed. It gives me such a warm, comfortable feeling.

"And do you believe what was said about them?"

"Meaning what?"

"About being evil, about summoning demons."

"Oh, that. I'm no peasant, Lord Merss. I was educated. At the school. I can read, and write, and do sums, and think. No, I don't believe that."

"What school?"

"There's been a school in Burz for years and years, to teach symbols and sums and citizenship."

"Citizenship?"

"Doing your duty to your country and county."

"Um. And what is your duty to your country and county?"

He made a face, and for the first time smiled a little. "That part didn't take so well. If they want me to fight their wars, they'll have to drag me there."

"I see. So the peasants here can read?"

"Peasants? No. It's not open to the peasants. Just children of mill workers."

"Mmm. What about children of merchants?"

He sniffed. "Father Noij teaches them."

"All right, then. So you don't believe in summoning

demons, or groups of evil witches. Then why did most of the Merss family leave?"

"Because the peasants believed in those things."

"You don't think much of peasants, do you?"

"They're ignorant. It isn't their fault," he added magnanimously.

Most people seem to take pleasure in feeling superior to someone. I'm not like that, which pleases me because it makes me feel superior.

"Why?" I said.

"Hmm?"

"Count Saekeresh. Why did he start a school?"

"It wasn't him, it was his grandfather. Because you have to be able to read to work in the mill, you see. It isn't just brawn, you need to use your head to make paper. At least, to make it right. The process—"

"All right," I said. "I get it." He sounded proud. He wasn't a peasant. He was superior.

That, too, was a piece of the puzzle.

Don't be distracted by shadows, Vladimir. Concentrate on the target.

There were shadows everywhere.

There were shadows covering the actions of people who didn't want what they did to be known; and there were shadows covering the minds of people who didn't want to see, and even shadows covering the minds of those whose lives became easier if they believed themselves to be powerless. Shadows, shadows everywhere. Don't let them distract you, Vlad.

In a town this size, you'd think that nothing could be concealed; that everyone would know everyone else's business. I'd mentioned that once to my grandfather, when he'd suggested Cawti and I leave Adrilankha and find a small town somewhere. He'd said it wasn't as true as people thought—that small towns were full of secrets. If he was right, it was just possible that—

"My lord?"

Saabo was looking me.

"Sorry, I was thinking. I was remembering things my grandfather told me about the East."

"The East?"

"This country. Fenario."

"What did he tell you, my lord?"

I shook my head on the pillow and stared up at the ceiling. I was getting tired of that ceiling. "Is there a house here?"

"My lord?"

"A house of, ah, I'm not sure what term you'd use. Boys and girls who, no, I guess it would be only girls here. Girls who, for money—"

"Oh!" First he blushed, then he gave me a puzzled look as if wondering how, in my condition, I could possibly make use of a place like that. Then he said, "No, my lord. But there are girls who work out of the Mouse."

"I see. And have you made use of their services?"

He didn't blush this time, he just shook his head. "I never wished to, my lord. In my youth I, ah, I never needed to."

I decided he wasn't lying, which was unfortunate, because it meant he couldn't tell me one of the things I needed to know. "Does the Guild run these services?"

"Oh, certainly, my lord."

"And it's legal?"

"My lord? Of course. Why—"

"My grandfather told me it was often forbidden by law, but ignored by custom."

"Ah. I see. No, there are no such laws here."

And at exactly that moment, with one of the best incidents

of accidental good timing of my career, there was the light tapping at the door that I'd come to recognize.

"That would be my physicker," I said. "Thank you for taking the time to visit a sick kinsman."

He managed a slight smile to go with his bow, and, hat in hand, walking backward, he left as Aybrahmis and the witch came in. I noticed that Aybrahmis nodded to Saabo, who gave him a smile of recognition as well as the polite bow he also gave the witch.

He wasn't all bad, was Saabo. But he was still a deferential little wretch I'd like to kick.

Some time later, Aybrahmis remarked that I was making good progress, and complimented me on being in generally good shape. For someone who couldn't even stand up to—couldn't even stand up, I didn't take it too seriously. The witch muttered and murmured and changed my dressings, and when they were about to leave I said, "A moment, please."

Aybrahmis got that look physickers get when they're prepared to reply politely to an enormity about your condition, or to an impossible-to-answer question about when you'll be able to do something or other. I said, "What do you know of the Art?"

"Me?"

"Yes."

"I know how to apply the dressings and poultices made by those who study it; I don't need more than that." He seemed slightly offended.

"Your pardon," I said. I used my friendly and sincere voice. "I've never entirely understood the relationship between the healing Arts and the Art of the witch, and it has become important that I do. In the Empire it is different. There are certain sorcerers who specialize in ailments of the body, and they are the ones we call physickers. Here, I don't know."

I looked back and forth between Aybrahmis and the witch. They both stood over my bed, both with hands clasped in front of them. Aybrahmis looked like he wanted to ask why it was important, but instead he said, "We cooperate a great deal. If I deem a patient requires some medication, a witch will create it. Also, certain urgent problems are best tended by a witch."

"So then, other than the most urgent things—such as, for example, me—you might enlist the aid of a witch to concoct poultices, medications—"

He nodded.

I kept looking at him. He flushed just the least bit, but didn't say anything. My nod I kept entirely to myself.

I said, "Are you familiar with something called *nemaybetesheg*?" You'll have to excuse me, but there's no word in the Northwestern tongue for it. My grandfather, however, made certain I knew the Fenarian word for it when he was drilling me for my first visit back here. "Hard for a physicker to cure, but easy for a witch to prevent, Vladimir," he'd said. Sometimes I wonder what he thinks of me.

The physicker's eyes widened. "I, of course I know it. I never thought to . . . what makes you think—?"

"I don't," I said. "I don't have it. I just wanted to know if you're familiar with it."

"Well, there are many of them, not just the Sheep Disease as most people think. And, certainly, I know something about it, but why—"

"Does it come up often in your work?"

He frowned. "I don't believe that is an appropriate question."

I laughed. I couldn't help it. "You look at me like this, and you don't realize that people did this to me? And that they might be willing to again? When I ask a question of you, it is because it relates to my condition, one way or another."

"How could it—?"

"No. I'm not about to tell you, physicker. And you wouldn't want to know anyway."

He thought that over, then nodded and addressed the witch. "I will join you shortly," he said.

"No," I said. "I need to ask him about this, too."

He took a deep breath and let it out slowly. "Very well," he said.

I mostly closed my eyes—the old trick of watching someone from under your lashes. You can't see all that well, and it isn't all that convincing a deception. But once in a while it can lull someone into thinking you aren't paying attention. I doubted I would fool Aybrahmis.

"Does it come up often in your work?" I repeated.

"No," he said. "Hardly ever. Once in a while, when a young man goes to the City, or a visitor . . ." He trailed off. I chuckled. His nostrils flared and he said, "I am not about to give you the names of anyone I have treated."

"I don't need to know," I said. "What I need to know is why."

"Eh?"

"I've been to the Mouse. I've seen the number of girls who hang out there, and I know what they are. How is it you aren't busy day and night with such treatments? Is there another physicker who handles it?"

"There are two others in town who are called on by some to—"

"Does one of them treat this disease among the, ah, the Velvet Ladies, as they're called where I come from by people I don't talk to?"

"Not that I am aware of." He enunciated each word carefully, the way you do when you feel it is beneath your dignity to be answering such questions at all. In Fenarian, the effect is much more pronounced than in Northwestern, because it takes all the flowing musicality out of the language. It was all I could do not to laugh.

"Do you do, ah, something to prevent such diseases? Or check for them?"

"No."

"Does one of your colleagues?"

"Not to my knowledge."

I said, "Then explain to me why such diseases are not a constant problem for you?"

"I don't know," he said. "It has simply never been a problem."

"And you never thought about it?"

"I'm sorry, Lord Merss, but I really think—"

"All right. Thank you. I found what I wanted to."

"Good day, then," he said. "I will see you tomorrow."

And I really had found out what I'd wanted to; I'd been watching the witch the entire time.

After they left, I realized how exhausted I was; but I didn't sleep. I sat there and tried to tie the last loose ends together in my head. I'm not all that good at that sort of thing. I mean, ideas come to me when I'm talking, or hearing things, or seeing things; and when I'm talking to Loiosh sometimes I can figure them out while I'm explaining things to him; but just sitting there trying to calculate how everything connects doesn't come naturally to me.

Still, I made a bit of progress muttering to myself, half out loud. "Well then, if they did that, he must have been doing *that*, which is why I thought *that* . . ." And so on. A lot of it came together that way, and the pieces that didn't, even if I didn't know how they fit, I could tell they belonged on the same table.

I was still putting things together when I was interrupted by Loiosh saying into my mind, "*No luck so far, Boss. How long do you want me to stay with it?*"

"Oh, sorry, chum. Might as well come back now. Should be almost time for food."

"Back to it tonight, or is there something new?"

"I don't know about something new, but no, you won't need to keep looking for Tereza."

"You found her?"

"No. And you won't either. Sorry, I should have told you when I figured it out. She's dead."

16

BORAAN: *My dear, if I have, yet again, accidentally said the
one thing that gives you the entire solution, I'll . . . I'll . . .*
LEFITT: *Have a drink?*
BORAAN: *Of course.*
  [Lefitt crosses to liquor cabinet]
                              —Miersen, *Six Parts Water*
                              Day Two, Act III, Scene 4

Outside, it was mid-day, and they were hard at work in the mills,
and the peasants were doing whatever it is peasants do at this
time of year. Digging something, I suppose. The window was
open to let the stench in. No, I still wasn't used to it. Well, I
don't know, maybe I was; it was bothering me less than it had
before. But I didn't have so many other miseries before. Not
complaining, just stating a fact.

I had most of it. That is, I now knew who had been trying to
do what, and why they'd done it, and who had been stupid (that
was me, in case you're wondering). More, I knew what I could
do about it. In general. But you can't implement a plan "in

general." And, when you can't move from your sickbed, your options with regards to violence are, let's say, limited.

It was irritating. It seemed like I was so close to being able to deal with it, like I had everything I needed if I could just figure out how to get it started. I needed to kick the thing around with someone, to just have someone to bounce ideas off until the answer settled in. I needed—

Loiosh flew in the window, and before he'd even settled he said, "All right, what happened?"

"Asked some questions, got some answers, made some deductions."

"Deductions? You're making deductions? I leave you alone for four hours and you start making deductions?"

"I'm trying to find words to describe how funny that is."

"So, going to explain these deductions to me?"

"After that crack, I'm not sure. Besides, I haven't fit everything into place yet."

"But you're sure she's dead?"

"She has to be. They couldn't leave her alive with me able to talk, and right now they can't risk killing me."

"Who is 'they,' Boss?"

"Yeah, that's the big question, isn't it?"

"Now you're sounding smug."

"Uh huh."

"Smug and helpless isn't a good combination for you."

"Is that a threat?"

"Damn right it is."

"Okay. Just checking."

Rocza lifted her head and hissed. Loiosh turned to her and his head bobbed up and down in one of the things jhereg do when they laugh.

"What was that about?"

"You don't need to know, Boss."

"You know, Loiosh, I think I could get used to having you fly around and find out things for me while I just sit and do the thinking."

"Heh. In a year you'd weigh three hundred pounds."

"So?"

"Hard to run from the Jhereg when you weigh three hundred pounds."

"Okay, good point."

"Boss, think this might be time to let me know what's going on?"

"I think it's time to figure out what to do about it."

"I could help more if I knew."

"Yeah, but I'm enjoying keeping you in suspense too much. I'm an invalid, you must permit me my little pleasures."

"Boss—"

"Okay."

I thought for about a minute. "We have a three-legged stool: the Count, the Guild, and the Coven. None of them trust each other, none of them like each other, none—"

"You're going to kick one of the legs in."

"Exactly."

"How?"

"Still working on that."

"How did you know, Boss? I mean, about the stool?"

"Well, there are bits I still need to confirm."

Meehayi came in with my meal. Loiosh remained quiet, as he knows how much I hate talking during meals.

Meehayi didn't. "I saw old Saabo was here," he said as I laboriously used a silver spoon to bring stew from a wooden bowl—first time I think I ever experienced that combination.

"Yes," I told him after I'd swallowed. "We had quite a nice talk."

"Good."

"You don't like him, do you?"

He jumped back as if I'd slapped him. "What do you mean?"

I waited him out. "I, I mean, he's older than me, so he isn't a *friend* or anything." I kept waiting. "No," he finally said, setting his jaw as if daring me to object. "I don't."

I nodded. "I wouldn't either if I were you."

He seemed startled. "Why? What did he say about me?"

"Nothing. Your name didn't come up."

"Then why—?"

"Because you're a peasant, and he doesn't think much of peasants."

"Well it happens that I don't think much of—" He cut himself off.

"Don't blame you," I said. "But then, I can't say too much about him myself; he's kindred, after all."

Meehayi looked at me carefully. "Is he? I mean, really?"

"He is," I said. "He really is. And if more people had believed that—ah, never mind. Sorry. Thinking out loud."

He cleared his throat. "Lord Merss—"

"Vlad."

"Vlad. I haven't said it, but I'm sorry for what happened to you."

"Thanks. So am I. But it'll be set right soon enough."

He cocked his head. "It will?"

I nodded and took a sip of wine, pleased that I was able to lift it without difficulty. It was wonderful. "As sure as my name is Merss Vladimir," I told him.

He seemed to accept that, if I'm any judge of grunts.

I said, "Is it always like that?"

"Like what?"

"With Saabo. The mill workers looking down on the peasants."

"Yeah, well, we don't have a lot to say them, either. They stink."

"I noticed that you frequent different establishments."

"What?"

"You drink in different places."

"Oh. Yeah, most of us. Except sometimes some guys will go into the wrong place to stir up a fight. It doesn't usually happen, though. The Guild jumps on it pretty quick."

I nodded. "Yes, I suppose it would be bad for business."

I smiled to myself. Nothing new there, but confirmation of what I'd suspected was always nice.

Meehayi finished helping me eat and left again, still looking slightly bewildered.

After he'd gone, Loiosh said, "*All right, Boss. Care to explain?*"

"*I've got a sort of idea, but it won't work unless all three—Count, Guild, and Coven—are in each other's pockets, because otherwise I can't make it work. I'd suspected, but until today I wasn't sure.*"

"*Okay, Boss. What did you find out?*"

"*The tags in this area don't have a problem with Sheep Disease.*"

"*Which means?*"

"*Which means there is a business arrangement between the Guild and the Coven. Mutual benefit, mutual dependence.*"

"*Oh. What is Sheep Disease?*"

"*You don't want to know. You're a jhereg; you're immune. Be happy.*"

"*But—okay.*"

I tried to sit up; failed. I still didn't know how to knock out that one leg of the stool. Loiosh was silent as I went over what I knew yet again, and got nowhere.

Who should I go after? Dahni? His role in this, it turns out, had been one of the easier ones to figure out. But no, he was done. I couldn't use him. Probably no one could use him. If he was lucky, he'd have made his way out of the country by now. Orbahn? No, he was too smart; he'd put it together.

I tried to sit up again, and failed again; sat back sweating and breathing heavily. I scowled.

"Take it easy, Boss. You'll give the physicker heart failure."

"Thanks, Loiosh."

"For what?"

I didn't answer for a while. I just sat there and smiled while my brain went click, click, click—just like it had before, just like in the old days. Yes. They may have broken my body, but my brain still worked. If you think that isn't important to someone in my condition, your brain doesn't work.

I nodded to myself. Loiosh said, "Does it have to be now?"

"What?"

"I understand you want to settle things, Boss, but is there any reason you can't come back in a year and do it?"

"Funny you should say that. If you'd asked a few minutes ago, I'd have said forget it—just like I'm saying today—but a few minutes ago I wouldn't have been able to give you a good reason."

"Oh, I see. Okay, Boss. What's the great reason?"

"Now there's no need. I can settle things right now. Today."

"You can kick out the leg?"

"Yes."

"And be sure the right one wins?"

"There is no right one, only a wrong one."

"Who's the wrong one?"

"The Coven."

"All right. But how are you going to set this off from flat on your back?"

"I'm not. Meehayi is."

"I can't wait to see how that works out."

"I can't wait to be done with this, and out of this town."

"That's the first thing you've said that I've agreed with in more than a week."

"Yeah. Which reminds me; I need to arrange a fast exit from this place once my business is finished."

"And that's the second. Any idea how to go about it?"

"I think I'd like to speak with Father Noij."

"Huh?"

"He can do it, and he will."

"Uh, sure, Boss. I'll fly right out and get him."

I chuckled. *"I don't think that will be necessary."*

"Boss, why won't you just tell me what happened?"

I didn't answer.

"You don't want to tell me, do you?"

I didn't answer.

He said, *"They took you, didn't they?"*

I stared up at the ceiling for a long time. Then I nodded. *"I had thought someone was playing me,"* I said. *"I didn't realize that they were all playing me."*

"Oh. Working together?"

"No. That's the thing. On their own, independently. That's what threw me. But the effect was as if they were working together."

After that he let me alone for a while. He knew I'd have to tell him about it eventually, and he can be an understanding little bastard on occasion.

Everything I'd said was true, and I was confident of all my conclusions, and the plan that was formulating in my head seemed sound. But there was still that one factor that I couldn't control, couldn't see, couldn't anticipate, and certainly couldn't ignore: The Jhereg now knew where I was. Yes, I still felt a fair bit of confidence in all those things I'd said: A Dragaeran would stand out, and a Morganti weapon would most certainly stand out. But what I hadn't said was: Give them enough time, and they'll find a way around those problems. They're tenacious, they're brutal, and when they have to be, they're creative. I know, I was one.

Once a fellow I was after surrounded himself with such solid protection that bribing them all would have cost more than I was being paid for the job. So I hired an actor to play a legitimate Chreotha merchant, hired another to play a low-level boss from Candletown, a few others to play flunkies and lackeys, and spent eleven weeks constructing a phony business deal for the guy just to get him to a meeting—no bodyguards permitted, you understand the need for secrecy—at which I turned out to be the only one doing any business. The whole story—why he needed to go, how everything played out—is interesting, and I may tell it someday. It was elaborate, elegant, and, if I may say so (after some initial foul-ups and few scary moments here and there), perfect.

What it wasn't was unique.

My point is this: Give the Jhereg enough time, and they will find a way to nail you. Was I giving them too much time? I didn't think so.

I reviewed what I knew yet again, and finally said, "Okay, let's do this."

"Now?"

"Now. Think you could manage to open my pack and bring me something out of it? It should be in the box, or next to it."

"Maybe, Boss. I can try. As long as you promise not to make any opposable thumb comments if I fail."

"None for a week, Loiosh, either way."

"What do you want?"

"Do you know the little bottle that I keep tincture of lithandrial in?"

"Huh? Sure, Boss. Since I don't think you'll be satisfied giving anyone the nettles, I assume you have the backache. But shouldn't you ask the physicker—"

"Loiosh, at this point I wouldn't even notice the backache if I had it. Just get the thing, if you can."

He could, and presently I was holding it, and I learned that opening a tightly corked bottle is much more difficult than feeding yourself. I eventually got it open.

"*Now I need a cloth of some kind.*"

He didn't ask questions, just dug in the box until he found an old pair of—until he found some cloth. I couldn't be picky at that point. I poured a little dab on the cloth and applied it as best I could, wiping the excess carefully from my mustache.

"*Dammit, Loiosh. I wish I had a glass. How does it look?*"

"*Compared to what?*"

"*Never mind. It'll have to do. Get rid of this cloth. Put it back in the box and bury it.*"

"*With pleasure.*"

"*And never mind the wisecracks.*"

I lay back on the bed and spent some time recovering my breath and remembering not to lick my lips. "*Can you put the bottle back in the box too?*"

"*Boss, have you gone nuts?*"

"*Do not mock the afflicted, Loiosh. Not only am I a wreck, but as you can see, I've just been attacked by a witch.*"

"*You've—*"

"*See? Red lips? Witch's mark?*"

"*Uh, who are you trying to convince?*"

"*Sit back and wait. All will be made clear.*"

When Meehayi came in with my lunch, I was lying on the bed, either barely breathing, or not breathing at all. If you're curious, you breathe only through your nose, into your chest, quick short breaths; and you can do it forever, though it takes some practice to just breathe into your upper chest. Oh, and my lips, of course, had a pronounced reddish tinge.

Meehayi dropped the bowl of stew (which was, as far as Loiosh and Rocza were concerned, either an unexpected bonus, or the only value the plan had in the first place), gave a high-pitched sort of scream, and bolted out the door.

I relaxed and waited off-stage for the next act in which I would be needed, like the ubiquitous merchant in a mannerist murder comedy. What I liked about this was that, if it didn't work, there was no risk—what had I done? Why, I'd taken a backache remedy and then had a nap; everything else had just been an over-reaction by a superstitious peasant boy.

Unless, by some fluke, Orbahn happened to hear about it too soon, and figured out it was a fake; in that case I was dead meat. But you need to accept some risks. It was much more likely that he'd hear about it later, and either manage to put only part of it together, or else figure out the whole thing and not care. Either way, I was good.

The first to arrive was Aybrahmis, with a look of mixed anxiety and rage on his features. That was odd, I have to admit. I'd expected him to show up; he was, after all, a professional; I hadn't expected him to take it personally.

The first thing he did was hold a looking glass to my lips. Through lidded eyes, I decided I hadn't done a half-bad job. I said, "Physicker?" My voice was weak, pitiful, a man just barely on this side of the Great Night. Heh. I missed my calling. I wonder if Miersen would cast me as First Student.

"Lord Merss!" he said. "I thought you—are you all right?"

"What . . . happened?" I managed to whisper through my barely moving lips.

"What happened?" he directed back at me.

"I don't . . ."

"Lord Merss?"

I opened my eyes again. "I was lying here. Then I, I couldn't breathe. That's all I remember."

Fenarian, my grandfather told me, is a language rich in curses that don't translate well. Yes, indeed it is.

I managed, "What . . . ?"

"Witchcraft," he said grimly. "Someone made an attempt on your life."

I shook my head. "Can't. Immune. Natural—"

"It's witchcraft," he said firmly.

If you want to convince someone of something that is related to his field, but still outside it, first, plant the suspicion in his mind, then deny it is a possibility for an unconvincing reason.

"Boss? You know this won't hold up to scrutiny by a witch."

"I know. That's the beauty of it."

The witch he'd been working with (I never did catch his name) came in around then, and started to examine me, but Aybrahmis started in on him before he had the chance, glaring and hissing whispers as he took him by the arm and spoke to him in a corner. The witch kept shaking his head and making gestures of denial with his arms.

He attempted twice more to examine me, but Aybrahmis wasn't letting him near. Reasonable: It looked like the Coven had just tried to kill me. It appeared that the disagreement might get physical. My money was on the witch, but my concern was that they not fall on top of the sick guy.

I admit I felt a tiny bit sorry for the poor witch; he'd done his best to heal me, after all. But those infusions had tasted terrible, so I didn't feel all that bad.

Besides, I didn't have a lot of room in me for feeling anything at that point—that is, anything except the need to get the job done and be away from there.

The witch left, saying loudly that he would speak with his superiors, and the physicker would hear from them. And there went the leg.

Aybrahmis came back, and listened to my chest with a device that fitted into his ears and made him look like an elephant. He said, "How are you feeling?"

"Better," I managed weakly. "Breathing . . . easier."

He nodded. "Your immunity is a resistance, not a full immunity, as such things usually are," he explained. I love it when they get pedantic about things they don't know. "And this time," he added, "it saved your life. They attempted to strangle you from a distance. I am going now to see to it that no such attempt is made again."

I moaned and tried a couple of times to speak, eventually succeeded. "In case you . . . fail."

"Hmm? Yes?"

"Wish to see . . . Father Noij."

He gave me an understanding nod. "Of course," he said. "I'll have him sent for."

When he had left, Loiosh said, *"Well, Boss, if that was an elaborate method to see the priest, it worked, but wouldn't it have been easier—"*

"Wait and see," I told him.

"You think this will make the Count attack the Coven?"

"Not exactly. It's a bit more, ah, complex than that."

Aybrahmis was as good as his word: Father Noij appeared in less than half an hour. His expression was reserved and distant; he looked the way you'd look if you were to offer condolences to a dying or possibly dying man. He came up to the bed, and I don't know what he was about to say, because I cut it off with, "In the sacred name of Verra, the Demon Goddess who owns my soul according to the ancient pacts, I demand sanctuary."

When he could talk again, he said, "I thought—"

"Yeah. I'm not actually dying, as it were. Just a simple misunderstanding. Well?"

"Sanctuary?"

"That's right."

He looked uncomfortable. "My home is small, but—"

"But I wouldn't last sixty hours in it. And you'd probably go down with me, not that that takes up a big part in my calculations, to be honest."

"Then—"

"I need to get out of town, out of the county, to a safe place, and I need you to arrange it. In secrecy. Because, I swear to you in Verra's name, if word gets to the right ears that you even know where I am, they will kill you on the way to getting to me. And don't try to get it to them, because you don't have a clue who they are. And if you even think of crossing me, I will kill you, and do not for a minute imagine that I can't. If I am dead, my jhereg will eat your corpse. Are you clear on this?"

His lips worked, then he nodded. "Threats are not necessary, Lord Merss. You have invoked sanctuary in the name of the Goddess"—he made a sign here with his hand; maybe it's a priest thing— "and that is sufficient. Of course I will aid you with everything in my power. The first question is, where should you go?"

"Fenario."

"The city?"

"Hardest place for them to find me, even if they track me down."

He nodded. "Very well. Now, for getting you there—"

"A boat?"

"Yes, exactly. I can arrange that. When—"

"Tonight."

"*Yes!*"

"*Shut up.*"

"Then all that remains is deciding how to get you out of here."

"Meehayi will help. Ask him."

He nodded. "All right. When shall we say?"

"Two hours after sunset."

"Agreed. I will be here with Meehayi, and the boat will be ready."

"Look at me, Father Noij."

He did. "Yes?"

"Look me in the eyes, and swear by the Demon Goddess that you will not betray me."

He looked like he was trying to decide if he should get angry, but things were moving too fast for him. After a moment to salve his pride with a scowl (not bad, for an amateur), he said, "I swear by name of Verra, the Demon Goddess, that I will carry out our agreement, and I will not betray you, or may the Goddess take vengeance upon my immortal soul." Then he nodded to me. "I trust that will do?"

"Good enough," I said.

He sniffed and left; Meehayi came in before the door had time to close. "Lord Merss! Are you—?"

"Vlad," I told him. And, "I'm all right," I added, with only a hint of weakness in my voice so I wouldn't have to answer any embarrassing questions just then.

He fussed over me and puttered around the room looking for something to do, then remembered the stew, and asked if I could eat. I allowed as to how I could, so he got me food, and then busied himself cleaning up the mess on the floor. Loiosh and Rocza hadn't left much for him to do. I announced I needed to rest, and he didn't like the idea of leaving, but finally did.

When he had gone, Loiosh said, "It isn't that I'm not pleased, Boss, but do you trust him?"

"Meehayi?"

"The priest."

"Oh. Yes, I trust him."

"Why?"

"Because I'm not giving him enough time to come up with a justification for betraying his oath."

"You're sure that will work?"

"Yes."

"Are you lying?"

"I prefer to call it exaggerating."

"Well, if anything does go wrong, Rocza and I—"

"Won't be there."

"Um, what?"

"I haven't explained your part in all of this."

"I can hardly wait."

"You're going to love it."

"Are you lying?"

"I prefer to call it irony."

"All right, let's have it."

"Second, you'll be following Orbahn after he bolts."

"Uh, what's first?"

"You're going to watch it happen, so I can enjoy it."

"Boss, is this going to work?"

"You'll know when I do."

"What if it doesn't?"

"Then I come back and try something else."

"Boss—"

"Let's not worry about the what-ifs right now, all right? It's time for Rocza to do her part so she can be back here while you're doing yours, or at least soon after. She'll be all right?"

He didn't answer me, but she stood and flew out the window like she knew what she was about. In three minutes, Loiosh told me Orbahn had been found, right in the Pointy Hat, or Inchay's if you prefer, right where I'd first met him. As long as no one noticed her little head peeking through a corner of the window, we wouldn't be losing him. And he didn't, at least as far as she could tell, seem to be upset, alarmed, or have any idea of what was about to happen.

Good.

"All right, Boss. When should I leave?"

"Now. Things should be starting any time. As soon as you pick up Orbahn, Rocza can come back here, as we agreed. And if everything works perfectly, you might even be back before they come to get me."

"When was the last time everything worked perfectly?"

"Go."

He went.

I went over things in my head, trying to see if I'd missed anything, if there were big holes in the plan, or little things that might improve the odds. I couldn't come up with anything, and there probably wouldn't have been anything I could do about it if I did.

For now, it was all working.

We would see. Very soon.

"Okay, Boss. I'm there."

"You know what to do."

"Yeah, Boss. Ready when you are."

"Go," I said.

I relaxed, closed my eyes, and opened my mind to him.

Presently, there came visions.

INTERLUDE

I let the breeze take me up over the top, and there is a perch—too narrow to let my feet flatten, but too wide for a comfortable grip. It hurts, but there I stay and watch and wait. Food on four legs walks by below me, as do people, young and old, and I wait—

This is where it will happen, if it happens. Here, right here. It will or it won't; I will it to will.

—it happens quickly; I leave my perch and make a slow circle, so he/I can see better. Fighting men—

Soldiers

—too many to count—

Thirty or thirty-five

—moving around all over—

Some covering the rear; the captain seems cold and efficient, knows his stuff

—door knocked in, things flying, wood chips everywhere, nice! A few people gather to watch—

Pouring in neatly and efficiently; not a lot of room for mistakes. Good.

—no door, may as well see if I can fly in and watch the fun—

"*Careful!*"

—hee, yeah, good times! No blood, though, just—

Yes, make them lie on the floor. I'd rather kill them all, but I'm just in that kind of mood.

—lots of shouting and yelling—

Threats of repercussions, but I wish them luck with that. Unless the witches take a hand, and they'll have their own problems soon.

—and there's the one, arms held behind him, ohhhh, fangs deep, deep in—

"*No!*"

—not protesting, wants to tear and bite and rage, know that feeling, me too—

Yeah, the bastard is glaring. Poor son-of-a-bitch. That's right, grit your teeth and demand to see the Count. See the Count? You want to see the Count? I am Vladimir, Count of Szurke by the grace of Her Imperial Majesty Zerika the Fourth; you can see me, you lowlife son of a thrice-poxed street whore. We'll see how that works out for you.

—now, finally exchanging words with a man, harsh words, nearly spitting—

The captain is doing his job—well, okay, my job—he ignores the complaints and gives the order for Chayoor to be taken to the manor—

—He walks between two others—

Looking absurd as he tries to keep his dignity

—out the door—

To the manor, and onto the next act of our little play. If he even makes it that far.

—There's an open window, so out and around, stay close to the building, and far above eye level, because they hardly ever look up. There they are, walking toward a big clunky machine with four horses in front of it—

A coach with iron bars, yes of course. And the driver is in the uniform of a man-at-arms, no coachman for the criminal.

—And they are leading him in, and he suddenly twitches as if I'd poisoned him, but I didn't go near him! Honest!—

They didn't wait. Good. Die slow, you butchering, murdering, heartless, child-killing bastard. Die slow and in agony. Feel your heart stop, know what is happening and that you can't prevent it. See your life ooze away, and think about the crimes you've committed to bring this about, and may you rot forever in Verra's prismatic hells.

—men all confused, staring at the one who claws at his chest and turns red, he is breathing smoke, I can see it and smell it, a harsh acidic-smelling smoke—

They picked the same way Zollie was made to look, and that I faked. Lack of creativity, or just a sense of irony? I don't much care. Yes, Loiosh, stay with him, I want to see every second of his death agony.

—eyes popping, face a terrible twisted thing, head shaking back and forth—

Yes, you miserable son-of-a-bitch, yes. Feel every second.

—and finally, at last, he is still, eyes open and staring at the sky—

I take a moment to relish, to enjoy. It heals my soul. It is nearly as good as I imagined it would be, though I'd have liked it to have lasted longer. If there is price for revenge, I'll pay it, and pay it again. Whatever horrid destructive thing this is supposed to do to my soul must have been done long ago, or else if it just now happened I didn't notice.

—they stand around the body, looking all about them for what isn't there—

They look helpless. But they know what happened. Time to move on, Loiosh, it's all over here.

—and up and over the town, people and food and places getting small, smaller, tiny—

"Boss?"

"Yes?"

"You knew that would happen?"

"Not that quickly. I wasn't sure I'd have the pleasure of watching."

"How—"

"The Coven. They're trying to cut their losses. They're trying to figure out if they can blame this on someone else, or maybe just get out of town."

"Will it work?"

"It might have, if I had let it."

—her form flying up, couldn't help but loop once, chase each other, only quickly, then she was gone, and claws grip hard into wood—

Yeah, there's the smug bastard, standing now, talking, gesticulating, and glancing at the door. He's heard something of what's happened, but still doesn't know.

—and he goes outside; so do I, up, seeing him again, circling once, just a harmless jhereg high in the sky, nothing here to see, then back—

He's standing outside the Guild hall, staring at Chayoor's body. Will he panic, or think it through? Doesn't matter either way.

—standing, staring at the body, circle now, high up, no need to take chances—

Looks like he's thinking it through. Fine. Think all you want, bastard. I remember when you first walked up to me and introduced yourself. I knew then something was wrong with you. But you shouldn't go trampling over people's lives like that; sometimes they take offense, and sometimes they can do something about it. And now *you're putting it all together, making sense of it, realizing what must have happened. Are you realizing, too, that it's too late to do anything about it? How are you feeling about now?*

—And he turns and walks eastward, fast, almost running, pace increasing, now he is running, only I fly much faster—

Yes, toward the woods. Probably the same place he was before. No other choice, either; whether he panicked, or reasoned it out, he has to run to his Coven. And it seems he did both. He figured out what was going on, and his reaction was right; in the same way a man is right to scream when his leg is being twisted to the breaking point. Or so they tell me.

—under the eaves of the woods, trees appearing as white streams of air that flow about them showing the path—

Oh, a different place, then. They have more than one, or different entrances?

—and bushes move, and a hole, air flowing hot from it, but there is room to—

"No! That's enough! Wait there."

"Okay, Boss. Whatever you say."

But I knew how he felt; I wanted to get my fangs into him, too.

17

BORAAN: *Now now, my dear. Don't take on so. You know there will always be another body.*
   [Curtain]

—Miersen, *Six Parts Water*
Day Two, Act IV, Scene 6

I realized that Meehayi was there, and had been talking for some time.

"I'm sorry," I told him. "I was distracted."

"I was telling you what happened."

"The Count has broken the Guild and arrested its leaders. Chayoor is dead, apparently killed by witchcraft. Are we ready to go yet?"

He stared at me.

I love doing that to people. It's a weakness.

"How did you—?"

"Are we ready to leave?"

"Almost," he said. "I'm just waiting for Father Noij to let me know the boat is ready. How did you know what had happened?"

"I have sources," I said. "I suspect people are also out looking for the Coven."

He nodded, his eyes still wide.

"Would someone in the mob out there like to know where the Coven leaders are right now?"

His eyes widened some more and he nodded. "East of town about three-quarters of a mile, where the road suddenly makes a sharp right, if you continue straight, there is a path that leads down a hill to a brook."

"Ostafa Creek," he said.

"Cross the creek and bear left for about three hundred yards. When the creek turns left, look to your right for a clump of bushes. Move them aside and there is a hole in the ground with a ladder."

He gave me a look I couldn't read, and went out.

I could now hear commotion in the street outside of my window; I imagine there was a panicked meeting of all the shopkeepers, wondering what they were going to do now, and mothers gossiping about what had happened, which was already starting the transformation from news to history to myth. Five hundred years from now, there will have been a great battle between the witches and the Evil Guild, in which they slaughtered one another, and would have laid waste to the region if the Young Count, riding at the head of his army, had not arrived in the nick of time.

My name would never appear, which was as it should be. We assassins are not big on appearing in news accounts or history books.

The street became quiet.

Meehayi came back in a few minutes later. "They've gone off," he said. "To—"

"Are we ready to leave?"

"There was a little delay."

"What sort of delay?"

"Father Noij was trying to talk them out of going to see the Coven."

"Ah," I said. "Did he have any luck?"

"They ignored him. He should be here soon."

I nodded and tried to wait patiently. It was more difficult than it ought to have been; but this was the time when, if something were going to go wrong, it would. And being helpless has never been high on my list of favorite things.

I listened to my breathing and waited, not thinking very much about anything. My legs itched under the splints.

"Boss, a mob has just arrived. About thirty of them."

"Good. Come back."

"You don't want to watch?"

"I've seen enough."

"On my way, then."

Rocza, I noticed then, was already back; she had returned while I was watching through Loiosh's eyes.

It's a useful thing to be able to do—actually see through the eyes of your familiar—and something very few witches have ever mastered; but it can be dangerous as well, because you have no idea what's going on around you.

It was about a quarter of an hour before he got back, during which time Meehayi expressed concern about Father Noij and what was happening. I suggested he go find him and he went off to do so. While he was gone, Loiosh returned.

"We're waiting for Father Noij," I told Loiosh.

"I saw him with the mob, Boss. I think he's trying to stop them."

"Hmm. Determined son-of-a-bitch. Never figured such a low-life bastard to care about anything enough."

"Is this bad?"

"Probably not. Just delays us a bit. I hope."

No, I couldn't really see any danger. But I had had things

timed nicely, and this introduced places where something might go wrong: I didn't want the Count, for instance, insisting on seeing me and asking embarrassing questions. Or the physicker, for that matter. It could lead to complications.

It was, in the end, a couple of hours before Father Noij came in, looking unhappy.

"They've hanged six witches," he said. "Leaders of the Coven."

My eyebrows climbed. "Indeed?"

He nodded.

Meehayi was right behind him. "You didn't know?" he asked me.

"How could I?"

That earned me another Look.

"Who was 'they'?" I asked Father Noij.

"Members of the Merchants' Guild, mostly."

I nodded. "Do you know a fellow named Orbahn?"

He nodded. "He was one."

I half regretted not having Loiosh stay around to watch that, but, as I'd told him, I'd seen enough.

At that point, someone I didn't know came into the room. I tensed, until Meehayi introduced him as his big brother. He was actually a little smaller than Meehayi, but that still left a lot of room for big.

Father Noij himself picked up the box full of my things that had been taken when—that had been taken for me. I held the amulet in one hand, Spellbreaker in the other; if anything happened to the box, I'd get by all right.

I winced as they set in to pick me up, Meehayi sliding his arms under mine, his brother taking my legs; but it didn't hurt. I must be recovering quickly. The virtues of clean living.

Speaking of clean living, damn but those two were strong! They got me down the back stairs only troubled by the narrowness of the stairway and my size; my weight, as far as I could tell, they didn't even notice.

More important, as far as Loiosh, Rocza, or I could tell, no one saw us.

Once more out into the stench, and I was lying down in the back of a wagon. Meehayi climbed up and took the reins; Father Noij got up next to him, and the brother jumped in next to me. Meehayi gave a cluck, and the horse set off. Loiosh and Rocza flew overhead, watching.

The ride was all right; I bounced a lot but it wasn't too painful.

They unloaded me like cargo and put me on a small boat of some kind; I didn't get a look at it. I was placed in a hammock that was a lot more comfortable than I'd have thought. Father Noij left without a word, or even looking at me. There were sounds of footsteps around me and over my head.

Loiosh and Rocza were jumpy and nervous, but I wasn't, because if something had gone wrong there wasn't anything to be done about it at this point. A certain amount of fatalism is necessary in this business or you'll drive yourself nuts worrying about things you can't help.

I felt the boat push away, and the current take us, and I relaxed, thinking I was safe.

Well I was, for the most part.

I had done a bit of ocean sailing before, and I didn't especially like it; but this was an entirely different sort of experience. If I had my way, I think I'd live on a boat on the river, just to be able to sleep there. I wasn't able to watch us leave Burz behind, but I could imagine it, and I did. My dreams were good that night.

The boat trip lasted three days, during which time I never saw a crewman, nor, indeed, anyone except Meehayi, who brought me my food and helped take care of me in other ways.

He said little during that time, which was fine with me; I wasn't feeling especially talkative myself.

I asked him about our progress and he said we should be arriving tomorrow. I asked him if he'd ever been to Fenario before and he said no. I asked if he was excited about being there and he didn't answer. I had the feeling something was bothering him, but I didn't think I was in a position to ask him what it was if he didn't feel like saying.

That evening he came in with a tray with brown bread and a bowl of the fiery pork stew that they'd been serving every evening. As he approached with the food, Loiosh flew over and landed on the side of the bed, interposing himself between me and Meehayi, and hissed.

Meehayi stopped, looked at him, looked at me, and said, "How does he know?"

I don't know if my mouth dropped open, but it felt like it should have. "You were going to try to kill me?"

"I don't know," he said, looking me dead in the eyes without, as far as I could tell, any expression at all. "I was thinking about it." He half turned and lifted his shirt, and I could see the hilt of a very long, very big knife in a sheath around the back of his pants.

I stared at him. "Why?"

"Look at what you've done," he said. "You are an evil man."

"Okay, what have I done?"

"You had Master Chayoor killed, you had people in the Guild arrested, you, you must be behind what happened to the witches too. I don't know." He kept looking at me. "How many people did you have killed?"

It was strange. His voice was so calm. I swear, give me half a year with this kid and I'll make him an assassin. "I haven't laid a finger on anyone," I said.

"How many?"

"In Burz? Seven."

"You killed seven people. Just like that."

"You probably shouldn't kill me," I told him. "It'll make you as bad as me. Not that I think I'm that bad, really. And besides . . ." I nodded at Loiosh and Rocza. "I've got defenders."

"I don't know if I would have done it," he said.

"How did you know?"

"How did *you* know?"

"Oh," I said. "Yeah, I always figured showing away like that would get me in trouble. Well, do you have any idea why I did it?"

He shook his head.

"Would you like me to tell you?"

He hesitated, then nodded.

"Then back away a few feet so Loiosh can relax a little."

He did, and sat down.

"I left home," I said, "for reasons that don't concern you. My home is in the West, in the Empire. But my family is from Fenario. My fath—"

"But you're human."

"Yes, but I'm more Dragaeran than human now. Never mind. My father died when I was young, my mother when I was younger. I never knew her. I wanted to know who she was. Can you understand that?"

He nodded, just barely. He wasn't giving anything.

"I learned that her name was Merss."

"You learned?"

"That's not my name. Though it could be." I shrugged. "In any case, I wanted to find her family—my family. I learned of this town, with its paper mill, and that seemed the place to start looking, as long as I was leaving home anyway. So I came here, with nothing more in mind than seeing my family and introducing myself to them, maybe getting to know them a little."

I gave a short laugh. "Yeah, that was the plan. So I asked around, and none of the merchants would tell me anything about them; the name seemed to upset them. I met Orbahn, and he— well, it doesn't matter. I was suspicious of him. But he warned me about the Guild, and denied knowing where the Merss family was. Possible, but in a town this size I didn't believe it. A family well known enough that the merchants took the name as a threat, yet he didn't know them? No."

He nodded, still listening.

"Eventually, I found Zollie, who was willing to tell me about the Merss family. I went out to see them the next day, and they'd been killed. And I learned that the person who'd given me the information was also dead. Most interesting, someone had poisoned him, and tried to blame it on the Coven."

"You knew about the Coven?"

"I guessed, I didn't know. There's usually a Coven in a town like this, so my grandfather told me. They act just like a craft Guild, for witches."

"What is a craft Guild?"

"Like the Merchants' Guild, but without the disease."

"Disease?"

"The Guild in this town is sick, twisted, depraved, power-mad, and greedy."

"You say that like it's a bad thing, Boss."

"It is when they get in my way, Loiosh."

I continued, "A craft Guild is, well, it's an organization of people in a single craft. All the tinsmiths, say. Or all the masons. Or the glazers."

"What's a glazer?"

"Never mind. It was possible there was no Coven, since there were none of the other Guilds. But there are always witches, and they sort of need to band together sometimes, so it's hard for there not to be one."

"There isn't one now," he said accusingly.

"There will be again. Give it a season. You see, in a town like this—" I bit my tongue so as not to make any remarks about superstitious peasants. "In a town like this, if anything goes wrong, it's very easy to blame the witches for it, so those who practice the Art need to have some means of banding together to defend themselves, and so no one can play witches off against each other. So, I assumed there was a Coven, and someone wanted it blamed for Zollie's death."

"How did you know they hadn't killed him?"

"Red lips? A 'witch's mark'? There are a thousand ways to kill someone using the Art. Why pick one that would point right at them?"

He nodded and I went on. "Who wanted Zollie dead? And who wanted the Coven blamed for it? Whoever fit that was almost certainly who killed my family."

He looked down.

"Except that I was wrong."

"You were?"

"Yeah. I'll try to explain my thinking. My first idea was the Guild, just because they'd been ordering me—through Orbahn—to stay away."

"He told you he was with the Guild?"

"No, he tried to say he wasn't. I didn't believe him."

"Oh."

"I kept coming back to *why*. The Merss family lived here all their lives, for generations, and then I show up, and they're killed. What did I do? What did I say? Who did they think I was?"

I sighed.

"I saw the Count and got nothing but an invitation to visit the mill. I tested him with a story of coming from the Empire to see if he was the greedy sort, and he was. The invitation scared me; I didn't accept it. I was right to be scared, but it didn't help."

I was quiet for a while; I hadn't realized talking about it would hit me like that. He waited, not looking at me. I took a deep breath and let it out slowly. "I had a whole plan for pulling the information I wanted out of the people who had it. It got as far as my first contact with the Guild. You see, they knew my name."

He looked up. "Your real name?"

"Yes."

"How could they know it?"

"My name flashed through my head during the spell, so if someone was watching me, well, it could be done."

"What spell?"

"It doesn't matter. A minor Working." It was embarrassing, that part.

"Okay."

"So, the next question was, why was the Guild watching me so closely? By then, I was pretty much convinced they were the ones who had killed my family, and Zollie, but there were things about it that didn't make sense. To get my name, they had to employ a witch. Just what was the relationship between the Guild and the Coven? They ought to be enemies, because the Coven was the one craft Guild they hadn't absorbed. But if they were working with the Coven, why try to blame them for Zollie's death? And what about Count Saekeresh? Zollie thought being under his protection made him safe. Why was he wrong? So, I wasn't sure enough to act."

I shook my head. "It was quite the muddle."

He nodded.

"I'd learned some of the history, by then. You should too, sometime. Find Father Noij and shake him until he tells you the real history. It's something you should know."

He frowned, started to say something, but didn't.

I said, "I learned, at any rate, that the Merss family had been part of a group of witches with either a different Coven than the one that had survived, or no Coven at all. Covens like that frown on independent witches, and so they either die, leave, or give up practicing the Art, except perhaps in secret. The Merss family had, in parts, done all of those, including changing their name to Merss.

"And there was more, going back to when some poor bastard found an old, old manuscript, or engraving, or, well, something, that told how to make high-quality paper cheaply, in quantity. Up till then, there were different Guilds, like there are most places. But with the paper mill, most of those in the Guilds started working for the Count for cash. And what was left combined into one Merchants' Guild, both to make it easier for the Count to bargain with, and to have more leverage bargaining with him. It ended up functioning as the town government as well. The Guild has been fighting with the different Counts Saekeresh for generations—over laws that help trade versus laws that help industry, and over who has jurisdiction over what. The merchants are all Guild, which is what gives them any sort of power at all. The mill workers have His Lordship as their protector and enemy at the same time; an odd situation to be sure, but the cheaper he can convince the merchants to set the prices, the less he has to pay the workers. He has to protect them because he needs them. And, in all this, there are the peasants, who are caught in the middle because Count Saekeresh doesn't really need them anymore. He gets more money from the mill than he ever did from ground rent. To him, they're just a convenient way to feed his workers. And the Guild doesn't care about them at all; when I went into a shop and was taken for a peasant, I was treated as if I were a thief."

I shook my head. "What a mess. In the end, the only ones

the peasants had to turn to were Father Noij, and the Coven." I shrugged. "It's led to all sorts of conflicts between those working at the mill and those who still farmed—"

"That's why you asked me about that? To find out—"

"Yes."

He looked unhappy. I shrugged. "In the past—back when this started, it led to conflicts among the witches, the breaking up of the old Coven and the formulating of a new one. And it ended with a three-way balance of power. Three groups that didn't trust each other, that schemed against each other, tried to get the advantage over each other, and needed each other."

"Needed each other?"

"Each needed another to keep the third in check."

I gave him a moment for that. I could see him going over things he knew, looking at them from that viewpoint. Finally, he gave a hesitant nod.

"And that is the situation I, the most suspicious-looking fellow this town has seen in a hundred years, walked into, all innocence. Meehayi, do you know what 'paranoid' means?"

He shook his head.

"It's a mind-sickness. It's when you think that everything going on is a conspiracy against you."

He thought that over and nodded. "And that's what you believed?"

"Not enough. No, that's what everyone believed about me."

He shook his head. "I don't understand."

"The Count believed I had come to town to steal the secret of paper-making. The Guild, seeing my familiars, assumed I was with the Coven. And the Coven, when they realized that witchcraft wouldn't work on me, jumped to the conclusion that I was working for the Count."

"Oh. How did you figure out all of, well, that?"

"From the questions they asked me. The Count had me

first, and his questioner drugged me and asked me things that indicated he thought I was there to steal his secret." I snorted.

"Oh. But you couldn't tell them anything."

"No, and the questioner finally believed that, at which point he turned me over to the Guild. He'd worked with them to get me in the first place."

"How do you know that?"

"Orbahn was part of the set-up. And so was Tereza. They both work for the Guild."

"But you said Orbahn worked for the Coven, too."

"Yes, he reported to them, but he wasn't in on their councils, just a paid spy in the Guild. But that's how he learned that my jhereg would have to be distracted, and about making sure the amulet I wear had to stay on me."

"So, His Lordship was working with the Guild?"

"That far, yes. A deal. Probably something like, 'You help me take him, and I'll question him and tell you what I learn.' 'What if you don't learn anything?' 'Then you can have him, I don't care.' Probably a lot like that. And he carried out his bargain. The Guild's questioner had me when Saekeresh's was done."

He looked away. Then he said, "What did the Guild think?"

"At first they were afraid I was from the King; that the kingdom finally started caring about what happened out here in the West. Then they didn't know, and set about trying to find out. Of course, they didn't believe that I'd just come to visit my family. A flimsy story like that, who'd believe it? And the more I stuck to it, the more frightened they got."

He nodded.

"The other thing that helped me put it together was just the way they got me. It involved all of them: Saekeresh to lure me there, the Guild to play out a little comedy to distract Loiosh and Rocza, and the Coven, though all unknowing, to

give Aybrahmis the knockout drops to slip into my glass on behalf of His Lordship."

He stared at me. "The physicker?"

I nodded. "I surprised a flush out of him when he wasn't expecting it. And I knew the Coven wasn't involved directly, because they wouldn't have made the mistake of telling me my
familiar was dead without confirming it. But a witch was certainly involved on some level, because they recognized at least
some of what my amulet did and made sure I couldn't remove it.
Anyway, after that, it was just a matter of confirming it, and fixing it."

"Fixing it," he repeated.

"Yes. After I was taken out, we were playing a little comedy.
His Lordship isn't a bad fellow, really, and when he saw what
had been done to me, which he'd never planned on, he actually
wanted to help me recover. The Guild didn't dare do anything,
because Saekeresh was watching them, all ready to send his
troops in. The Coven couldn't do anything, because everyone
was suspicious of them for Zollie's death, and if I died too things
could get ugly for them. They sent their youngest witches to
help Aybrahmis; witches who wouldn't know enough to ask
about why the Art wouldn't work on me, but—"

"Why won't it?"

I shook my head. "Long story. Never mind. But the witches
did their best to cure me, and the Guild stayed out of the way,
and all of them hoped this would just blow over and things
could go back to normal. It didn't. Like I told—I mean, it was
like a stool with three legs, you know? Kick one in, it all goes
down."

He thought that over. He finally said, "Why didn't Count
Saekeresh destroy the Guild before?"

"They were protected by the witches."

"I thought the Guild didn't like the Coven?"

"They don't, but they needed each other to fend off Count Saekeresh. Saekeresh could take the Guild, but he knows his family history. His grandfather had a lot of trouble with witches, and he didn't want the same sort of trouble."

"Well, but why did the Coven need the Guild?"

I smiled. "They didn't exactly need them. The Guild knows that—excuse me for this—that peasants, even when they may practice witchcraft, don't trust Covens. They, you, tend to blame them for things. According to my grandfather, that's why the leaders of most Covens stay secret, because sooner or later there will be a bad year for crops and it'll be taken out on the Coven. So the Guild had managed to discover at least some of the leaders of the Coven, and so they had that to hold over their heads. Whenever they needed to keep the Coven in line, someone would die with a 'witch's mark' on him."

He thought that over, and finally said, "Oh." Then he frowned. "But you—"

"Yes. I gave myself the witch's mark, just as the Guild gave it to Zollie. Probably almost the same way, too, if I had to guess."

"So you used *me* to—"

"Yes."

He looked at me with an expression I couldn't read. Then he shook his head. "How do you *know* all this?"

"I confirmed it in different ways, talking to different people. I wasn't sure about the connection between the Guild and the Coven until I learned there are certain diseases common to prostitutes that aren't a problem here. To prevent it takes a witch. There you have the foundation of a business arrangement."

After a while he said, "But who, who was it who actually, that is, who—?"

"Who killed my family? Who lit the fire? That was witchcraft; natural fires don't burn that way. I couldn't say who did the Working. Maybe Orbahn. It was the Coven, though."

"But I don't understand why."

"None of them trusted each other. They were always watching each other, finding each other's spies, pushing for advantages, careful none of the others got advantages. So I came in with an obvious lie about looking for my family, they all 'knew' I was up to no good. And that was fine, they just watched me, none of them daring to touch me until they knew whose side I was on. I might, after all, be from the King, and getting the King mad at them wouldn't be in anyone's interest."

He was watching me, his eyes fixed to my face, listening in silence.

I said, "When I started asking questions about the Merss family, they thought it was just to look good, and they kept watching me to see what I'd do. But then—okay, here I'm speculating, but it makes sense. The Guild pointed me at Zollie. It was a test, I think—they wanted to know how far I'd push my cover story, or else they wanted to see what I'd do when I'd used that up by finding them. So they arranged for me to see Zollie, who they knew would direct me to the Merss family and answer my questions.

"The Coven heard about this, through their spy, Orbahn, and became scared. The Merss family, after all, had been, years and years ago, their enemies, and now a man they couldn't touch or investigate with witchcraft was about to make contact with them. They didn't know what I had in mind, but it couldn't be good, and so they acted."

He nodded. "And Zollie?"

"The Guild."

"Why?"

"For the same reason they killed Tereza later. Once the Merss family was killed, they panicked. They were still afraid to touch me and they knew I was going to come back to Zollie and ask more questions. They were pretty well convinced now that I was working for the King, and that I had wanted to see the Merss family to learn the history of area—and they didn't want me to know it. Bastards always hate people knowing history. It scares them. So they had Zollie killed, and tried to make it look like the Coven had done it. Not to fool Count Saekeresh, but to fool, well, you."

"Me?"

"People. Peasants. The mill workers."

"What could we do to them?"

"You could make things uncomfortable for the merchants, for one thing. For another, you're always a threat against the Coven, a good chance to keep them in line."

He chewed on his lower lip, then nodded. "How did you figure all of this out?"

"What you should be asking is, why didn't I figure it out sooner? I don't know. I guess because I've spent so much time around Dragaerans, that—"

"Who?"

"Elfs."

"Oh."

"I didn't think my people—humans—would be a serious threat. There is an entire family dead because I didn't start asking the right questions soon enough. I have to live with that. You think I'm bad because I killed those responsible. I think I'm bad because I didn't kill them earlier."

He looked down. "What are you going to do now?"

"Well, if you don't kill me, I'm going to hide until I can move again."

"Hide? From who?"

"The people who've been chasing me all along."

"Who are they?"

"I made an enemy of a large criminal organization among the elfs. They want my head."

"Oh."

"So I'll hide for a while, and when I can move again, I'll leave here and go back where I belong, back where I know the rules, and the only people I get killed are the ones who deserve it. I'll be a bad man among other bad men."

"I'm not going to kill you," he said.

"That's good to hear. Because it might be that you could right now, and there aren't many I've said that to."

"But what you did is still wrong."

"Is it? Why? Who says someone should be permitted to hurt me with impunity?"

"It's bad to carry hate around with you."

"I'm not carrying it around. I got rid of it. I put it to good use."

"All those people you killed."

"What about them?"

"They had family. Mothers. Brothers. Lovers. People who cared about them, and who didn't do anything to you, and who you've hurt."

"Let them come for me, if they care to try. In a year or so, anyway."

"That isn't the point."

"I know."

I dropped it there, because I didn't have a good answer. I still don't. I won't play the hypocrite and make some crap-filled remarks about how sometimes people get hurt and it's just a necessary part of the cost. I don't know, and I don't care. I know those bastards couldn't get away with what they did, and they didn't, and I'm happy about it. Whatever that makes me is what it makes me. You decide; I'm done thinking about it.

"Do you want some more food?"

"In a while. Right now, I just want to close my eyes."

I did so, and presently I heard his footsteps, then the door closing.

"*Was that true, Boss?*"

"Eh? Most of it."

"*No, about hiding for a year, then going back.*"

"Oh. Almost."

"*Almost?*"

"I'm not quite done with the town of Burz. There's still Saekeresh."

"*Boss—*"

"Relax. It'll be half a year at least, probably more before I'm in shape. And I know the town now. No one will even see me."

"*Okay, Boss. If you have to kill him, okay. But—*"

"I'm not going to kill him, Loiosh. That would be much too kind."

I think I fell asleep somewhere in there; when I woke up again, we had arrived in the City.

EPILOGUE

TADMAR: *Noble Boraan and good Lefitt have*
Once again this eve
Shown that murder cannot prevail—
If that's what you believe.
Our criminal led off in chains
The stern Magistrate to face;
While here the jars of gratitude
Are in their accustomed place.
For when all the lines have been spake
Though to distant towns we've ranged
We return you now to a theater plain
Amused, we hope, and changed.
We introduce the players now
Who have delivered each their lines
So we may at last get off our feet
And you off your—chairs.

—Miersen, *Six Parts Water*
Curtain Call

I like to think the Jhereg assassin—whoever he was—had something all set up, and if I'd remained in town an hour longer he'd have had me. I like to think that. It appeals to my sense of the dramatic. In fact, I have no idea; all I know is that I got out of town still breathing.

That was three years ago, and they haven't gotten me yet.

Meehayi helped me find a hiding place—not that hard in a big city—and stayed with me until I could walk well enough to find one he didn't know about; then I gave him some gold and sent him traveling. I suggested he wait at least a couple of years before returning to Burz.

Apparently one of the things the witches had been giving me was for pain, and when they stopped giving it to me things got unpleasant. There are a few months in there that don't bear thinking about or talking about, but I got past it.

It was, in the end, just about a year that I was in hiding in Fenario, before I felt like myself again. Then I returned to Count Saekeresh's manor, and snuck in one night, found the vault in the basement, opened it, took what I wanted, and left. I honestly have no idea if Her Imperial Majesty Zerika the Fourth has the least interest in a process for mass-producing high-quality paper, but it is now in her hands, courtesy of the Imperial Post, and the idea tickles me. I think even Meehayi would approve; not that I care.

In all, it was a year and a couple of weeks from when I had stood on Mount Saestara and failed to see the future that I stood there again, and, I imagine, did no better. But I was well and whole; well, almost whole. For as stupid as I was, I guess I got off lucky.

"Loiosh, do you remember that peasant who helped us bury the Merss family?"

"Sure, Boss."

"He started to say something about them. About how one winter they did something or other."

"*I remember.*"

The wind was very cold.

"*I wish I'd let him finish the story,*" I said.

I stood on the mountain and didn't look back. Looking ahead, I couldn't see my future at all, which I figured was probably just as well.

ACKNOWLEDGMENTS

Thanks to Dr. Flash Gordon for medical consultations, and to Anne K. G. Murphy for a very useful emacs macro. Thanks to my first readers, Kit O'Connell and Reesa Brown, for much useful feedback. And a very warm thank-you is due, as always, to Robert Sloan, who created so very much of the background of Dragaera.